BY WAY OF THE WILDERNESS

BOOKS BY GILBERT MORRIS

THE HOUSE OF WINSLOW SERIES

1. The Honorable Imposter
2. The Captive Bride
3. The Indentured Heart
4. The Gentle Rebel
5. The Saintly Buccaneer
6. The Holy Warrior
7. The Reluctant Bridegroom
8. The Last Confederate
9. The Dixie Widow
10. The Wounded Yankee
11. The Union Belle
12. The Final Adversary
13. The Crossed Sabres
14. The Valiant Gunman
15. The Gallant Outlaw
16. The Jeweled Spur
17. The Yukon Queen
18. The Rough Rider
19. The Iron Lady
20. The Silver Star
21. The Shadow Portrait
22. The White Hunter
23. The Flying Cavalier
24. The Glorious Prodigal
25. The Amazon Quest
26. The Golden Angel
27. The Heavenly Fugitive
28. The Fiery Ring
29. The Pilgrim Song
30. The Beloved Enemy
31. The Shining Badge
32. The Royal Handmaid
33. The Silent Harp
34. The Virtuous Woman
35. The Gypsy Moon
36. The Unlikely Allies

CHENEY DUVALL, M.D.[1]

1. The Stars for a Light
2. Shadow of the Mountains
3. A City Not Forsaken
4. Toward the Sunrising
5. Secret Place of Thunder
6. In the Twilight, in the Evening
7. Island of the Innocent
8. Driven With the Wind

CHENEY AND SHILOH: THE INHERITANCE[1]

1. Where Two Seas Met
2. The Moon by Night

THE SPIRIT OF APPALACHIA[2]

1. Over the Misty Mountains
2. Beyond the Quiet Hills
3. Among the King's Soldiers
4. Beneath the Mockingbird's Wings
5. Around the River's Bend

LIONS OF JUDAH

1. Heart of a Lion
2. No Woman So Fair
3. The Gate of Heaven
4. Till Shiloh Comes
5. By Way of the Wilderness

[1]with Lynn Morris   [2]with Aaron McCarver

05C

GILBERT MORRIS

LIONS OF JUDAH

BY WAY OF THE WILDERNESS

BETHANYHOUSE
MINNEAPOLIS, MINNESOTA

Published by Bethany House Publishers
11400 Hampshire Avenue South
Bloomington, Minnesota 55438

Bethany House Publishers is a division of
Baker Publishing Group, Grand Rapids, Michigan.

Printed in the United States of America

Library of Congress Cataloging-in-Publication Data

Morris, Gilbert.
    By way of the wilderness / Gilbert Morris.
        p.   cm. — (Lions of Judah ; bk. 5)
    Summary: "Gilbert Morris now turns this biblical saga to the story of Moses with a compelling vision of a holy, personal God"—Provided by publisher.
        ISBN 0-7642-2920-6 (pbk.)
    1. Moses (Biblical leader)—Fiction.   2. Bible. O.T.—History of Biblical events—Fiction.   I. Title.   II. Series.

    PS3563.08742B9   2005
    813'.54—dc22   2005012616

To Johnnie

Exactly fifty-six years ago from the time I write this, you walked down the aisle of a small church and put your hand in mine.

For all those wonderful years, you have never taken your hand nor your heart from me.

Thank you from the depth of my heart for the joy you have brought to my life.

GILBERT MORRIS spent ten years as a pastor before becoming Professor of English at Ouachita Baptist University in Arkansas and earning a Ph.D. at the University of Arkansas. A prolific writer, he has had over 25 scholarly articles and 200 poems published in various periodicals, and over the past years he has had more than 200 books published. His family includes three grown children, and he and his wife live in Alabama.

PROLOGUE

A circle of flimsy huts made of reed poles and palm leaves huddled together near the banks of the Nile, surrounding a single campfire that serviced several families. Next to this circle of huts stood another just like it, and on and on as far as the eye could see. Such was the Hebrew slave camp in the land of Goshen, a makeshift city of impermanent dwellings, consisting of whatever materials could be dragged up from the river. The only furnishings inside each humble abode were woven rush mattresses lying on the bare earth. Passersby could easily look inside most of the homes through open doorways and slits between the palm leaves that let in air. Some of the huts were covered with a lightweight cotton material to reflect the intense heat of the Egyptian sun and to serve as a door covering that provided a modicum of privacy.

Miriam, the daughter of Amram and Jochebed, had never known any bed throughout her twelve years of life except the mat she rested on. She slept deeply, comforted by the night sounds of the camp to which she was so accustomed—the shrill cries of crickets, the distant howls of wild dogs, the quiet voices of those in the shelters close by.

But suddenly the regular sounds of the camp were broken by a piercing scream that came from some distance. Miriam sat straight up, her eyes wide open, and she caught her breath. "Soldiers!" she whispered. Rising at once, she left her family's shelter and ran through the camp toward the screams, weaving through the endless circles of huts just like her own. Whole families were emerging from their dwellings, some listening and waiting, others running in fear. Miriam continued in her reckless race toward the screams, and as she drew closer, she could make out words. The silver moon was high in the sky, its ardent beams revealing all that lay below.

Dodging behind a hut for cover and peering out, she saw two Egyptian guards manhandling a woman and laughing at her attempts to get free.

"Silence, woman! We just want to dispose of your accursed boy baby!" one of the guards sneered. The burly guard held the baby high in the air with one hand, out of the mother's reach, his blunt features smiling in devilish amusement as the woman managed to free one hand and clawed for his eyes. She only managed to rake her fingernails across the side of his face, but her action drew blood, and the guard cursed and shoved her onto the rocky ground. Before she could struggle to her knees, he grabbed his dagger from his belt and plunged it into the struggling baby.

The mother's cry rent the night as he tossed the dead infant onto the ground by her feet.

"Next time have a girl. They're safe enough. Come, Lanon," he ordered the other guard, "let's get away from this pathetic sight."

As the guards turned to leave, another woman emerged from her hut and cried out, "You can't kill all the seeds of Israel!" she cried. "For every boy you kill, we'll have ten more!"

The burly guard turned toward her, his face twisting with rage, but his companion grabbed his arm. "Ignore her, Mako! These Hebrew women are crazy. Come on. We've got more work to do tonight."

Seeing the guards heading in the direction of her own home, Miriam flew over the ground ahead of them. When she reached her shelter, she found her mother awake, cradling Miriam's baby brother in her arms, her face tense as she tried to calm the baby's cries.

"Is it the guards?" Jochebed choked in her distress.

"Yes, Mother. They're coming this way."

"Take the baby and run, Miriam. Hide him until they're gone."

"Yes, Mother."

Miriam took the infant and continued her flight, darting through the slave camp until she reached the outer edges, where she found shelter in a grove of date palms. Her heart pounding, she sank onto the ground, gasping to catch her breath. She looked into the red face of the crying infant and began to soothe him. Running her hand over the silky black hair, she whispered, "Don't cry, my little brother. I won't let them get you."

———————

Amram was older than his wife, but he looked even older than his years due to the terribly oppressive labor at the brickyard. He was emaciated—his ribs protruding, his face a mere skull. The incessant labor in the blistering heat of the desert sun was designed to break the Hebrew men down.

Jochebed remained silent until her husband had finished his meal, then said, "I have saved a little of the milk from the goat."

"Good," Amram muttered. He took the cup and slowly sipped the sour milk. "That's good," he whispered. His eyes were closing in sleep, so Jochebed quickly spoke.

"Husband, we must find a way to hide our son."

Amram opened his eyes and stared at his wife, his expression distraught. "You trouble me with this again, woman? What can we do? There's no place. No way to hide him."

Jochebed was a strong woman. Her face was etched with the fatigue that all the Hebrews bore, but still there was a light of fierce determination in her eyes. "I have thought of a way, and I have prayed to the God of our fathers to preserve our son."

"Other mothers have prayed for that, but still their sons died. Some things we cannot change."

Jochebed had more faith than her husband, whose spirit was broken by the years of terrible labor. Though she always gave her husband appropriate respect, she knew she would have to take authority in this situation.

"I prayed to the God of our fathers, and in a dream He has shown me a way."

Amram's eyes opened, and he looked at her doubtfully. "Dreams. We cannot run our lives by dreams."

"This was not any dream, my husband. It was from the God of Abraham, the God of our fathers," Jochebed insisted. "He has told me that our son will live and that he will grow to be a strong man."

"What is this dream of yours, wife?" He leaned forward and listened as Jochebed spoke quickly, and when she had finished, he spread his arms in a helpless gesture. "If this is a message from God, it must be so, but I don't understand at all how such a thing can be."

"We may do it, then. You agree?" Jochebed leaned over to pick up her son from the reed basket that served as a cradle and gave the infant to her husband.

Amram cuddled his son in his arms and ran his rough finger down the smooth cheek. "Yes, wife. We will trust God as you say."

———

Miriam walked closely behind Jochebed, glancing anxiously in all directions. The guards had been out in strength today, and as the mother and daughter made their way toward the Nile, both of them were fearful.

"Come along, Miriam," Jochebed whispered, "we must hurry."

When they reached the river, Jochebed plunged in at once, disappearing into the tall reeds that covered the bank, the mud of the Nile squeezing between her toes. Miriam followed, her heart beating even faster. When her mother stopped and turned, she whispered, "Mother, are you sure this is what we should do?"

"Yes. God has promised me," Jochebed said. "Put the basket down in the water."

Miriam put the basket in the water and turned to watch her mother, who kissed the infant frenziedly; then with tears streaming down her face, she gently laid him in the basket. She turned to Miriam and said, "You must push him out into the river."

"I, Mother?"

"Yes. I cannot bear it." Without another word, Jochebed turned and moved back toward the bank.

Miriam looked down at the face of her baby brother. Her heart broke as she took in his dark eyes, lustrous and clear, the jet-black hair and the smooth complexion. Leaning over, she kissed him again and again and then said brokenly, "I . . . I must do it, baby brother. God will be with you." She put a fragment of blanket over the baby to shield his face from the sun and then waded through the weeds until she reached the broad expanse of the Nile. "God be with you, baby," she whispered as she pushed the basket out into the current, where it began to move swiftly downstream.

Miriam quickly made her way back into the shelter of the reeds along the bank and followed the basket. As time passed she caught glimpses of the tiny vessel as it floated downstream.

The sun was dropping low in the sky when Miriam came to a bend in the river where a group of women had gathered. She could hear their voices and laughter and knew by their clothing they were upper-class Egyptian women. They wore rich fabrics of scarlet, green, blue, and purple, and she caught glimpses of the silver and gold ornaments around their necks and on their fingers and arms as they glinted in the sunlight.

She realized the basket was passing right by these women, and she hurried to where she could watch them without being noticed.

"Look, what is that?" one of the women asked as she spotted the floating basket.

"It seems to be some kind of a boat, princess."

"Go fetch it to me."

Miriam recognized the woman who had first spoken as Princess Kali, daughter of Seti I, the pharaoh of Egypt. Pharaoh Seti had many daughters and only one son, but it was well known that Kali was his favorite child. Her face was long, and she had almond-shaped eyes. Her skin was the color of alabaster, and she had the straight nose, thin lips, and slender throat of the aristocracy. Miriam had seen her many times in ceremonial processions, but this was the first time she had been close enough to hear the princess speak.

Princess Kali waited until her handmaids had brought her the basket. She rose and stepped forward. Leaning over, she removed the cover and exclaimed, "Why, it's a baby!"

"Yes, your highness, but not an Egyptian one."

"No," the princess said. "This is one of the Hebrew boy babies. No doubt the mother has tried to save his life by this means." She reached out a slender finger, and the baby's hand touched it and grabbed it. A smile turned the corners of Kali's lips upward, and she said, "He is strong. He will be a strong man."

"But the guards will take him, will they not, princess?" one of her maids inquired.

At that moment Miriam almost stopped breathing. Would the Egyptian princess turn the baby over to the guards to be killed? Then she was overjoyed to hear the princess say, "The Nile has given me this infant. He is my son. I will name him Moses."

"One taken from the water," the maid said with a smile. "But will the great pharaoh allow it?"

"He will not deny me a son."

Indeed, Kali had yearned for a son. She had had a brief marriage before being widowed, and no children had resulted. She had chosen not to marry again, so without a husband there was no way for her to have the son she so wanted. She did not hesitate to choose this baby for her own son, the child given to her by the great Nile. "He will be a prince in Egypt," she said.

"But he is too young to be weaned, princess."

At that instant Miriam knew why she had been brought to this place, and she stepped forward to make her presence known. The princess turned at the sound of her footsteps.

Miriam bowed down, touched her face to the ground. "Your Highness," she said, "I saw you take the baby from the water."

"Who are you?"

"My name is Miriam. My father is Amram."

"What do you want, child?"

"The baby will need a nursing mother."

Kali nodded. "Why, that is true enough."

"Shall I bring one of the Hebrew mothers? I know one who has recently lost her baby. She would be glad to nurse your child."

"Yes," Kali said. "That is necessary. Go at once and bring her here."

As Miriam turned and ran away, running with all her strength, she knew now with certainty that God was in the life of the baby that the princess had named Moses. Somehow the great God of Abraham and Isaac and Jacob had given Moses back to his family, and she could not wait to tell her parents the news. "Mother will have her baby to nurse and to raise—at least for a while," she murmured as she ran on toward the slave camp.

PART ONE

EGYPT

CHAPTER

I

Being the favorite daughter of the pharaoh, Princess Kali had several residences, one of which was an apartment in the harem of the pharaoh. There she could visit with her unmarried sisters, who their father kept in the harem for the purposes of making political alliances. He had done this with Kali herself before she was married, but when her husband died, he had welcomed her back, for she was the most intellectual of all his daughters—and the one who pleased him the most.

Kali enjoyed the harem and the friendship with her sisters and with the pharaoh's concubines. She had come to her apartment today to visit with her sisters. Her quarters were close to the main gate and were surrounded by flowers of all kinds, which she herself had planted. Bright murals decorated the walls with images of falcons, fish, and the residents of the harem itself.

Kali had been speaking with two of her sisters when suddenly the cry was heard, "The pharaoh is coming!"

All three girls quickly rose and faced the door. When the pharaoh entered, they bowed low, and the pharaoh smiled to greet them. "Well, girls, are you glad to see your father?"

"It is always good to see you, Father," Kali said.

"Good. I must talk with you, Kali. You girls run along."

As soon as the sisters were gone, Kali asked, "Can I get you some refreshment?"

"No, I think not." Pharaoh Seti I took his seat on one of the curved benches padded with leather and leaned back against the wall, closing his eyes. He was a small man, and people who met him for the first time were always shocked that the god of Egypt could be so insignificant in appearance. But however insignificant Seti might appear outwardly, he was a shrewd man. He had to be in order to rule over Egypt, with its powerful armies of well-trained soldiers, another army of slaves, and enemies on the borders who sought every opportunity to break through and steal the riches of Egypt.

"Moses is returning," Pharaoh said. He opened his unusual slate gray eyes and looked pointedly at Kali. "Have you had any messages?"

"Yes, Father. He sent a runner to tell me he would be here soon."

Pharaoh closed his eyes but did not seem to relax. He opened them again and said, "He has proven himself to be an able soldier."

"Yes, I am very proud of him."

"You always were." Seti sat up straighter and leaned forward. "The most difficult thing for me to understand is your attachment to this man. It has always been a mystery to me."

"I always wanted a son. My husband did not give me one, so the gods did."

"You think Moses is a gift of the gods?" Seti smiled suddenly. "The priests would not agree with you."

"No, they would not."

In fact, the priests had no use at all for Moses. They called him "The Stranger" and spread tales about him. They dared not attack him, for he was the adopted son of Pharaoh's favorite daughter, but they hated and feared him. After all, the pharaoh had only one son. If that son were to die, it was not impossible that Moses, the adopted Hebrew son of Pharoah's daughter, might be in line for the throne.

"They are envious of him," Kali said with a smile. "He excels them all in the arts and sciences of Egypt."

"Indeed he has. It might have been better for him if he had not been quite so accomplished. He would not be such a threat to them if he were stupid."

"It's a little late for Moses to become stupid, Father."

"I agree. But I must warn you that the opposition from the priesthood is growing stronger. He does not reverence the gods properly, or so they say. You must have noticed it yourself."

Kali hesitated. Indeed she had noticed that Moses was not overly religious. She had cautioned him on this already, but now she studied her father, wondering if his message meant more than it appeared to. "Do you think he is in danger?"

"Yes, I do, and I have come to tell you that you must help him join himself to our people and our ways."

"I have tried, but he is a stubborn man," Kali said. "He is a strange mixture of sweetness and stubbornness. He will do any-thing for me except what I ask him to do!" She laughed. "Maybe all strong men are like that. You're like that yourself, Father."

Pharaoh Seti laughed too and stood to his feet. He came over and put his arm around Kali and said, "You must teach him, daughter."

"Teach him what?"

"Teach him to at least go through the motions of religion. It may mean the difference between life and death."

"Yes. I will try. And I'm grateful to you for giving me this counsel."

Pharaoh kissed her on the cheek and shook his head. "Sweet and stubborn. Try to talk him out of the stubbornness. He needs to be sweet if he's going to pacify those priests of mine."

Amram's family had gathered, along with many others of the slaves. It was one of the rare occasions when the slaves were granted time off from the brickyard, in this case to help celebrate a victory. The Egyptian army was coming back from a conquest, and the overseers had been commanded to line up the slaves along the road down which the conqueror and his troops would come.

In this case the conqueror was none other than Moses, Prince of Egypt. Amram and his family had not spoken to Moses since he had been taken away from them. As soon as he was weaned, the princess had sent for him to be schooled in the palace, where he was thoroughly trained to be a soldier and a scientist, as well as to learn the difficult art of writing.

Amram and Jochebed had grown old, but their children, Miriam and Aaron, were now fine-looking adults. As the family stood along the parade route, Miriam cried out, "Look, they're coming."

Every eye went to the procession that began to pass. First came the infantry, their spears glinting in the bright noon sunshine. Hardened by warfare and training, they were strong men, their faces burned by the sun.

Next came the archers, with their bows and quivers on their backs. More soldiers followed in a seemingly endless procession until finally a cry went up, "There he is! Moses the prince!"

Miriam fixed her eyes on the approaching chariot and stepped out in front of the crowd. The movement caught the eye of the tall, powerful man who stood in the chariot beside the driver. Moses wore the uniform of a general, and the sunlight made his golden armor flash. Their eyes met, and she saw Moses draw back his head in a strange motion, almost that of recognition. She had seen him before, but it was always from a distance. Every time Moses appeared in public, Miriam made it a point to be there and be seen by him, so she knew he must remember her face by now.

Moses turned his head as the chariot passed, keeping his eye on Miriam, and then he suddenly snapped around, shaking his head as if to clear it.

"He recognized you, Miriam," Aaron whispered. "All the years of putting yourself before him have paid off."

"Yes, I saw him look at you, daughter," Amram said.

They watched the procession sadly as lines of captives shuffled past in shackles—more slaves to make bricks and build Pharaoh's cities. Old and young, strong and feeble, these prisoners of war appeared dazed, confused, and exhausted. Bruised and wounded from their battles, they dragged by in weary resignation of their fate: They would die in this land and never again see the homes from which they had been callously stolen.

When the procession of Egypt's triumphant spoils of war was over, Amram turned to go home, and the family followed him back in silence. When they reached their hut, Miriam prepared a simple meal for them.

Aaron was thinking about Moses as he ate. "I can't get over the way he recognized you, Miriam. I wish he had looked at me."

"He will someday," Miriam said.

"That's not likely," Amram muttered, his mouth stuffed with soft bread. "He will never be a true Hebrew."

"He *is* a true Hebrew, Father," Miriam said firmly.

Jochebed studied her daughter. "You've believed for years that the Redemption will come through your brother."

The *Redemption* was the way the Hebrews described their future hope and dreams of freedom. The more devout among them, at least, believed that a day would come when they would no longer be slaves but free men and women in their own land. Miriam was one of those devout. There was no doubt in her mind of a glorious future for her people, though many had given up any hope and succumbed to a life of despair. Her own father had little faith in the promised Redemption.

"Yes," Miriam declared boldly. "I do believe that Moses will be used as an instrument of God to bring about our Redemption."

"I think you're right, sister," Aaron agreed, excitement dancing in his eyes at such a wonderful idea. "He's close to the pharaoh. He can have great influence."

"He doesn't even know we're alive," Amram grumbled.

Miriam kept quiet, feeling it useless to argue with her father and wanting to be alone with her thoughts. She was not of Aaron's mind that Israel would be set free through political maneuvering. God would do something else, something startling. She had heard the old stories of her forefathers—of Abraham, Isaac, and Jacob—and it seemed God never did what people expected. His actions were always beyond human reasoning or imagination. She kept all this in her heart and said no more, but she thought constantly about the Redemption and how God would bring it about.

———————

"Moses, you're here!"

Kali jumped from her couch and came running as Moses

entered her apartment. He reached his arms wide and enclosed the small, fragile woman in his embrace, holding her almost like a child. "Yes, Mother, the conquering hero has come."

She pulled him over to the couch and said, "Come sit down. You must tell me everything. Don't leave out any detail."

Moses laughed as he sat down beside her and studied her face. "You're looking well," he said.

"Your mother is growing old, Moses."

"No, you'll never be old."

The constant care of her maids had kept Kali looking almost like a young woman, but Moses could see a weariness in her face that troubled him. "You must take care of yourself," he said, holding her small hand in both of his large ones. "What would I do without my mother to take care of me?"

Moses and his mother had always been very close—closer even than many natural-born sons and their mothers. As Kali felt the strength in his hands and looked into his gentle eyes, she reveled in his youthful vigor, the breadth of his shoulders, the strength of his corded neck. He was a virile, handsome man, and she once again wondered, as she often did, why he so insistently refused marriage. There had been plenty of prospects, with many beautiful young women of royal birth vying for his attention.

She reined in her thoughts and focused on Moses' story. He was not as good a speaker as many, but he was full of the adventure and could make the battles come alive for his mother. He spun his tale of military conquest while the servants brought and served them a meal. He continued talking with his mouth full, barely pausing long enough to chew and swallow.

Kali reveled in hearing his exploits. Ever since pulling him out of the Nile as a helpless infant, her life had become focused solely on him. She thought of that long-ago moment now as he sat beside her, glowing with health and strength, and she stroked his hand, proud and happy in his success.

Finally the story drew to a close. Kali begged for more, but Moses shrugged his shoulders. "That's all, Mother. Do you want me to think up some lies to tell you about how brave I was in battle?"

"You don't have to lie, my son. I've heard from your lieutenants how very brave you are."

Moses laughed. "They wouldn't dare speak ill of their commander, would they?"

"No, that is true." She paused. "Son, there's something I must speak with you about."

"I think I can guess what it is, Mother."

"Yes, you probably can, but I have to say it anyway. You must be more careful in your observance of our ceremonial laws."

Moses knew his mother was going to say this, and he sighed with frustration. For reasons he could not explain, he had no interest in the vast pantheon of Egyptian gods. He knew he was not an Egyptian by birth—Kali had not kept that information from him—but being a prince, he had tried his whole life to accept the gods and make them his own. The more he tried, however, the more he hated them all.

He did not know why he had such a deep aversion for the gods, particularly for Osiris, the Lord of Death, seated on his throne ready to judge the souls of the dead when they were brought before him. He also despised Horus, the son of Osiris, with his falcon head. It was Horus that, according to Egyptian theology, brought the dead before Osiris, took out the heart and weighed it. Then the dead man was either taken to some sort of paradise or transformed into a black boar. Moses saw in Egypt's religion nothing but death. The pharaohs spent their lives building tombs and collecting riches to go in them, believing they could enjoy the death they could not escape.

"You know how I feel about this, Mother," Moses said. "We've discussed it many times. Why are you bringing it up now?"

"Because I think you could be in real danger."

"I know that Jafari despises me," Moses said. "He may be the high priest of all of Egypt and almost as rich and powerful as Pharaoh himself, but he is not going to touch the pharaoh's own grandson, is he?"

"You cannot assume that, my son," Kali insisted. "He is a dangerous enemy. I have been aware of his hatred for you for a long time."

"Why do you suppose he hates me so?"

"Because you are a threat to him. He hates anything he cannot control."

"Well, he can't control *me*," Moses said, his eyes narrowing in anger. Then he saw the troubled look on his mother's face and could not bear her anguish. "I promise you, Mother, that from here on I will be more attentive to the ceremonies of the gods."

"But you don't believe in them, do you?"

"No, I do not. I wish I could. It would make life much simpler." He looked at her and turned his head to one side. Reaching out, he put his hand on her cheek and asked quietly, "Do *you* believe in them, Mother?"

"What else is there to believe in?"

"I don't know," Moses said slowly, gazing out the window at the distant horizon. "But there must be more than the gods of Egypt."

Kali shook her head at her son's musing. Why was it so difficult for him just to accept what was? But nonetheless she was relieved to have gained at least one concession from him. It was a beginning, and it emboldened her to speak of another of her concerns. "I have one more thing to speak to you about. Why haven't you married?"

"We're back to that," Moses said with a shrug. "I really don't know, Mother. I simply have no answer for you."

"You could have married many women, Moses—beautiful, wealthy women with royal blood."

"That is true, but I have desired none of them. If I could find a woman like you, I would probably change my mind, but I doubt if there is one." Moses' face clouded, and he said gloomily, "I've thought about this myself so many times, but the best way I can put it to you is that I believe I have some purpose in this life that is greater than marrying and having children."

"How can you say such a thing?" Kali lifted her hands in frustration. "Nothing is more important than having a child to carry on your name and your very life. How else can you continue to be a part of this world after you've gone to the next one?" Kali reached out for his hand, capturing it between her two small ones. Her love for him radiated from her eyes. "You are my whole life, Moses. You are a prince of Egypt now, and you must think about the future."

Moses shook his head sadly. He knew his mother would never understand what was inside him. He had a restlessness that drove him daily to wonder where his life was going, what was he here for? He knew he would never be satisfied with all the wealth and power that Egypt had to offer him, and when it was suggested once that he might one day become the pharaoh, he had merely laughed. "Who would want such misery?"

Those who had heard his shocking answer had repeated it to others, until the matter had reached the ears of the high priest, Jafari. Suspicious of everyone, Jafari had demanded that his subordinates be on the constant lookout for heresy and immediately report any of it to him. That such disbelief and arrogance existed in the highest echelons of the land infuriated him.

"I am begging you to be careful, my son," Kali went on. "Jafari does not like your strange independence. He believes it is not fitting for a prince of Egypt, and he will not hesitate to remove you by any means."

Moses gave her another warm embrace. "Don't worry so, Mother. I will be fine. I do not believe that Jafari's power is as great as he thinks it is."

Kali said no more but could not hold back her tears over her son's stubbornness. She was convinced that his bravado was going to get him killed someday. She clung to him now, deeply troubled that she could not convince him to conform to the conventions expected of a prince of Egypt.

CHAPTER

2

Moses inhaled deeply of the intoxicating river air. It was like wine to him as he stood in the prow of one of the royal boats that had come to hunt for hippos in the Nile. As the boat plowed through the waters near the shore, the air exploded with the sounds and sights of hundreds of birds rising into the sky. Many varieties flew out of the rushes together, including the black-and-white ibis, sacred to the goddess of the river, as well as great blue herons, geese, and ducks.

Glancing down, Moses saw movement in the water beneath the hull. He held up his spear with its eight-inch head, honed to razor sharpness. His heart beat faster as he saw a huge form walking along the bottom of the river. The massive animal moved rapidly, even underwater, and Moses shouted to the oarsmen, "Pull! Pull for your lives!"

Shouts of pleasure and excitement rose from the other boats. The priesthood kept a strict account of the number of hippos living in the river and set a limit on how many could be killed. This day the limit was twenty, which would provide a much needed supply of meat to the Egyptian population, but it would also leave enough of the huge beasts to keep the river's edge free of the choking weeds that grew so rapidly.

Directly in front of Moses' boat, a monstrous form burst through the surface about thirty feet from where he stood in the prow. Moses lifted his spear and shouted again to the oarsmen, who bent their naked, sunburned backs to the task as they sent the craft shooting straight toward the beast.

Without warning, the monster turned, and Moses found himself looking directly into gaping jaws, jaws big enough to swallow a man whole. Moses lifted his spear high as the animal bore down upon him. He brought his arm forward, and the spear went directly into the huge maw of the monster. It responded with a frightening cry of fury as great fountains of blood spewed forth from its mouth. With its final breath, the dying animal lunged at Moses' craft, striking it and sending it reeling backward, spilling Moses and his four crewmen into the water.

As the water closed over Moses' head, he had one chilling moment of fear. He had known desperate times in battle, but the thought of being cut in half by the huge beast was different. His arms beat wildly as he struggled to the surface. He glanced around to see the oarsmen floundering and making for the shore. Quickly he turned and saw that the hippo was dead, its body rolling upside down, its four legs sticking up like pillars.

"Stop!" Moses commanded his oarsmen. "Get back in the boat and we'll tow this fellow to shore."

The oarsmen returned and attached ropes to the dead beast so they could drag him up onto shore. Moses stood off to one side, watching with interest. Although normally only the priests were allowed to eat the flesh of the hippo, one exception was made during the ten days of the festival of Ra, when the common people— including the Hebrew slaves—were permitted to share in the beasts that were killed in the Nile.

Moses watched as teams of men worked to attach ropes to the huge beasts that had been killed by the entire hunting party and dragged them ashore, ignoring the deadly threat of crocodiles that lurked along the river's edge. That was foolhardy, for the scaly creatures were known to rush out on shore and seize children playing near the water's edge and women washing their clothes.

Moses sat on a large flat rock, letting the sun dry his wet garments. He watched as the men, women, and children on the lowest scale of Egypt's social strata lined the shore. He was aware of the stories concerning his birth, for his mother had told him how she had found him as an infant in a basket in the river. The story was no secret among the people either, and everyone knew that Moses was not an Egyptian but one of the Hebrews, whose male children the pharaoh was determined to eradicate.

During his growing years, his mother was unable to tell him very much about his Hebrew origins, but he was intensely curious to know more about the Hebrew people. He did not think of them as "his" people, for having been raised in the royal palace, he saw himself as an Egyptian prince. Nevertheless, he had paused many times to watch the slaves as they hewed out massive stone blocks to build the pharaoh's pyramids, and in the marketplace he would sometimes watch the emaciated, bent bodies of the slaves and wonder what it was like to live their lives.

Now he watched those slaves being allowed to haul out one of the hippos. The daily diet of the slaves was monotonous, and the prospect of fresh meat stirred the people to a frenzy. Men and women alike, and even the older children, hauled at the ropes to draw in the carcass. As soon as they reached the shore, the Hebrews swarmed over the hippo, their knives and axes flashing in the sun. Blood and bone flew as the blades cut and sawed. Moses saw more than one of the Hebrews get a serious wound as they slashed at the flesh of the beast with razor-sharp knives.

Moses, who had never known a hungry day in his life, wondered what it was like to have this kind of hunger. He knew that normally months would pass between one mouthful of meat and the next for these slave families, but this festival was a time when normal restraints were thrown away. He watched as a woman hacked and sawed at the hippo, opening up a tremendous cavity. She was plastered with blood, and reaching down inside, she drew out the liver, which she threw to her children, then went back to pulling at the flesh of the beast. A fire had been built on the shore, and the oldest children threw the liver on the coals while the younger watched, crowding around and yelping like wild beasts themselves.

Soon a man and woman, who were presumably husband and wife, grabbed the scorched liver off the fire and threw other chunks of meat on it. The flesh of the hippo was delicious in Moses' opinion, and he watched as the people, who were starved for animal fat, went wild gorging themselves, cramming the juicy, fatty meat into their mouths. While the people were still carving out the meat, the priests were going around collecting the ivory teeth, which belonged to the pharaoh and were as valuable as the elephant tusks brought from the land of Cush far to the south. The hides were given to the army to be turned into leather war shields. The meat that could not be consumed on the riverbank would be pickled in brine, smoked, or dried. Much of it would be used to feed the army, the lawyers, the keepers of the temple, and other civil servants.

"Quite a sight, eh, Lord Moses?"

Moses turned to see Majal, his chief lieutenant, who had come to stand beside him. Majal was a short, muscled individual with gaps between his teeth and a pair of bright, snapping black eyes. He was an expert soldier, and if he was afraid of anything on earth, no one ever found out about it.

"Have you wondered, Majal, what it would be like to be a slave?"

Majal stood stock-still for a moment, his black eyes fixed on Moses. "Why would I think about that?"

"I think about it," Moses said. "Look at them. They're starving to death. That is probably the first meat some of those children have ever seen."

Majal shifted uneasily. He knew Moses' history, and now that Moses himself was referring to the Hebrews, he had a sudden thought. "You can't think about things like that," he said. "People are born according to the will of Ra."

"You really believe that?"

"Well, it's what the priests tell us."

"Don't believe everything you hear," Moses said.

Moses watched the archers in the boats killing the crocodiles that swarmed to the fresh blood of the slain hippos. Harpooners were driving their lances through the tough, scaly hides. Many of the harpooners were so skillful that it took only one thrust to kill the beast, but if they missed, the croc would roll, twisting the harpoon and dragging the men under the water with it. Moses saw at least two men killed by the crocodiles.

Majal watched Moses for a while, thinking what a strange master he had, then said, "I'm going to find me a woman. Come along."

"No, I'll stay here, Majal."

Majal shrugged his massive shoulders and sauntered off. Moses had been seized by a feeling he could not understand, a feeling that he was being watched, and his eyes searched the seething crowd as they feasted on the meat. He spotted a woman who took no part in the festivities. She was tall and thin and wore the typical garb of a slave woman. She was not beautiful, for a lifetime of hard labor had etched itself into her face.

Nonetheless, her eyes caught at Moses, and he realized he had seen her before. Memories came rushing back, and he knew that this woman, whoever she was, had sought him out many times. He remembered seeing her when he was a very young man, when he would often wander through the streets of the city. He had thought little of it then, but now something in him responded to her.

Her eyes were light brown, her skin roughened by blowing sand and exposure to the blistering Egyptian sun. He could see that her hands were hard and calloused, but it was not her physical appearance that held Moses there. Rather it was the intensity of her gaze.

Impulsively he started toward her, but after two or three steps he stopped. Something passed between the two of them as each ignored the yells and laughter and noises of the crowd. Moses seemed to be drawn into the woman's eyes and could not understand why.

Why is she watching me? he thought. An irrational fear seized him. Without another word he turned and moved away, keeping his back to the woman. He did not turn to look at her but could feel her eyes boring into his back, and he hastened his pace to get away from her as quickly as he could.

———————

"This is good, daughter," Amram muttered, savoring another piece of roasted hippo meat. He could not chew but enjoyed sucking out the juices. His eyes were alight with pleasure as the fat ran down his beard.

Jochebed laughed, staring at her husband. "You're a pretty sight," she said. "You eat like an old crocodile, snapping at your food."

"Say what you will," Amram grunted, ignoring his wife's taunts. "We don't get meat like this very often."

Miriam and Aaron had been able to procure a goodly portion of the meat, and Miriam and Jochebed had roasted it, preserving the grease in which to soak the thin flour cakes she had baked over the coals.

Miriam had said little during the meal, but when everyone had finished and her mother rose to gather and clean the wooden dishes, she said, "I saw Moses this afternoon . . . and he saw me."

Aaron turned to face her, his eyes alight. "Did he speak to you?"

"He started to," Miriam said with a nod. "He turned, saw me, and our eyes met." Her voice was soft, but there was an excitement in it. "He recognized me, I'm sure."

"He should," Jochebed said, staring at her daughter. "You've pursued him all of his life."

"You should have spoken to him before this," Aaron said.

"What would I say?" Miriam countered.

"You could ask him how he feels having his family in slavery while he lives in the palace."

"That's enough of that!" Amram quickly admonished Aaron. "God spared his life."

"Spared him for what?" Aaron said with irritation. "So he could wear fine clothes and eat the best of food while we starve?"

It was an old argument in the family. Aaron, for years, had tried to convince Jochebed and Amram that they should approach Moses. His argument had been that Moses was wealthy, the son of the daughter of Pharaoh. It would be nothing to him to give a dozen golden rings to his family. He would never miss them. Jochebed, however, had refused, and she refused now.

"It was God who saved him, and God will have to do whatever must be done."

"I think we should speak to the elders about my brother."

Miriam had spoken quietly, but the three members of her family turned to look at her. "What would we say?" Amram asked.

"I don't know, but it might be that they will know better than we what to do about Moses."

Amram fell silent, and his head dropped. Grease from the meat stained his beard, but he paid it no heed. Finally he lifted his head and stared at Miriam. "You may be right, daughter. I will go to the elders and see what they say."

"Good," Aaron said, his eyes sparking with excitement. "Now maybe we'll get some good out of what God has done in the life of my brother."

The elders of Israel were holding one of their regular meetings. Korah, the head elder, was a heavyset man with a round face and a black beard that covered most of his features. His eyes were also black and conveyed a sense of power. He sat within the circle of elders and dominated any decisions they made.

Like all the Hebrews, Korah was a slave, but he had managed to accumulate some property, and this fact gave him power in this nation of slaves. The other elders were also better off than most of the slaves, wearing garments that were not tattered and appearing far healthier than most of the Hebrew men. These were men who through cunning had won certain privileges with the Egyptians and now served as overseers under the Egyptian overseers. The Hebrew slaves resented having some of their own people as overseers, but they also feared and respected them for having gained such a position.

Korah had just said, "We will do no more today but tomorrow—" He never finished his statement for the cloth door of the hut suddenly opened and Amram walked in.

"What is it, Amram?" Korah said with irritation. "Can't you see we're having a meeting?"

"Yes, I know. That is why I came." Amram bowed low and said quickly, "There is a matter I would bring before the elders of Israel."

"Well, what is it?" Korah snapped impatiently. "We don't have time for small things."

"I have come," Amram said hurriedly, "to speak of my son Moses."

Instantly every eye turned toward the old man who stood before them. He was bent and frail and had no authority, but every one of the elders knew the story of his son and how he had been delivered from death and become part of Pharaoh's family.

"What about Moses?" Korah demanded.

"My family and I have been wondering if he would be willing to do something to help our people."

Korah's face flushed. "If he had wanted to help us, he would have done it long ago."

Eli, one of the elders, said, "Perhaps he doesn't know who he is."

"Of course he knows!" Korah snapped. "Everybody in Egypt knows. Why should he be ignorant of his origin?"

"Amram may be right," Jacob, a tall thin man with hawklike features, spoke up. "We need all the help we can get, and he has the pharaoh's ear."

"That's right," Eli said eagerly. "One word to his mother, Princess Kali, would be all it would take."

"Yes," Jacob agreed, nodding vigorously. "The pharaoh listens to her."

"Why would he listen to a woman?" Korah said with displeasure.

"That is hard to understand, but in this case I know it is so," Jacob insisted.

Korah stared around the circle of elders and then turned to face Amram. "What would you have us to do?"

"I would not know how to advise you. You are the wise men of our people. Surely you can think of some way that Moses can be of help to us."

Korah stared at the old man, then shook his head in disgust. "Expect no help from your son. He has had years to give it to us, and he has not even once acknowledged that you are his family and that we are his people. Speak no more of this, Amram."

"It shall be as you say," Amram said.

He bowed to the elders and left the hut, and a lively discussion ensued. Jacob and Eli joined together to try to convince Korah and the other elders that there might be some wisdom in what the old man had suggested.

"After all, what would be the harm in trying?"

"We have other things to do," Korah snapped. "I will hear no more of this." He rose and the meeting was over.

Jacob and Eli left together, discussing the meeting as they returned to their homes. "Korah is jealous of any authority that might threaten his own," Eli said. "He is afraid he will lose his power if Moses comes to help us."

Jacob looked around and said, "I wouldn't speak those words if I were you. Korah has long ears."

At the insistence of his Egyptian mother, Moses made an effort to show more interest in religion—not because he had any faith in the gods of Egypt, but for her sake. It also made sense to placate the high priest, Jafari, the most powerful man in Egypt next to the pharaoh. Moses knew that to cross him would invite disaster.

The sun was shining brightly, and the temple areas were busy. Moses made his way down the crowded streets, passing by many of the temples. For the Egyptians, a temple was the home on earth for the god or goddess to whom it was dedicated. Normally only priests and priestesses went inside, while the worshipers themselves went only as far as the entrance.

The temple before which Moses paused was colorful, the outer wall painted with images of the gods and scenes of the pharaoh's conquests. Two large sphinxes—carved figures with a lion's body and a ram's head—guarded the entrance. Two scribes sat at the temple gates. If someone wanted to ask the god a question, they asked the scribe to write it down and then this was taken inside the temple.

Moses moved closer and noticed that there were several figures placed against the temple wall. These small clay objects were carvings of the god, with two ears carved into them, and served to remind the gods that they were to listen to the person's prayers.

Moses' lips twisted with disdain as he stared at the objects. *Why would a god have to have clay ears?* he thought and shook his head. He was about to join those who were praying outside the temple when suddenly the same eerie feeling he had felt during the slaughter of the hippos came to him. Turning quickly, he saw the same woman staring at him. She made no attempt to speak, but her eyes seemed enormous.

Anger seized Moses, for he was always angered by things he could not understand. But his anger turned to a determination to speak with her, and he strode over to where she stood. Though she was a tall woman, he towered over her and she seemed frail as she stood before him.

"Why do you always watch me?" Moses demanded. He kept his voice low, for he knew Jafari's spies followed him constantly.

Showing no fear, the woman lifted her head and stared directly into his eyes. "Because you are my brother," she said quietly.

The words were spoken in a whisper, scarcely audible even to Moses, but they rocked him to the very depth of his soul. He knew the story of his rescue from the Nile as an infant, but his mother had never told him any more than that about his origins. He had always wondered how it had come to be that the son of Hebrew slaves had escaped certain death and now occupied a high position in the Egyptian world. For a moment he even felt light-headed, and a faint hope came to him.

"What do you mean I am your brother? That's impossible." He waited for the woman to answer the charge, to argue, but she said nothing, simply stood looking up at him. Moses saw something in that look he could not identify at first, but then it came to him. The light he saw in her eyes was love, and this shocked him more than anything else.

"I am your brother?" he asked. "How do you know?"

"It was I who put you into the basket in the Nile. My name is Miriam."

Moses stared at the woman, and though everything in him fought to rise up in doubt, there was something so simple and plain in the woman's expression that he could not speak for a moment. When he did his voice came hoarsely. "Take me to my family!"

CHAPTER

3

The camp within the land of Goshen where the Hebrews lived was alive with movement. Many of the shelters were only three-sided to allow the occupants to stay cooler in the searing Egyptian sun, but such structures also allowed for little privacy. Moses wondered as he followed Miriam through the camp what it would be like to live with your life always on display. Even with all the difficulties he had in his mind with his life at the palace, he knew suddenly that these people—his own people—had suffered as he could not even imagine.

Miriam took him along a winding path where women were hard at work in little gardens, no more than ten feet square. Others were cooking over fires. Women and young people were laboring up from the river with pots of water, either on their heads or suspended from a yoke. Several women were grinding corn by pounding the grain with a rock.

The activity of the camp stunned Moses, and he gazed about him with hungry eyes, wondering again how it came to be that he was not among these people. He saw children of every age, but he also became aware as they moved through the camp that boys were a rarity. He felt sick when he realized that many of the Hebrew boys had been killed as infants, and that the Hebrews feared him in his Egyptian dress, feared that more of their sons would be taken and were now hiding their sons from him.

Finally the two arrived at their destination. This area was much better cared for than much of what he had seen. The gardens were larger, with rows of cucumbers, leeks, garlic, beans, oats, and barley all neatly arranged.

Everywhere were animals, mostly goats and sheep, but also ducks and hens, clucking and pecking at the ground. A small pond had been created to give the ducks a home, the larger ducks being followed by a line of tiny yellow ducklings.

Moses saw that Miriam had stopped in front of a dwelling built of reeds, the entrance of which was covered by a woven rug.

"In here," Miriam whispered. She drew the covering back, and Moses stooped to step inside. The interior was lit by a candle, and sunlight streamed through slots on three sides, illuminating the scene before him. Moses was startled to find himself fearful in these surroundings. He had faced the horrors of battle and the threat of death many times, so why should he be afraid in this slave hut? He could not explain it, so he stood quietly, noting that the woman had stepped inside too. She touched his arm. "This is your family, Moses. This is your father, Amram. Your mother, Joche-bed—and your brother, Aaron."

Moses scanned the three quickly, his gaze coming to rest upon his mother. She was worn and burned by the sun, and her eyes were netted with red veins. She had lost most of her teeth, and her arms were thin as sticks. She was not beautiful, yet Moses could not take his eyes off of her. He bowed and saw that all three of them were speechless. He turned then to face his father. "I am your son?" he whispered.

"Yes. God has preserved you marvelously."

"You are welcome, Moses," Aaron said. "I have long wished to speak with you."

Moses studied Aaron, his mind working slowly in his confusion. "I cannot understand any of this," he said finally. "I know nothing of you or of your lives. All I know is my life in the royal court."

"That is natural," Aaron said, apparently speaking for the family. "How could you know us when you have never been with us?"

"Tell me about yourself, about the Hebrews," Moses said.

"What do you already know?" Aaron asked. He was a sharp-eyed man, highly intelligent and eager to speak. "Do you believe that we are your family?"

"Everyone knows the story of how I was found—taken out of the Nile by Princess Kali, who became my foster mother."

"Then you must know, son, why we did this," Jochebed said. Her voice was thin, and her eyes seemed enormous as she gazed at her tall and robust son. "So many boy babies were being killed. I prayed, and God told me what to do."

"Which god?" Moses asked.

"There is only one God," Aaron said quickly. "The God of all the earth."

Moses considered this, then asked, "Where did all of you come from?"

"Our family came to Egypt many years ago to escape a famine in our land. Our ancestors were men of great wealth, and for a time we prospered here, for one of our ancestors had risen high in the pharaoh's sight. But when that pharaoh died, another pharaoh came, and gradually we were enslaved by the Egyptians."

Moses studied his brother, who was tall and well built, with a neatly trimmed black beard. "Why is it that you are not permitted to worship the gods of Egypt?" Moses asked.

"We came here not as prisoners but as free men at the invitation of the pharaoh himself," Aaron explained. "We have kept our identity as Hebrews and worship the only God. We have records of every child that has been born."

Moses was astonished by this. "Every child? But that must be thousands."

"Yes, the records are extensive, but it is necessary to preserve the history of the family lines. We keep them in secret places out in the desert."

"Why do you maintain your family lines so carefully?"

A glow appeared in Aaron's eyes, and he lifted his hand in a victorious gesture. "Because one day, Moses, we will no longer be slaves. Our forefathers have prophesied to us that the day of our redemption will surely come. Every true Hebrew looks forward to the day that our servitude in Egypt will be over."

"How can you know all this?"

"As I told you, we keep records. Our elders have now reckoned that the four hundred years foretold by one of our forefathers, who was a prophet, is almost finished. When the end of that period comes, we will be redeemed from our slavery."

"What is the name of your god?"

Moses saw his family react oddly to this. Amram shook his head slightly but did not speak. His mother explained, "We never speak His name, but He is the only God."

Moses studied his mother and said finally, "There once was a god in Egypt like that. A pharaoh wanted to replace all the gods by a single god named Aton, but after that pharaoh died, all the temples he had raised to Aton were destroyed and his name was rooted out."

"The God of our fathers is not like the gods of Egypt. They are made by the hands of men or created in the minds of men. The God of our fathers is the only God. He is the God of our forefathers Abraham, Isaac, and Jacob."

Moses had a burning desire to know more. "Please tell me more of the history of our people."

Miriam cried aloud with delight. "*Our* people! You believe, then, that we are your family and you are of the Hebrews?"

"Yes, I know it is so," Moses said, "but other than that, I know so little."

"Our elders could teach you everything," Aaron said. "I myself could teach you much, but it would be dangerous for you, Moses."

"Yes, it would," Miriam agreed. "You are watched constantly."

"I know," Moses said. "The high priest hates me, and the people do not trust me. They call me 'The Stranger,' yet I must know more. Teach me now, my brother."

Moses sat down on the dirt floor, and Aaron sat facing him. Aaron's face was alight with pleasure as he began to speak. "Our history begins with a man called Abraham. He was an idolater and had no children, but the only God spoke to him and promised that his offspring would one day be as numerous as the stars in heaven. . . ."

Moses found himself returning to the Hebrew slave camp often, spending many hours each time with his brother. He soaked up the stories of the forefathers of the twelve tribes of Israel, men like Abraham, Isaac, and Jacob. He was amazed at the detail Aaron knew of these ancient ancestors. Indeed, careful records had been kept over the centuries, for the Hebrews believed that their god had chosen them for a special purpose.

Moses was drawn to the Hebrews in a way he could not explain to himself, but he realized this interest had always been inside him. He had never felt like an Egyptian, no matter how high his position in the court, and now the stories of the heritage of the descendants of Abraham and the concept of one god over all things and all people consumed him.

One afternoon as he walked along the streets of the Egyptian capital, lined with its palatial homes and elaborate temples, he looked around at the opulence he saw and could not help contrasting it with the poverty and misery of the slave camp. He was stirred with a feeling he could not identify, but he knew it had something to do with the injustice Aaron had spoken of. *The Hebrews have been unjustly enslaved,* he thought. *They were not captives of war but came here as free men, at the invitation of the pharaoh, and yet now their lot is miserable.*

His thoughts were interrupted by his mother's voice: "Moses, come here."

Looking up, he saw Princess Kali and went to her at once. She was the one thing of Egypt that he loved and honored. He took her hand and bowed low before her. "Mother, how are you?"

"I am worried, my son. Where have you been?"

Moses suspected that Kali already knew. "I have been to the slave camp to speak with my brother, Aaron."

"Do you not know that the priests and his spies are well aware of your frequent visits there?"

"It doesn't matter."

"Of course it matters. They are looking for something to use against you."

"Then they will have to use it, because I must go back."

Princess Kali started to speak but realized it would be useless. Since the time he was very young, Moses had been obedient to her slightest whim—except for a few instances. She had seen an iron will in him and knew that at this time it would be useless to try to talk him out of his visits to the Hebrews.

"There's someone I want you to meet," she said instead.

Moses gave her a quick look. "And who is it, Mother?"

"A princess from Babylon. Her name is Olani."

"Let me guess," Moses said with a smile, then laughed loudly. "She's here looking for a husband."

"She's merely here on a visit."

"Oh, come now, Mother. Pharaoh wants to make an alliance with Babylon. We both know that. Everyone knows that."

"That has nothing to do with this young woman. She's a very lovely creature."

"I am sure she is. Bait is often quite attractive."

"Moses, you must meet her."

"Very well. I will if you insist. But I will not marry her."

Princess Kali heard the finality in her son's voice. "Very well," she said wearily, "but you must stop your visits to the slave camp. It's too dangerous." When he did not answer, she shrugged. "Come, then, and meet Princess Olani."

CHAPTER

4

As a member of the royal court, Moses had long been aware that the economy of Egypt was largely based on slave labor. He had often paused to watch the slaves building Pharaoh's palatial cities and gigantic burial pyramids, but he had never seen them as human beings. They had seemed more like oxen or donkeys.

Since Moses met his family, however, his perspective had changed, and when he went out at midday the day after Olani left for Babylon, he was drawn by an irresistible force to the brickyards where the materials for the construction were created. As he approached from the height of a slight hill, he saw the long lines of slaves below, appearing like serpents snaking across the brickyard. He could not make out individual workers from this vantage point, but as he moved closer, he took in the endless lines of slaves bearing yokes on their shoulders, some of them were bringing water from the river and others bringing clay from the banks.

Moses smelled the sweat of thousands of emaciated bodies toiling under the sun, but he also sensed the broken spirits of the men. He walked toward the pits where the loam was dumped and straw added to it. Water was poured in, and the bony slaves began treading out the materials, their naked bodies practically immersed.

When this was completed, other slaves drew the clay mixture out from the pit in buckets and hauled them to the brick makers, who fashioned the clay into bricks and laid them out to bake in the blazing sun.

Moses moved silently among the laborers. From time to time a slave would lift his eyes but would quickly avert them from Moses' gaze. Several times Moses would see an Egyptian taskmaster raise his whip and beat the naked back of a slave until the blood ran down to mix with the clay. *These men put their own sweat and blood into these bricks,* Moses thought.

He talked to one of the taskmasters, who boasted to the prince that the failure to produce the assigned number of bricks was not charged to any single worker but to an entire group, and at the end of the day the entire group was lashed if the tally was lacking. The daily count of bricks was carefully kept by scribes, who never failed to inform the taskmasters when the count was low. A chill went through the prince's soul as he listened to the callous bragging of the man.

The more Moses witnessed, the more his heart swelled with anguish, and his eyes blazed with such anger that he had to lower his head to keep his feelings from showing. Another thing he discovered, and which chilled his heart even more, was that not all of the taskmasters were Egyptian. Some of them were Hebrews. Every line of slaves had a Hebrew guard, and these guards drove their fellow Hebrews on as cruelly as the Egyptian overseers. His thoughts screamed out the injustice of it—*Hebrews helping to make slaves out of their Hebrew brothers! This is wrong!* The cry rose from his heart, but he did not allow it to drop from his lips.

Moving away from the brick-making area, Moses discovered another form of servitude. Slaves with matted hair and sweat pouring down their bodies were harnessed to each other by long ropes, throwing their combined weight into the task of pulling an enormous stone to which the ropes were harnessed. Atop each stone sat an Egyptian scribe, shouting commands to drive the slaves onward.

In the past Moses had observed such work from a distance but had never allowed his heart to acknowledge that the massive group of slaves was actually made up of human beings. Now as he moved among them, he discerned individuals. One man had lost an eye, another a hand—but they still performed their tasks. Even as Moses watched a frail old man with white hair who was assigned to throwing in the chopped straw, the slave suddenly reeled under the relentless heat of the sun and fell to the ground. When he could not be roused, one of the guards cursed and struck him in the head with a metal rod with a large metal ball on the top. The old man's skull broke, and the bright crimson blood stained his white hair. Gritting his teeth, Moses watched as the Egyptian continued to curse the man even after he was dead, kicking the lifeless body as if the old man had done something terribly wrong.

Most of all Moses was shocked by the faces of the slaves. Through long tangles of hair, their eyes were fixed expressionlessly on the ground, like the eyes of beasts enduring cruel torture. From time to time Moses saw the signs of rebellion in a slave, in his eyes or in his stiffened back, but the taskmaster was always quick to pick up on such behavior and apply additional whippings. By day's end, several slaves lay dead from the intense labor under the hot sun.

The visit ignited a flame in the heart of Moses, Prince of Egypt. Were these his brothers? His flesh and blood? His kin? Why were they subjected to such cruel treatment? The injustice of it flamed within him, and his anger turned on himself for letting so many years pass without a thought of his people. His lips trembled as the fury in him burned like a glowing furnace. He had heard tales from those who traveled widely of mountains that for centuries had appeared serene and idyllic but had without warning exploded, casting fire and burning mud high into the air and destroying everything about it. Now Moses felt like one of these mountains. He would not be able to contain the anger in his heart that was smoldering unseen. Sooner or later it was going to burst forth.

———————

"Prince Moses is here, sire."

Jafari, the high priest, was having his evening meal. He hated to have his meals interrupted, for he had a fierce appetite, his corpulent body even sweating from the effort. "Show him in," he grunted.

As soon as Moses entered and bowed, the high priest snapped, "I sent for you yesterday! What took you so long?"

"What can I do to serve you, master?"

"I have evil reports of your activities," Jafari said. He tore the meat from a bone with his teeth, chewed it fiercely and then washed it down with red wine, allowing it to spill over and run down his chin and clean-shaven chest. He did not allow even one hair to remain on his body, for parasites might lodge there and hence defile the high priest of Ra.

"You have been negligent in your temple duties. Weeks go by without a single visit from you."

"Have you been told this or have you seen it for yourself?"

"Don't be insolent to your priest!" Jafari shouted. "You well know I speak the truth. Your offerings have been sparse." Jafari swept the food away with his arm, and the silver dishes clattered onto the stone floor. A slave scurried to clean them up, cowering from Jafari's shouts of rage. Finally the priest mastered himself and said more quietly, "I have another charge. It is reported to me that you are spending time with the Hebrew slaves."

"I have been studying the brick-making process."

"For what purpose?"

"To see if it could be made more effective."

"More effective? The brick-making has always been effective."

"If you will permit me, I would like to offer a suggestion."

"A suggestion? What is it?"

"We have better sense than to wear out our animals. We keep them well fed, and we let them rest. We are not so wise with the slaves. They burn out quickly. This is not good economy."

Jafari grew silent then, his eyes narrowing to slits. "Slaves are different from animals."

"I am glad you see that, sir."

"Don't be insolent! They are different because they are capable of rebellion. Animals are not. We must keep the slaves weak or they might overcome us."

"Personally, O Priest of Ra, I am not afraid of what starving slaves might do."

It was a bold statement, and Jafari's face flushed red. "I will not argue this with you! You are being watched, Moses. I am giving you this warning. You think you are protected because your mother holds her hand over you, but you go too far."

"I am sorry you should say so," Moses said.

"Out! Get out! Amend your ways!"

Moses bowed and left without another word, his head held high, his body proud. As soon as he was outside, Jafari motioned for a tall, hawk-faced man with glittering eyes. "Nodi, watch him."

"We always watch him, sire."

"Find some fault that would bring him before the pharaoh. He must not live."

"We will watch him, sire."

Aaron listened intently as Moses repeated the essence of his visit with the high priest of Ra. When Moses was finished, Aaron shook his head. "You must be careful, brother."

"How can one be careful when our people are dying by the hundreds? They are starved and beaten as if they were animals!" Moses cried.

The two men were sitting alone at some distance from the Hebrew slave camp. Moses had gone to Aaron to tell him what he had seen and what he was thinking. "Something must be done, Aaron. I know that I am not the one to speak, for I have ignored my people for years, but now I see with fresh eyes all of the indignities heaped upon our people."

"You are an impulsive man, Moses, and this is good . . . and bad. Sometimes there is need for immediate action, and that is where you specialize. But I am different from you in that way. All my life I have watched the injustice of the Egyptian lords as they grind our people into the dust. I have waited, and now I believe your return to us is a sign." Aaron leaned forward and studied Moses' face. Finally he said, "You must use your influence to help your people."

"Influence? But I have none."

"Ah"—Aaron nodded emphatically—"but you could have. Your mother is the favorite of the pharaoh. He listens to her."

"That would never free our people, Aaron," Moses said. "Surely you must see that."

"I think it might. You are in too much of a hurry, Moses. You must be patient."

"Patient? Our people have been patient for hundreds of years."

"That is what God told the prophets long ago—that we would be slaves for four hundred years. But He also promised that we would be set free."

The two men talked earnestly, Aaron doing most of the talking as he explained the ancient prophecies.

Moses finally turned and put his inquisitive dark eyes on his brother. "What do you want, Aaron, for yourself and for our people?"

It was the opportunity Aaron had been waiting for. "Our people need a form of religion they can see and handle. It is not enough that God is a spirit. Men must see things."

"See what? If your god is a spirit with no body, what could they see?"

"They could see ceremonies that would be pictures of the qualities of God," Aaron said eagerly. He had thought this out carefully, and now words spilled from his mouth. "The Egyptians know this well. That is why they have so many ceremonies, so many temples, so many—"

"So many idols," Moses interrupted. "Surely you can't mean this."

Aaron was a perceptive individual and knew he had gone too far.

"Well, of course we do not want idols. But there is nothing wrong with ceremony. It gives people something to cling to. Now, back to the question at hand. Go to your mother. Have her beg the pharaoh to lighten the load on our people."

"That is not what I want. I want them to be free."

"That will come. One step at a time, brother—one step at a time!"

———

Moses was no longer sure of who he was. All his life he had known himself only as Moses, Prince of Egypt, but now another identity had suddenly arisen within him. Moses the Hebrew. Moses the servant, not of the gods of Egypt but of the formless god whose name could not even be spoken aloud but who had made all things.

Moses struggled with this intently, and he found much relief while sitting at the feet of the oldest of the elders. Zuriel was older than anyone knew, more than a hundred. He was kept as a treasure of the Hebrew people, for he remembered sitting at his great-grandfather's feet, and his great-grandfather could remember as a small child the Hebrews serving under the elderly Joseph's benevolent reign.

Day after day Moses went to Zuriel, soaking up the stories of his ancestors. Zuriel's body was frail, but his mind was still alert, and he remembered the stories in great detail. His old eyes were faded, but they glowed as he spoke of Abraham and Isaac and Jacob.

Moses sat still as a stone, listening intently as Zuriel spoke of Jacob's death.

"He was not as good a man as his grandfather Abraham," old Zuriel said, nodding his head constantly. "But he was a crafty fellow. He had twelve sons, and his twelve sons became the twelve tribes of Israel." He looked over at Moses and smiled toothlessly. "We know you are of the tribe of Levi, one of those sons."

"How do we know all this? It was so long ago."

"We are not a strong people in many ways, but we Hebrews are strong on tradition," old Zuriel said. "We guard what we have heard and repeat these stories over and over to keep them firm in our memories. We pass these along to our sons, and they pass them to their sons. Our traditions are everything to us."

"Tell me about the other sons of Jacob out of which our tribes came."

"Reuben was the firstborn and would have been the leader of Israel's sons, but he forfeited his birthright by sleeping with his father's concubine. Had he become the leader of Israel, his tribe would have been the most significant, but that never happened."

"Which one of the sons *did* receive the birthright?" Moses asked.

"Ah, you go right to the point. It was Judah." The old man

began to chant in a voice that was weak at first, but grew stronger as he recited the ancient prophecy:

"Judah, your brothers will praise you; your hand will be on the neck of your enemies; your father's sons will bow down to you.

"You are a lion's cub, O Judah; you return from the prey, my son.

"Like a lion he crouches and lies down, like a lioness—who dares to rouse him?

"The scepter will not depart from Judah, nor the ruler's staff from between his feet, until he comes to whom it belongs and the obedience of the nations is his."

Moses straightened up, relieved to hear this. "Well, I do not have to worry about being the leader of Israel, for I am not of the tribe of Judah."

Zuriel's old eyes blinked; then he leaned forward and whispered, "There is one coming who will be the Great Redeemer. He will be like no man we have ever known. But until the Great Redeemer comes, God will use men of flesh and blood to serve and to save His people." Zuriel reached out his hand, and Moses took it in his strong hand. The old man's hand felt as fragile as the bones of a tiny bird, but they suddenly tightened on Moses' strong hand.

"I think you are one whom God has chosen to be *this* kind of redeemer."

The words sent a tremor of fear through Moses. "I have no desire to be a leader."

"That has nothing to do with it. Abraham had no desire to leave his homeland, but God commanded him, and he had no choice but to go. Others of our family have also been chosen when they did not expect it. God has reached out and touched them and put them in directions they never dreamed. You, I think, will be one of these men, Moses of the tribe of Levi!"

———

Princess Kali listened as Moses repeated the story of what he had been doing. She had already been warned by her spies that the high priest had given instructions that Moses would be followed and every word he said carefully scrutinized.

Now she leaned forward and took both his hands in hers. "Oh, son, why must you pursue this?"

"I must help my people."

"Perhaps we could work together. I will speak to Pharaoh. The burden of the slaves could be lightened with one word from him."

"That is what Aaron said, but I am not interested in lightening the load. The Hebrews came to Egypt as free men, and they have been enslaved by the pharaohs. They must be set free."

Fear came into Kali's heart and was reflected in her eyes. "That can never be."

"Perhaps not, but I must go join my life to those of my brothers. If they suffer, I must suffer also."

Kali did all she could to persuade Moses not to follow this course. She felt frightened for him, but finally she saw there was no changing his mind.

Moses put his arms around his foster mother and held her tightly. "I love you dearly, my mother, but something that I cannot explain is pulling at me. I must go and join the fate of my brothers."

CHAPTER

5

Despite the miserable lives of the Hebrews, they maintained a reverence toward marriage unknown in Egypt. This irritated the Egyptian taskmasters.

One of the most loving couples among the tribes were an older man called Yagil and his wife, Berione. Yagil was some years older than his wife and had been in declining health for years. Berione was an attractive woman, despite her hard life as a slave, and often had to fight off the attentions of the Egyptian taskmasters who sought to seduce all the attractive young Hebrew women.

Yagil had awakened early and attempted to get out of bed, but when he sat up, he began to cough furiously. He grabbed for a cloth that he kept by his mat and put it over his face, his body racked by spasms.

Berione was already up, and coming to her husband's side, she knelt beside him waiting for the coughing to subside. She took the cloth and saw that it was spotted with blood. She put her arm around him and said, "You cannot work today, husband."

"I must. The taskmasters will not let me lie idle."

"But you can't work if you are sick."

"What do the Egyptians care if a Hebrew is sick?" Yagil fought off the impulse to cough again and got to his feet. He took a deep breath and shook his head. "I must go."

"Here. I have fixed your breakfast."

Yagil sat down cross-legged and took the bowl of soup that

Berione had placed before him. He had little hunger, for the wasting disease that had struck his lungs had sapped his appetite. He ate what he could and got up, trying to hide his weakness from Berione. "I will go. If I do not, our whole group will be punished because I'm not there to help make up the count."

Berione put her arms around him and kissed him, then stood at the opening of their hut as he slowly walked out. She watched as he joined the group of men who trudged silently toward the brickyard, then turned back inside the hut, her heart filled with apprehension for her husband.

"You don't look like you can work today, Yagil," one of the men said to him, but Yagil only shook his head. "You're sick," the man insisted. "You need to be in bed."

Yagil did not have the strength to answer. He only shook his head and continued walking, each step a misery for him. Several times he had coughing spasms, and the rag that he kept to wipe his face was now thoroughly soaked with his blood.

When they reached the brickyard, Yagil climbed down into the pit and began the endless treading of the clay.

The day passed interminably for the old man, and by late afternoon he had lost all feeling in his lower body. He had coughed until his ribs were hurting, and finally he felt himself slipping down into the mud.

But he did not fall, for strong arms held him up. Yagil's body was racked with coughing, yet still he turned to see who had picked him up. He did not recognize the face, which was healthy and strong, not weak and bony and starved. The eyes of the man were what Yagil noticed most. They were almost like twin beams of light, and the voice was different from the voice of slaves.

"Brother, you cannot do any more. I will help you."

"Who are you?"

"A friend."

Twenty minutes later one of the guards came to check on the workers in the mixing pit. He looked down and saw Yagil being supported by a tall, muscular man. He did not recognize the slave and shouted, "Let that man go!"

Instead the tall figure turned and said, "He is too weak. I will do his work for him." Without another word he picked Yagil up as if he were a child, carried him out of the pit, and set him down in the shade of a scrub tree.

The guard stared at him in astonishment. "I do not know you."

"You know that the work will be done, for you will watch me."

The guard lifted his whip, but suddenly the eyes of the strange slave burned, and the overseer took a step backward, his eyes filled with alarm.

"What do you care who does the work as long as it gets done?"

The guard watched as the strange slave slipped back into the pit. He looked out of place there, his limbs muscular and rounded, his neck wide and strong. The guard watched for a time, then shrugged. "Maybe he's right. What do I care as long as the work's done?" He walked over and looked at the frail body of Yagil and saw the blood mixed with mud on his chest. "He won't last long anyway."

———————

Berione looked up, shocked to see her husband being helped along by a stranger, a tall man who did not appear to be a slave, yet was dressed in a slave's loincloth.

"Husband," she cried, rushing to his side, "what is it?"

"He was too sick to work," the man supporting him said. "I took his place."

"Put him down over here."

Moses put the limp form down on the mat and watched as the wife bathed his face and body with water. Yagil was panting, unable to get his breath, but he turned to the man and managed to ask in a weak voice, "What is your name?"

"I am Moses . . . of the tribe of Levi."

"The tribe of Levi?"

"Yes. I am the son of Amram and Jochebed."

Both Yagil and Berione stared unbelieving at Moses. They knew his story, as did all the Hebrews.

"But you are not a slave. Why are you here?" Yagil asked in astonishment.

"I am a Hebrew. I must join myself to my people."

Moses turned to leave, but Berione said, "Wait. Stay. I have food fixed."

Moses turned and smiled at her. "Thank you. I am hungry."

The meal that Moses sat down to was simple—a watery stew with little meat in it. He did not ask what it was. He watched as Berione urged more food upon her husband, but the man seemed uninterested in food.

"I was surprised that the guards permitted you to work for me," Yagil said.

"Why did you do such a thing?" Berione asked.

"Because my brother here was sick and I wanted to help."

"All of our people are sick," Yagil said huskily. His voice was weak and reedy, and an unhealthy pallor discolored his complexion. "You cannot work for all of us—even as strong as you are."

"No, I cannot, but I will do what I can," Moses said.

Then he rose and nodded to the couple. "I will come back in the morning. I will find the guard to tell him that I am working in your place. You must rest, my brother, until you are well."

But Yagil was studying Moses with the eyes of one who knew his fate. "It is too late for me, but I will pray that the strong God we worship will help others who are stronger than I."

After Moses left, Berione said, "I've never seen anyone as strong as he is."

"Yes, strong in body but even stronger in spirit. When he put his eyes on the guard, I thought the guard would run away. He is the one sent to help us. Not just you and me, Berione, but our whole people."

———

After the day's work had been completed and the evening meal consumed, Korah called a meeting of the elders to order. He stared at Moses, displeasure in his eyes.

"Your brother has done a foolish thing," Korah said bluntly, directing his words to Aaron. "You should have counseled him better."

"He did counsel me." Moses spoke up, wearing a simple linen garment around his waist, the muscles of his arms and chest standing out in stark relief. He stood with his legs slightly apart and his arms crossed in the Egyptian manner.

"That is right," Aaron broke in. "I have tried to convince Moses that he could do more good in other ways."

"We all agree with that," Korah said. "Do we need more slaves? There are enough of us as there are. Why have you done this thing, Moses?"

"I have joined my people," Moses said simply. "I should have done it years ago, but I was thoughtless."

"What good will your death do?" Jacob demanded. A tall man with thin features and an anxious look, he was second on the council next to Korah. "Sooner or later the Egyptians will recognize you. Then what will they think?"

"That's right," Eli enjoined. "What will happen to us then?"

"If anything happens, it will be to me," Moses said calmly. He saw the resistance among the elders and asked abruptly, "Why are you so afraid for me to join you? I am of your own flesh and blood. It is true that I was raised in the court of Pharaoh, but I should have recognized my heritage. Indeed, I have been at fault, but I have come now to join you and must suffer along with my brothers."

Korah shook his head, and the fat of his jowls and neck quivered. "That is foolishness, man, absolute foolishness! You have a high position in Egypt. You can do much to alleviate our suffering."

"Exactly what I told him, Korah," Aaron cried. "You must go back to the palace, Moses."

"I will not," Moses said firmly, and his voice was like the closing of a stone door.

Korah shouted in frustration, "You are a fool! What good will your death do to us? Be gone with you!" He rose to his feet and, with a gesture, scattered the council.

As soon as they were outside and on their way back to their parents' hut, Aaron began to remonstrate with Moses. "You should not have been so arrogant before the council."

Aaron's words surprised Moses. "Me, arrogant? I did not think I was."

"Why, of course you were. You told the chief elder that he was wrong."

"Well, he *is* wrong."

"Who are you to say that? What do you know?" Aaron cried in despair. "You come among us for a few weeks, and you think you know more than the entire council of elders."

"The council has gotten used to slavery. They wear it like a garment," Moses said. He was not an arrogant man, although he had developed a certain pride in his place. He was rapidly losing this, however, now that he knew his true nature and heritage. He was shocked at how Aaron and the council and many others could simply accept slavery as their fate. It was true that they expected freedom to come for their people someday, but they could not find it in themselves to rise up and resist the Egyptians now.

When Moses and Aaron reached their parents' house, they listened to Amram and Jochebed argue on the side of the council.

"You should pay heed to the council, Moses," Amram insisted. "They are wise men."

"I'm sure they are, but they have forgotten what it's like to be free," Moses said. "Or more to the point, they have never known freedom." He suddenly realized that this was the truth. He was talking to people who had never known freedom. That was why they were willing to bargain for an extra benefit or two, another extra morsel of food, or half a day off from time to time—they had no concept of trying to free themselves from their captors. Moses, on the other hand, had known nothing but freedom, and he knew in his heart what it was like never to have to answer to the lash of the taskmasters.

"Leave him alone," Miriam said suddenly, and her parents and Aaron turned to stare at her in shock. Her eyes were open wide and fixed on Moses. "My brother Moses is right. What good will it do us if the Egyptians give us a little more food or a little time off? We will still all die in Egypt as slaves. Do not listen to them, Moses."

Moses smiled and moved over to put his arm around Miriam. "You have followed me all of my life to see this day, haven't you?"

"Yes. I knew when I saw the princess pick you out of the water that you were going to redeem Israel from slavery."

Jochebed suddenly began to cry. "I remember how very hard it was to give you up that day."

"But now," Moses said, "God has given me back to you." He stood tall and strong, and his parents saw the burning light of strength in the eyes of their broad-shouldered son. "God will deliver our people."

When Moses stopped by the hut of Yagil and Berione early the next morning, he saw a guard named Magon, one of the cruelest of the taskmasters, outside the hut taunting Berione. He was holding her by the shoulders and laughing as she protested. Yagil came out of the hut and said, "I will go to work today. Leave her alone."

Magon reached out and struck the old man a terrible blow in the chest. It drove Yagil backward, and he began gagging and choking.

Berione tore herself loose and went to her husband. She fell down and put her arms around him, calling his name. Moses moved forward, and as he did, he heard her cry, "He's dead! He's dead!"

"Then you need a man now," Magon said with a cruel laugh, grabbing Berione's arm and pulling her up. He had begun to tear at her clothing and Moses knew he had to do something.

"Let her go."

Magon turned to see a large figure coming at him swiftly. He dropped Berione's arm and plucked a dagger out of his belt, holding it out menacingly. "On your way, fellow."

But Moses continued to advance. "You have killed him," he said.

"And I'll kill you!" Magon growled in a guttural tone. He had killed many of the slaves, and though this one was bigger, he had no doubt he would kill him as well. He leaped forward, thrusting the dagger out, intending to pierce his opponent through the heart.

But Moses' training in arms stood him in good stead. With a quick motion of his wrist, he turned the blow of the dagger aside, then closing his hands over the fist that held the dagger, he put his leg behind Magon and threw him to the ground. The breath rushed out of Magon, and he saw the dagger in his own fist coming down toward his throat.

"No—no!" he cried out.

But it was too late. Inexorably the dagger came down, piercing the throat of the Egyptian, scraping on the bone until it was down to the hilt. Scarlet blood exploded from the struggling man's neck, and a filmy red mist floated from his mouth. He tried to speak, but his mouth was filled with blood.

Moses stood up and watched as Magon made a feeble attempt to pull the dagger out. But it was too late. He shuddered, kicked the ground with his heels, then went limp and still. With one look at Berione, Moses knew he had to get rid of the body of the Egyptian or she would pay the price.

"Here. Let me help you move Yagil inside and then I will come back and see to his burial." He carried the fragile body into the hut and then, with an easy motion, scooped up the body of the Egyptian. He threw it over his shoulder and hurried away. He looked carefully for witnesses but saw no one, for it was very early in the morning, the light barely dawning. By the time full light had come, he was standing beside a grave he had scooped out with his bare hands and dumped the body of the Egyptian in. He looked down at the man in disgust, feeling no compassion or pity for him. "You will kill no more Hebrews," he said, then turned and went back to see what he could do for his dead brother.

———

For several days Moses was apprehensive that someone might have seen him. He half expected one of the Egyptians to arrest him, but nothing happened. A week later he began to relax. Although he kept up his work as a slave, it all seemed futile. How could he help his brothers by trampling out mud to make bricks? They needed a redeemer, and he was obviously not the one.

Late in the afternoon one of the Hebrew overseers glanced at the tally and began to yell, "You are two hundred bricks under your quota! You want to get us all beaten to death?" He picked up a stick and began to strike the naked backs of the men. They covered their heads and accepted their punishment mutely.

But once again Moses intervened. He grasped the wrist of the Hebrew, crushing it as the man screamed in pain. Moses said furiously, "Why are you hitting your brother?"

The taskmaster wrenched his arm away. He looked around and saw several Egyptian guards coming and muttered under his breath, "Who made you a prince and a judge over us? Do you intend to kill me as you killed the Egyptian?"

Startled, Moses took a step backward and saw triumph in the overseer's face. Without a word, Moses turned and fled. He did not stop running until he returned to the palace. He went at once to his old quarters, ignoring the cries of his former attendants, and bathed and put on fresh clothes. His jaw tensed as he moved through the palace toward his mother's apartment. "Tell my mother I'm here," he said to the attendant.

"Yes, master."

Moses waited until the servant stepped out and gestured; then he entered his mother's apartment.

She gave a glad cry and rushed to embrace him. "Moses, you're here!"

Moses stood absolutely still, not able to return the embrace, knowing what he had to say would crush her.

Kali looked up, troubled, trembling as she saw his stern face. "What is it, my son?"

"I must leave this place."

"Tell me why," Kali whispered. She listened in horror as he told her what had happened.

His voice was thick with misery as he explained, "I can do no good for my people here. I am not an Egyptian. I must leave, Mother."

"But where will you go?"

"I do not know." He suddenly threw his arms around her and held her tight. "Don't be afraid. I will go find this god that the Hebrews talk about. I must know him, for I have no god."

Then Princess Kali wailed in grief, knowing that all was lost. She held him tightly, as if to keep him with her forever, but finally she pulled her head back and looked up. "When you find him, Moses, come and tell me where I can find him too."

Moses kissed her and left without another word. As he hurried out of the palace, he knew he was saying good-bye to the only life he had ever known. But somewhere out beyond the palace walls, beyond the magnificent streets and buildings of the Egyptian capital, he was certain he would find the god that the Hebrews worshiped.

CHAPTER
6

After fleeing the city, Moses walked alone through a sandy wilderness that stretched away in all directions, not exactly sure where he was heading. As he made his way through the desert, he thought constantly of the idea of a God of righteousness. Though he did not understand Him, Moses now believed that—unlike the gods of Egypt—the God of the Hebrews was worthy of his allegiance and service. He had a hunger in his heart to know this unseen, silent God who seemed to have a hand on his life. He had no final objective or goal in mind except simply to leave Egypt. His mother had seen to it that he had plenty of food, supplies, and money, and he had studied a map and decided to head first for the oasis city of Kadesh-Barnea in Midian.

Night was now almost upon him, so Moses made camp, ate a little of the food he had brought, then lay down and looked up at the stars. He remembered the story Zuriel had told him about his forefather Jacob. Jacob had been a fugitive, even as Moses was, and on his journey away from his home, a lone man, Jacob had dreamed a strange dream. In the dream, a ladder reached all the way to heaven, and angels were on that ladder, ascending and descending. Moses longed for such a dream as this. He had asked Zuriel what the dream meant, and the old man had answered, "It means that there is a connection between men on earth and God in heaven. There is a coming and going of the servants of the Great Spirit, so be careful. You may encounter an angel."

"I wish I might see an angel." Moses spoke aloud, and his voice seemed to shatter the night. He looked up at the stars and thought of how he would rejoice if the Great Spirit would let him know that He existed.

He thought of Jacob, who was not the best man who'd ever lived but was a man to whom God spoke. Somehow this God of Jacob was calling him. Until now Moses had known only the sterile religion of the Egyptians. He had always hated their worship of death, and now as he made his way toward Midian, he was determined to find the God of Jacob, the giver of life.

Suddenly Moses found himself on his knees, his arms stretched toward the stars of heaven, and crying out, "O mighty God of the Hebrews, you who have no visible form, I call out to the One I cannot see and the One I cannot hear. You know my heart, for you know all things. I have prayed, O Great Spirit, the only God, that you would free my people, and I pray also that I might be one with my people."

Moses prayed for a long time, his voice echoing in the silence of the desert. At times the howls of wild dogs and the cries of night birds joined with his voice. Moses waited, hoping to hear a voice, to see something, but he heard nothing and he saw nothing. Finally he lay back down and went to sleep without having met the God of Abraham.

After a long and dangerous journey, Moses reached the area of Ezion-Geber. He was aware that this was not the safest place in the world for him. It was a meeting place for caravans and travelers, a Red Sea port that served as a base for the pharaoh's ships. It was always possible that someone would see him, recognize him, and report his presence to Pharaoh.

Moses skirted the village, and when he approached a still smaller village, he came to a well just outside the settlement. He had been walking in the cool of the night, and it was early morning, before sunrise. He sat down within sight of the well to wait for daylight before entering the town.

As had become his habit, he lifted his thoughts to the God of the Hebrews. "I wish I knew your name, O Great Spirit, great God of Abraham. Show yourself to me," he prayed. "Let me see and hear you."

He thought again of how Jacob had had to flee his father's house, and the first person he saw after getting to a strange land was a young woman. He fell in love with her at once, and they eventually married, but only after much difficulty.

Moses longed for clear evidence of God's hand on him, as Jacob had experienced. "O God of Jacob, put your hand on me as you did on your servant Jacob."

Even as he prayed, he looked up and saw a flock of sheep approaching. He paid little attention to the sheep, however, for his eye was on the young women who were leading them. The tallest of the group was in front. Her black hair fell about her shoulders, and she walked proudly.

For a long time Moses sat there as the women drew water out of the well for their sheep. He had an impulse to go speak to them, as Jacob had done in his encounter with Rachel, but he knew that this situation was different. Rachel was Jacob's relative, while he was a stranger in this place.

The women were laughing and talking and had not noticed Moses, who was inconspicuous from his seat under a tree. They suddenly became upset, and Moses sat up straighter and saw that a group of rough-looking shepherds had come and were shouting at the women to get out of the way. They had brought their own sheep with them. The black-haired woman argued with him, and one of the roughest-looking of the shepherds shoved her away, so that she fell down.

Moses was on his feet, flying over the ground without thought. He halted before the shepherd, his eyes blazing. "You call yourself a man, yet you treat helpless women like this?" Moses' hand shot out, and he grabbed the man's throat. The man struggled like a fish on a line but was powerless against Moses' strength. "Take your mangy sheep and get away from here before I break your neck!"

Moses flung the man backward. The shepherd fell in the dirt and scrambled to his feet. He gave Moses a murderous look, but then looked at his two companions, who were watching him.

"Come on. There are other wells," he muttered.

Moses turned to the young woman, who by now had gotten to her feet. She was dusting the sand from her garment, and she smiled at him, saying, "Thank you, sir."

"Let me help you collect your flock." Moses helped the young women as they gathered their sheep and watered them. When they were finished and started to lead them away, Moses said, "Go in peace," and the tall young woman smiled at him and nodded. "Yes. We will go, and we thank you, sir, for your help."

———

Moses had dozed beside the well, thinking of how very similar his encounter with the tall, black-haired woman was to that of his ancestor Jacob. It pleased him to think this, although he did not know why. Finally hearing the sound of feet, he looked up and saw that very woman approaching. Her face was flushed and her eyes were bright. He stood up at once, and she said breathlessly, "Our father, Jethro, sent me to get you. Please come with me so that you may break your fast and eat bread under our father's roof."

Moses was pleased. "I will be happy to." As he went with her, he asked, "Who is your father?"

"He is the priest of Midian. I am Zipporah, the oldest of my father's children."

They reached the dwelling of Jethro, and a close-shaven man came out to greet them. He bowed low before Moses and greeted him. "My daughters have told me how you kept them safe from the men at the well. Please come into my house and take bread with us."

Moses bowed also, gave his name, and then went inside. The meal was excellent, and after it was over, Jethro said, "You have an Egyptian name, but you do not look like an Egyptian."

"No, I am not. My people are slaves of the pharaoh."

Jethro's eyes flew open. "You are a Hebrew?"

"Yes. I'm surprised that you should know them."

"Why should I not know the descendants of Abraham, the father of the Hebrews?"

Moses stared at the man in shock. He could not believe that

here in the desert he had found those who knew the God of his people and of his people's history. "How could you know such a thing?"

"How could I know Abraham, you ask? Why, who does not know him? I know his entire history. Are you indeed a descendant of Abraham?"

"Yes. I was raised as an Egyptian, but I am a Hebrew, the son of Amram of the tribe of Levi." He wondered how much to tell this man and finally decided to tell the whole truth. He related the parts of his story that he felt were good for Jethro to know, and finally said, "And so I am a fugitive."

"Then you may stay with us," Jethro said firmly. "I do not have any sons, only daughters, but I am the priest of Midian. Since you are trained in the arts of the Egyptians, you might become a priest also."

"Not I," Moses said hastily. He had seen enough of the priesthood in Egypt that the very idea offended him. Then a thought leaped into his mind, and he said abruptly, "I will tend your flocks and your herds. My forefathers were shepherds, and I have a yearning to know their trade. I will keep your sheep."

"And what shall be your reward?"

Another idea came to Moses. He was not usually given to such impulses, but he was very taken with the black-haired Zipporah, and he said to Jethro, "You may have heard the story of my forefather Jacob."

"I know it well."

"Then you know that when he left his father's house and came to a strange land, the first person he saw was a young woman, and he loved her. Give me your daughter Zipporah for my wife, and I will serve you for seven years, even as Jacob served for Rachel."

Zipporah had not said a word through this interchange. She did, however, have her dark eyes fixed on Moses, and her lips were slightly parted.

Moses turned to her and said, "Of course, I would not take you against your will, but if you will have a stranger for a husband, perhaps God will be good to us."

Zipporah's eyes were locked with Moses' own, and she said

quietly but with certainty, "I will have you for my husband."

"That is good!" Jethro exclaimed. "I will have a son after all. My daughter is yours, Moses, and one day the sheep will be yours too." The sisters excitedly gathered around Zipporah, whispering to her and hugging her.

As Moses rose and went over to his betrothed, the sisters separated, their eyes envious. He held out his hand, and Zipporah put her hand in it. "This is very sudden, Zipporah. You do not know me, nor do I know you."

"But I will be your wife, and a wife will know her husband."

"You are marrying a strange man," Moses said. "I give you fair warning. You would be better off with another."

But Zipporah shook her head. "No," she said. "I take you for my husband."

"And I take you," said Moses, "for my wife. We will go to the desert and keep your father's flock. We will have many children." He put his other hand over Zipporah's and smiled. "Our lives will be simple, as simple as those sheep that we care for."

PART TWO

EXODUS

CHAPTER

7

"There now, my little one, don't wiggle—let me help you."

The young shepherd who was watching Moses attempt to free a scrawny lamb from the grasp of a thornbush shook his head in disgust. His name was Gili, and he spent a great deal of his time wondering what sort of man his master was. Now he snorted impatiently, "That lamb's going to die anyway, master. Just break its neck and spend your time on more important things."

Moses turned to look at the shepherd. Gili was a tall, stringy individual, almost emaciated but tough as a piece of dried leather. Two of his front teeth were missing, which gave his speech a whistling quality, but despite the missing teeth he considered himself quite a catch for the young women he pursued. Moses shook his head. "You're a hardhearted young man, Gili."

"Hardhearted?! Why it's just a worthless lamb!"

"Nothing is worthless in God's sight." Moses' big hands moved carefully and gently pulled the thorns away from the twisted, stringy wool of the lamb. "The Great Creator made this lamb the same as He made you."

"That's ridiculous! It's just a dumb beast—while I, on the other hand, am a human being."

Moses did not answer for a moment. He had removed the last of the needlelike thorns from the lamb's wool and now stood up, cuddling the tiny creature in his arms. He stared at Gili, trying to think of a way to make the ignorant young man understand something about the God he himself longed for so desperately. For nearly forty years now he had wandered in the desert, tending the sheep of his father-in-law, Jethro, but it seemed to him that God was even more evasive than when Moses had been a prince of Egypt. Still, the years in the desert had not weakened his intense desire for the God whose name he did not even know.

"Haven't you ever looked up at night and seen the stars, Gili?"

"Seen the stars? Why, of course, I have. What about them?"

"Have you ever wondered who made them?"

"No. They're just there. That's enough for me."

With a sigh, Moses rose to his feet, stroking the woolly head of the lamb, who was bleating piteously. "You're hopeless, Gili," he said. "Somebody had to make the stars, just as somebody had to make you and me and this little lamb."

He turned and walked toward the camp with Gili following, peppering him with questions. It was the one trait of the young shepherd that got on Moses' nerves. He himself loved the peace and quiet of the desert, but he could enjoy little of it with Gili around. The lad seemed to have a compulsion to talk constantly, and when he asked a question, he immediately forgot Moses' answer.

When they reached their rough camp, which consisted of a pile of rocks made into a fireplace, some bundles of hides to sleep on at night, and a small store of food kept in a wooden box held together by pegs, Moses opened the box and got out a small clay jar. Taking out the stopper, he dipped his fingers in the ointment and began to apply it to the wounds of the tiny beast.

"What does one lamb matter?" Gili demanded. "He's going to die anyway."

"You never know what's going to be important, Gili. The Great Creator put me here as a shepherd. It's my task to care for these sheep, and this little one is important."

Gili stared at the tall form of Moses. He admired the strength of the older man intensely, and, indeed, Moses had become a magnificent figure. He had always been strong, but now his years in the desert roaming the hills had hardened him, burning his skin a deep, coppery hue that accented his fiery eyes, which, though soft and gentle at times, could flash like lightning during periods of anger.

"I don't know why you want to waste your time out here with these sheep," Gili said. He watched as Moses put the little one down and the tiny animal staggered around. "He's hungry," Moses said. "We need to get him back to his mother."

Gili ignored the instruction and moved around to where he could face Moses directly and repeated his question. "Why do you want to fool with these sheep? You've got money enough to hire shepherds. You could do anything you wanted to." When Moses didn't answer, Gili shook his head in disgust. "People say you're strange."

Suddenly Moses' face broke into a smile. "You mean they say I'm crazy."

"Well, some say that. Some say you can do magic—Egyptian magic."

"That's foolishness."

"That's what they say."

"People will say anything."

Gili shrugged and went over to pick up the lamb and go in search of a ewe that was missing its baby. When he found her, he plunked the lamb down in front of her. "Now, you better take better care of this one. The master thinks he's important."

Gili returned to Moses' side, then opened a box, reached in, and got out a handful of dried figs. He tossed one into his mouth and began chewing. "Mmm . . . good figs," he said.

"Save a few for me, will you?"

"So you can't do any magic. Then why do people say you can?"

Moses hesitated. Ever since he had become Jethro's son-in-law, stories about him had swept through the countryside. Many believed he had magical powers, that he could heal the sick or even raise the dead. This had worked to Jethro's advantage, for he had quickly learned that the skill and the knowledge his son-in-law had stored up in Egypt came in handy out in the desert.

Moses admired his father-in-law—or, at least, respected him—but he had quickly discovered that Jethro, the priest of Midian, pretty much believed in all gods without giving total allegiance to any of them. He dealt with amulets and magic formulas, performed rudimentary medical care, including even a little minor surgery. Jethro, as priest, was also called upon to settle disputes among the tribes that he ministered to. Here, too, Moses was called into service for the Midianites, who had an almost reverential awe of him.

Moses lived among the Midianites, sired two sons, and had a genuine affection for his wife, Zipporah, but his heart was constantly searching after God. As he sought for the God whose name he did not know, he studied the people around him. Although he had led a lonely life, he somehow knew, deep in his heart, that the Almighty would someday reveal himself. Moses did not worship the local gods, nor did he observe any ritual for his own God. It was out in the loneliness of the desert, in the intense and almost palpable silence, that he tried desperately to open up his heart and soul so that the God of Abraham and Isaac and Jacob would come to him. So far it had not happened—even after almost forty years—but Moses knew he would die seeking God.

An hour after the lamb had been rescued from the thornbush, Gili cried out, "There they come. It's Paz and Zimra."

Moses looked up and listened as Gili railed at the two men for being late. Paz was a fat young man with a round, moonlike face and a foolish grin. Zimra was an old man, whose leathery skin was baked and lined by the desert sun. As Moses gathered his things to go back to his home in the village, Gili winked at him and said, "Don't forget your lamb over there. It's a valuable creature."

The old man Zimra stared at the scrawny lamb. "What's valuable about him? He probably won't even live."

"Our master Moses says he's an important beast, and you know Moses is always right."

Moses paid little heed to Gili's taunts. He nodded to Paz and Zimra and gave them a few instructions, and then, without another word, walked off into the desert. Gili followed alongside him, pestering him with questions.

Paz stared out of his rheumy eyes at the two as they walked off, then shook his head. "Moses worries about a lamb that's nearly dead."

"He's crazy!" Zimra said. "Anybody'd have to be crazy that would stay out here in this heat when he could be home in comfort. Why does he stay out here?"

Paz nodded wisely. "Well, living with his wife is worse than living out here. She never gives him a minute's peace."

"He ought to beat her."

"Yes, he should—but he never will. He's too tenderhearted. That's a serious flaw in a man."

As Moses entered his house he found Zipporah sewing a garment. She had grown rather heavy over the years, and her once black hair now had threads of silver, but her eyes were still sharp and her voice was even sharper.

"So you finally decided to come home."

"We had to go farther than I thought to find pasture," Moses said defensively. He walked over and sat down across from Zipporah. "Where are our sons?"

"They've gone to a wedding feast with their friends."

Moses stared at Zipporah for a moment, but then asked, "Which friends?"

Immediately Zipporah was angry. She threw down the garment she was sewing and got to her feet. "They have to take their friends where they can find them! I'll fix you something to eat."

Moses sat back on a bench and leaned his head against the wall. He closed his eyes and tried to prepare himself for the time he would spend at home. Over the years Zipporah had gotten more difficult to live with. He never offered a word of criticism to her, but he knew she was disappointed in him. His two sons, Gershom and Eliezer, were also critical of him.

"You can come and eat now."

Moses got to his feet, walked over to the table, and sat down and began to eat. The food was sharp and seasoned with garlic and leeks and onions, and he smiled at her. "This is good."

"If you'd stay home more, you could have more good cooking."

"I have to take care of the flocks. You know that."

"You could hire someone to do that." Zipporah pulled at her

hair, which hung down her back. "You let my father take advantage of you."

"No I don't. He's always been goodhearted and kind to me."

"You should demand your share of the profits."

"All right, I will."

"No you won't. You ought to think more of your family. What's going to become of us?"

Moses had been through this many times. Indeed, he had been a help to Zipporah's father, but he had no plans to make any claim whatsoever for money or position. Jethro had one son, who had been born a year after Moses married Zipporah, and Moses was content that he would be the heir. Zipporah sat down and watched Moses eat. She could not be quiet for long, and soon she got back to her favorite theme. "Have you thought any more about going back to Egypt?"

"I could never go back there."

"Why not?"

"That life's closed to me."

"Your foster mother is a sister to the pharaoh. She's rich. You could have anything you wanted. I don't understand why you don't go back and claim what's rightfully yours."

Moses had long ago given up any attempts to explain his background to Zipporah, and he did not try now. He knew she was unhappy, and his mind went back to the time when he had first seen her. She had been happy then, and he remembered the dark beauty of her eyes and her hair, her trim form. It seemed like another lifetime to him, and he felt a sudden twinge of guilt because he had not provided for Zipporah the things she seemed to require.

"Why don't you become a priest like my father?"

"I could never do that, Zipporah."

"Why not? You know all about the gods."

"There's only one God. I've told you that many times."

"You could do so much more with yourself." Zipporah leaned forward, and her mouth twisted with anger. "I can't understand why you're content to stay out in the desert and ignore your inheritance in Egypt."

Moses had become accustomed to Zipporah's railings, and now he almost welcomed the sound of footsteps. As his father-in-law, Jethro, stepped in, he said with some relief, "Well, I'm home, Father."

"I know. Gili told me you'd come back. How are the sheep?"

"We'll have one of the best crop of lambs in years. Many fine young animals."

"Sit down, Father, and let me feed you," Zipporah said.

Jethro sat down, and she put a huge bowl of the soup before him. Grabbing a wooden spoon, he began to shovel it down, making noises of pleasure. He was a glutton, and it was only when he had finished the bowl that he turned to Moses, belched loudly, and patted his stomach. "Well, Moses, have you thought any more on what I talked to you about?"

"Not really."

"You ought to." Jethro leaned forward. "You could become the head of the whole Midianite nation. All it would take would be a little effort on your part."

"I'm a shepherd."

"We can hire shepherds by the dozen," Jethro snorted impatiently. "I'm talking about your future. You could even be a king."

"I don't want to be a king."

Zipporah gave a disbelieving cry and shook her head. "If you don't want to be a king, what do you want to be?"

Moses wearily put his spoon down and tried to think of an answer, but he had none. Finally he said, "I will never do more than herd sheep." He saw the look that passed between Jethro and his daughter and knew he would never please either of them. "I'm going to bed," he said. "I'm tired."

———————

A month had passed since Moses' return from the wilderness, and during that period of time he had been miserable—as he usually was when he was at home. When he could get away from the house, he prayed all the time. He tried to spend time with his sons, but their interests were so different. They cared nothing even for the gods of the Midianites, and as for an unseen god, they merely laughed at him.

"We have to have a god we can see," Gershom said. "How can we know he is there if we can't see him?"

Moses had never been able to make his sons or his wife or Jethro understand what it was he was searching for. During the past month he'd had a strange feeling he could not define. It was as if he were rushing toward something up ahead. He could not see what it was. He could not sense it with any of his physical senses—but, finally, he could no longer bear it.

"I'm going to go find new pastures for the flock."

"You can never be happy here at home, can you?" Zipporah said sadly. She felt she had failed as a wife, and she knew her tongue was too sharp, but she could not seem to help herself. "Don't run off. Spend some time with Gershom and Eliezer."

"I asked them to go with me, but they claim there's too much to do at home." Moses knew that was not so, but he had not argued with the two. "I shouldn't be too long this time," he said defensively.

"Go on, then! If you love your sheep better than your family, go to them!"

———

Moses looked up and saw Mount Sinai, which broke the horizon ahead of him. The sharp, pointed mountain was the highest in the Horeb range, and Moses' eyes scanned from Sinai's craggy peak to the lower rises surrounding it. The Midianites had always considered Sinai a sacred place, and Moses found himself heading toward it, even as his shepherd's eye kept a lookout for pastureland or springs.

Silence rested over the land for the most part, but as Moses drew closer to Sinai, occasional reverberating echoes thundered down from its peak. Moses took it to be falling rock, despite the Midianites' superstitions about the gods of Sinai. Moses had never believed their stories.

Struck by the silence of the land, the old shepherd stopped and fell on his knees to pray. "O God of Abraham, Isaac, and Jacob, look down on your servant. Remember your people, Lord, who are still in bondage in Egypt."

His voice began to break, and he wept. Finally he rose and wiped the tears from his eyes, then continued on toward Sinai. He had reached the base of the mountain, and as he looked up its rocky slopes, his eyes narrowed at something unusual in the distance. He began to climb toward it and saw that it was a bush on fire. This in itself was not unusual, because in this arid climate, a dry lightning strike could set a bush on fire. But watching carefully, Moses was puzzled to find that the bush was not consumed. He thought to himself, *I will go over and see this strange sight—why the bush does not burn up.*

As he walked toward it, a voice calling his name struck him with the force of a blow.

"Moses! Moses!"

The voice had come out of the burning bush. He stopped dead-still, staring at the bush as it blazed. Finally he cleared his throat and said hoarsely, "Here I am."

The voice came out of the bush again. It was like no voice Moses had ever heard.

"Do not come any closer. Take off your sandals, for the place where you are standing is holy ground."

Moses quickly kicked off his sandals and stood there trembling. He seemed hot and cold at the same time, for he knew he was hearing the voice of the God he had sought for so many years.

"I am the God of your father, the God of Abraham, the God of Isaac and the God of Jacob."

Overcome with fear, Moses fell on the ground and hid his face against his forearms, but he still heard the voice coming strong and clear.

"I have indeed seen the misery of my people in Egypt. I have heard them crying out because of their slave drivers, and I am concerned about their suffering. So I have come down to rescue them from the hand of the Egyptians and to bring them up out of that land into a good and spacious land, a land flowing with milk and honey—the home of the Canaanites, Hittites, Amorites, Perizzites, Hivites and Jebusites. And now the cry of the Israelites has reached me, and I have seen the way the Egyptians are oppressing them. So now, go. I am sending you to

Pharaoh to bring my people the Israelites out of Egypt."

Moses was so stunned he could not answer at first, but after a while he cried out in a high voice, "Who am I, that I should go to Pharaoh and bring the Israelites out of Egypt?"

The voice spoke reassuringly: "I will be with you. And this will be the sign to you that it is I who have sent you: When you have brought the people out of Egypt, you will worship God on this mountain."

Moses could not think clearly, so he voiced the question that had been on his heart for years: "Suppose I go to the Israelites and say to them, 'The God of your fathers has sent me to you,' and they ask me, 'What is his name?' Then what shall I tell them?"

The voice that spoke to Moses was warm and tender and full of power. "I AM WHO I AM. This is what you are to say to the Israelites: 'I AM has sent me to you.'"

Moses thought his heart would burst on hearing the name he had so longed to hear. The eternal God who created all things was actually speaking to him! Moses was alive with every part of his being as he continued to listen to God's instructions.

"Go, assemble the elders of Israel and say to them, 'The Lord, the God of your fathers, the God of Abraham, Isaac and Jacob, appeared to me.'"

Moses was trembling so much he could barely keep his mind on all that the voice was telling him. He struggled with doubts over the wisdom of his going back to Egypt as he was being instructed and telling the Hebrews that he had heard from God. How could they possibly believe such a claim? Finally he blurted out, "What if they do not believe me or listen to me and say, 'The Lord did not appear to you'?"

And the voice said to him, "What is that in your hand?"

"A staff," Moses replied.

"Throw it on the ground," God said.

Moses did as he was told, and the staff became a snake. Moses cried out and ran from it, but the voice continued: "Reach out your hand and take it by the tail."

Moses gingerly picked up the snake by the tail, and jumped in amazement when it became a staff again.

Then God said, "Put your hand inside your cloak."

Moses obeyed, and when he pulled it out, it was spotted with white leprosy. He gasped and thrust his hand away from him, but the voice spoke again: *"Now put it back into your cloak."*

Moses obeyed this command. As he drew his hand back out, he nearly cried to see the leprous hand restored to its normal state.

Again Moses' attention was drawn back to the voice coming from the burning bush.

"If they do not believe you or pay attention to the first miraculous sign, they may believe the second. But if they do not believe these two signs or listen to you, take some water from the Nile and pour it on dry ground. The water you take from the river will become blood on the ground."

Moses had never been a leader or a good speaker, and he simply could not fathom how God could be asking him to do such a task. He did not have the skills he would need for such a monumental accomplishment! So he protested, "O Lord, I have never been eloquent, neither in the past nor since you have spoken to your servant. I am slow of speech and tongue."

The Lord replied, *"Who gave man his mouth? Who makes him deaf or dumb? Who gives him sight or makes him blind? Is it not I, the Lord? Now go; I will help you speak and will teach you what to say."*

But still Moses protested, begging God, "O Lord, please send someone else to do it."

Now the voice grew harsh with him. *"What about your brother, Aaron the Levite? I know he can speak well. He is already on his way to meet you, and his heart will be glad when he sees you. You shall speak to him and put words in his mouth; I will help both of you speak and will teach you what to do. He will speak to the people for you, and it will be as if he were your mouth and as if you were God to him. But take this staff in your hand so you can perform miraculous signs with it."*

On hearing these words, Moses was filled with joy. He did not want to anger God by protesting further. God had provided a way for him to carry out His instructions, and he dared not disobey. He knew he had finally found the God he had sought for all of his life.

Moses rose in quiet awe as the voice fell silent and the bush ceased to burn. He felt a rush of cold wind sweeping down the mountain and swirling about him, whipping his robes and stinging his face with sand. But the warmth inside of him from his encounter with God glowed with such intensity, he barely felt the chill of the wind. With confidence now that God was still with him, even though unseen and unheard, Moses slipped his sandals on, turned, and headed back toward his home in Midian.

———————

Moses thought Zipporah would be happy to hear the news that he was going back to Egypt, but instead she hurled insults at him.

"You wouldn't go when *I* told you to go, but now you're willing because your god has told you to!" she griped. "I think you just want to get away from me and find a younger woman. That's why you are going back to Egypt."

"No," Moses said patiently, "I am returning because my God has commanded me to. He has work for me to do there."

"And I suppose your family is so unimportant to your god that he has told you to leave us all behind." Zipporah's eyes glared at him with her challenge.

Moses thought for a moment, then said, "There is no reason why you cannot come. We will all leave together in the morning."

Zipporah bit her lip in anger but did not have a comeback for this unexpected offer from her husband. She whirled on her heel and went off in search of her sons.

———————

The next morning, Moses and his family left together for Egypt. Jethro wished him well, saying as they parted, "She'll get over it, son. And you will do your work there and come back to us a wealthier man."

"I don't think so, Jethro," Moses said quietly. "None of us knows exactly what will happen in Egypt. I hope to see you again someday, and I thank you for your many kindnesses."

As Jethro watched his son-in-law leave with Zipporah and their two sons, he rubbed his favorite small idol and prayed, "Go with them, and bring them back to me soon!"

CHAPTER

8

The tribe of Judah had produced no better man than Caleb, the son of Jephunneh. He was a natural-born leader, a fearless man with the strength and courage of a lion. Ordinarily Caleb was a man of basically good nature, but his face was twisted with anger one day as he hurried through the slave camp, his eyes darting right and left. He ignored the greetings of those who spoke to him until he finally caught sight of Joshua, his friend from the tribe of Ephraim. Joshua was the son of Nun, and at twenty-five was younger than Caleb. Even though he came from the tribe of Ephraim, the two were fast friends.

Caleb marched up to where Joshua was engaged in a sword fight with one of the younger men. Joshua was stripped to the waist. His deep chest glistened with sweat and his eyes sparkled as he smashed his opponent's defense. They were using wooden swords since the Egyptians did not allow the Hebrew slaves to have any weapons, but now Joshua laughed, his white teeth flashing against his bronzed skin. "That's it, Eli. You're a dead man."

"Let me try again, Joshua," the young fellow begged.

"No. That's enough for now." Joshua half turned, and he smiled. "Why, Caleb, I didn't see you."

"Come with me. We have to talk."

Joshua was accustomed to Caleb's abrupt manner of speech. He moved quickly into step with Caleb, and the two made their way through the camp to a place beside the river where they would not be overheard. "What is it, Caleb?"

"It's Bezalel," Caleb said shortly.

With a sigh, Joshua shrugged his muscular shoulders. "What's he done now?"

Ignoring the question, Caleb turned to face Joshua. "Have you seen him?"

Joshua hesitated, for he and Bezalel were close friends.

Caleb noticed this at once. "Don't try to cover up for him, Joshua," he warned. "He's in trouble this time."

"I haven't seen him today," Joshua admitted. "He doesn't come down here too often."

Caleb nodded shortly. "If he does, grab him and hold him. Send for me."

"Why? What's he done?" Joshua demanded. "He's not a bad fellow, you know."

"He's a spoiled brat! He'd be better off working down in the brickyards," Caleb stated flatly. His eyes were hard as agates, and he shook his head. "I knew there would be trouble when he went to work in the house of that rich Egyptian."

"It's an easy life." Joshua shrugged. "I don't blame him for taking it. With a talent like he's got, it was inevitable."

Bezalel was the son of Uri, who had been married to Miriam's best friend, Illa. The boy's parents had both died years ago, and out of devotion to her friends, Miriam had raised young Bezalel. He had been a difficult youngster to raise, always into trouble of some kind. He had good looks, was highly intelligent, and had a talent for art. Early in his life he had revealed an almost miraculous talent for molding clay into statues. He made caricatures of some of the leaders of the tribe of Levi, and Miriam had been forced to stand between him and the angry leaders. The statues had not been flattering!

Working with clay had been just the beginning, however. As soon as it was discovered that the young fellow had a talent for making almost anything in silver, gold, and bronze, he had been taken out of the brickyards and was trained by some of the Egyptian metal workers. They valued such things, and less than a year ago, Bezalel, at the age of sixteen, became a highly valued apprentice in the hire of a wealthy Egyptian.

Caleb shook his head. "He would have been better off working down here in the pits."

"He's got it pretty easy. And he makes life easy for Miriam and the family. You know he gives most of his earnings to them."

Caleb gnawed on his lower lip. He was a tall man, lean and muscular, given to quick movements. "He's too clever and it will get him into trouble."

"He'll be all right. He's just a little wild."

"You've got to talk to him, Joshua. He'll listen to you."

"I doubt that." Joshua grinned dryly. "What has he done?"

"He's chasing around with Adila."

"You mean the daughter of old Hezmiah?"

"Yes. That's the one."

"But she's betrothed to Laaman."

"You think that makes any difference to Bezalel?" Caleb demanded.

"I'm sure Bezalel doesn't mean anything by it. He's just high-spirited, but it'll make a difference if he has trouble with Laaman. That man's a beast!"

Caleb shook his head. "He's driving Miriam crazy. I'd like to break his neck. He's like his father was, a trifler."

"You're right about that!"

Caleb stood in the hot sun, and finally he said grimly, "You'd better go looking for him. If Laaman finds him with his woman, he'll break his neck."

"So far he's had plenty of luck not getting caught," Joshua said.

"If Laaman catches him," Caleb said, "he'll need more than luck!"

———

The marketplace was busy, and Bezalel was pleased with himself. He was walking alongside Adila, and from time to time she would stop and admire something in one of the booths. The young woman was beautiful. She was from the tribe of Dan, the tribe with the worst reputation among all the sons of Jacob. They were easily led into idolatry and had caused a great deal of trouble back in the past. Adila was small but well shaped, with a pair of full lips enhanced by red paint. Her father was one of those Hebrews who had managed to become as well off as a slave can be, and she wore an attractive garment of light green silk.

"Oh, Bezalel, look. Isn't that precious?"

Bezalel stopped and looked at a small statue Adila was pointing at. It was a figurine of one of the hundreds of Egyptian gods. He studied it for a moment and shrugged. "It's very poor workmanship. But look—the eyes are made of a precious stone. Do you want it?"

"Oh, I would never buy an idol!" She laughed and turned and leaned against him so that he smelled her perfume. "But look at that ring there. I would love to have that."

Bezalel turned to the tradesman who was listening to all this and began a lively barter. Finally he bought the ring, and Adila at once stuck out her hand, spreading her fingers. Just as he was slipping the ring on her finger, they heard a harsh voice calling out her name, and the young couple turned. Adila let out a whimper. "It's Laaman. You'd better run."

"Run? I'm not running," Bezalel said with an arrogant shrug. "We're not doing anything wrong."

"But he's so jealous, Bezalel. He'll beat you."

"We'll see about that."

Laaman approached, and he was a fearful-looking sight. He was half a head taller than other members of his tribe, and his swelling muscles revealed his trade, which was moving the huge blocks of stone for the pharaoh's massive building projects. He was wearing a band around his head that kept his long black hair out of his face, and his lips were twisted in a snarl. "I told you to stay away from her, Bezalel."

"We're just walking through the marketplace," Bezalel said. "No harm in that."

"You don't hear too good." Moving quickly for such a big man, Laaman stepped forward and swung his huge, knotty fist.

Bezalel did not see it coming until it struck him right over the left eye. He was driven backward, and his world turned to stars. As he fell, he heard Adila crying out, "Laaman, don't kill him!" Then he felt more blows raining down on him. He struggled to get up, but it was hopeless. A final blow caught him in the temple, and his world turned to utter blackness.

———————

When Aaron entered Miriam's hut, the first thing he did was ask, "How is Bezalel?"

Miriam passed a hand over her face. She looked weary, and lines showed the strain she had been under. "He's asleep."

"He's lucky Laaman didn't kill him."

"He's beaten up badly. I think he may have some broken ribs, and his face is all swollen. He looks awful."

Aaron marched past Miriam and looked down upon the still form of Bezalel. "He looks like he was hit in the face with a tree."

"I'm worried about him. I've sent for Marneen. She's good with broken bones."

Aaron shook his head in disgust. "Some man's going to kill him for sure if he doesn't keep his hands off of other men's women."

"He doesn't mean any harm."

Aaron turned to Miriam and studied her. The two had always been very close. "I'm worried about you, sister. You should never have taken on raising Bezalel. He's been too much for you."

"It was something I wanted to do for my friends. I couldn't let their son be homeless."

"I know. You're always taking in strays, but Bezalel hasn't worked out."

"He'll be all right."

Aaron came closer and looked down at her. "You look tired. You do too much."

"I'm all right," she said. "Come. Have a drink of water. It's cool from the well."

The two sat down and spoke for a time about the work there was to do. Finally Aaron drained the cup and got up. He stopped before he left and turned and asked, "Do you ever think of Moses?"

"Every day of my life."

"We'll never see him again. You should forget him."

Miriam shook her head and looked directly into Aaron's eyes. "God saved him from death for a purpose. If Mother and I had not put him in that basket, he would have been dead." She reached up and put her hand on Aaron's chest. "He'll come back one day, brother, and then we'll see the Redemption!"

Aaron stared at his sister, then reached down, patted her shoulder awkwardly, and left the hut. Miriam walked back to where Bezalel lay sleeping. She began praying for the young man, who was the only son she would ever have. He was of the tribe of Judah. She was of the tribe of Levi. But he was her son in everything but blood. She leaned over, put her hand on his dark, curly hair, and prayed, "O Almighty God, put your hand on my son, heal and protect him."

Bezalel's twisted, swollen features twitched slightly, and he muttered a few words but did not awaken. Miriam knelt down beside him and took his hand in hers. She kissed it and held it against her cheek. "Please do something, Lord. Take care of my son," she whispered softly to the God she had never seen.

CHAPTER
9

A sharp pain struck Bezalel in the side, bringing him out of a fitful sleep. He gave an involuntary grunt and put his arms around his middle as if to protect himself. Opening his eyes, he saw that the dawn had just begun to break, sending gray streaks of light in through the small window to his right. Cautiously he took a deep breath but found that this was more painful than he had anticipated.

"He must have broken some of my ribs." He whispered the words and tried to sit up, but he could not stand the pain this caused. He lay back on his bed, a thin pad on the dirt floor of the tiny hut he shared with Miriam. From the outside came the sounds of the camp beginning to stir—chickens clucking, dogs barking, cattle lowing, and muted voices babbling as the Hebrews awoke and began their busy lives.

Realizing there was nothing to get up for anyway, Bezalel lay on his back and bitterly reviewed the circumstances that had earned him a beating. "I should have known better than to fool with that woman. Everyone told me so, but I was too stubborn to listen."

It was a rare admission of guilt and one that he would never have made publicly. Young Bezalel was a proud young man and with some reason. His grandfather was Hur, the leader of the tribe of Judah for many years. This gave Bezalel some honor among his tribesman, despite the fact that his father, Uri, had been a rather worthless individual. He had been handsome, to be sure, but not a father to be proud of. Bezalel had received his good looks from his father: a wealth of curly black hair, lustrous, dark eyes, widely spaced and well shaped, with eyelashes any woman would have been attracted to. He had a sensuous mouth that was full and wide, and he had not been cooked by the blazing sun of Egypt as had most of his childhood companions. He could thank his artistic talents for this, for he had been pulled out of the terrible labor of making bricks and placed in the home of one of the wealthiest Egyptians, who had put him under the tutelage of the best teachers, intending to make a prize slave out of him.

Once more Bezalel made an effort to sit up, and this time he succeeded, gasping for breath with each small movement. He heard Miriam moving about outside, no doubt preparing food for him at the fire, and he dreaded seeing her. He felt guilty for the trouble he had brought to her and did not want to listen to the inevitable scolding he would receive. He would have risen and left, but that was out of the question in his present condition.

Miriam appeared at the doorway; then her face drew into a tight mask and her lips pressed tightly together. She came to stand over him and said without preamble, "Well, I hope you're proud of yourself."

"Please don't start on me, Mother. I don't feel up to it."

"Well, I should think not! Bezalel, you should have better sense. When are you ever going to grow up?"

"Could I have something to eat and some water, please?"

Miriam glared at him but shrugged her shoulders and moved across to where the drinking water was stored in a jar. She poured him a cupful, came back, and handed it to him. Stooping down, she watched him, her eyes intent. When he finished drinking noisily, she took the cup and said, "Son, don't you know you're breaking my heart?"

Every time Miriam called Bezalel "son," it touched him. She had been his mother's best friend and had been like an aunt to him while his mother was alive. He was only eight years old when his mother died, and his father had died earlier, so Miriam had taken him into her little hut and raised him as her own. She had never married, so it was just the two of them, and Bezalel knew she had poured herself into him as his real mother would have done had she lived. Trying to think of some reasonable answer to her question, he realized there was none. "I'm sorry, Mother," he said. "I was a fool."

"Well, everyone knows that," Miriam snapped, "but *why* were you a fool? There are plenty of fine young girls looking for a husband, but you have to chase out after a harlot like that one. Sometimes I think you don't have any sense at all!"

Bezalel dropped his head, unable to meet her eyes. He listened, knowing there was no logical explanation he could give her, for he had indeed been a fool. He was relieved when she finally got up and said, "I've fixed you something to eat."

Bezalel sat there wondering how long he would be unable to get up and pursue his normal activities. "I'll have to send word to my master that I've been hurt."

"He's probably already heard it," Miriam said as she brought him a bowl of stew.

"He wouldn't be interested in the affairs of slaves, Mother." Rishef, the wealthy Egyptian who had taken Bezalel into his service, took no thought for his servants' private lives—indeed he was unaware that they had any. He would be angry, however, if Bezalel did not come to work. "Could you get word to him, Mother?"

"I'll send someone to tell him this morning." She looked up as the door flap opened and smiled at her brother. "Hello, Aaron."

"Good morning, Miriam." Aaron crossed the room and stood over Bezalel. He was a formidable figure, tall, strong, and with a masterful air. "Well, I suppose you're proud of yourself brawling in public over a strumpet."

"Uncle, I'd appreciate it if we didn't have to discuss this right now." Bezalel suddenly felt very weak and carefully lay down, hoping he could avoid his uncle's tirade.

Aaron laughed shortly. "I'm sure you would, but everybody else is talking about it, so why shouldn't we?"

"What are they saying?"

Suddenly Aaron laughed. He was not a man of much humor, and it took something extraordinary to amuse him. "You're not the only one who got a beating."

"What are you talking about, Uncle?"

"Laaman gave that worthless woman a beating too—not as severe as yours, of course—then dragged her right to the priest and married her on the spot. I must say, I think they deserve each other."

"I can't believe it," Bezalel whispered.

"That's because you don't know anything about people. All you know how to do is to make statues for the Egyptians. Aren't you ashamed of the way you have brought disgrace to your family?"

Bezalel sat glumly, unable to meet Aaron's stern glance. He could not shut out the penetrating voice, and he could not get up and leave, so he merely endured it.

"I hope this will be a lesson to you to stay away from women like that—especially married women. I think a member of the tribe of Judah would have more pride," Aaron added stridently. "Get yourself a wife of your own and stop chasing after other men's women."

He turned and left the hut abruptly, and Bezalel tried to smile. "He has a rough way, my uncle."

"He loves you," Miriam said. She came over with a bowl of water and a cloth and began cleansing the wounds around Bezalel's face. "You have so many gifts, son, and we fear you are wasting them."

Bezalel tried to think of a response to that, but nothing came to him. Indeed, he knew that his aunt and uncle were right. He could not understand himself, so how could he explain it to Miriam?

Finally Miriam finished bathing him and asked, "Do you want to sit up again?"

"Yes. I think I will."

Miriam helped him sit up and propped him up with some cushions. She set a cup of drinking water by his side and left the door flap open so he could watch the goings-on in the camp. "I've got to go over to help Tabia. Her baby's coming, and she needs help. I don't know how long I'll be gone, but I'll make sure Rishef is notified that you've been hurt."

"That's all right, Mother," Bezalel said, nodding. "If I get tired, I'll just lie down again."

"You'd better not try to move around too much. Those ribs need a chance to heal." She came over, looked down at him, and said, "Try to be a good man, son." She leaned over, kissed him, and picking up a basket in which she had put some food and items to help care for a newborn, she left.

Bezalel waited until Miriam was gone and then managed to stand up. He bit his lip, for it hurt terribly to move. Crossing the small room, he went to a box where Miriam kept her cooking supplies. He opened it and pulled out the jug of wine that she always kept there. Going back to his mat, he sat back down against the cushions, removed the stopper from the jug, and took several long swallows. He expelled his breath and sat back, the wine jug at his side. At first he thought of Adila, but he soon dismissed her. The woman had really meant nothing to him. She had simply been a challenge. As he rested against the cushions, sipping the wine occasionally, he thought bitterly of how Laaman had beaten him as if he were a child. For a time Bezalel thought of his friend Joshua. "He wouldn't have beaten Joshua like that," he said aloud, but Bezalel was no Joshua. He was not a fighting man but an artist, grown soft from good living in the home of a wealthy Egyptian, whereas Joshua was as hard as granite.

Bezalel hated to be bested at anything, and the thought of being publicly beaten by a brute like Laaman left a bitter taste in his mouth. He was honest enough with himself to acknowledge that his pride was hurt. For a long time he sat sipping the wine until he grew sleepy. He struggled to his feet once more, replaced the wine jug, and went back to lie down on the pad. His last thought before drifting off to sleep was, *You may have married her, Laaman, but let's see how long you can keep her from me!*

———

Aaron awoke with a start. His body jerked and his eyes flew open. He almost cried out but managed to restrain himself. His movement awakened his wife, Elishiba. "What's wrong, Aaron? Are you sick?"

"No, I'm not sick."

Elishiba reached over and touched his face. "You don't have a fever?"

"I'm all right, I tell you." He lay in the darkness, trying to collect his thoughts. "I had a dream of some kind."

"Well, it's gone now. Go back to sleep."

Aaron did not answer. He found that he was filled with a nameless dread. Although highly intelligent, he was a man of little imagination—he liked things well organized and in order. The dream had unsettled things. He tried to recall it, but it was elusive, like a fleeting shadow, and it would not come back to him. A message from the dream stayed with him, however, and this is what troubled him. He wrestled with it as he lay in the darkness and finally said, "Elishiba?"

"Yes, Aaron?"

"I must leave."

"Leave?" Elishiba sat up on the pad that she shared with Aaron. "Why, it's the middle of the night!"

"I know, but God has spoken to me."

"What are you talking about?"

"I had a dream, and I can remember only one thing about it— a voice was telling me I had to go to the wilderness."

"To the wilderness? Why, you can't do that! There are wild beasts and bandits there. The wild desert men will kill you."

Aaron was not a man blessed with dauntless physical courage— such men as Caleb and Joshua possessed this quality—but his strength lay in his orderly mind and his solid determination once he had his mind made up. He rose suddenly in the darkness and began to dress himself.

"Aaron, you can't do this," Elishiba said in a panic. She got up, and the tiny lamp that they kept burning cast shadows about her face. She was a nervous woman, given to fears, and now she begged him to stay.

Aaron paid her little heed. "I've got to go," he said. "That's all there is to it."

"Well, at least take Nadab and Abihu with you."

"No. I must go alone. I know God said that much."

"Aaron, I'm afraid!"

Aaron had finished getting dressed and stood irresolutely for a moment. He had always questioned that God spoke to men in dreams, at least for himself. He had heard that other men had such dreams and had often wished that God would speak to him as He did to others. But now that God *had* spoken, it seemed a frightful thing to go out into the darkness. "Fix me something to eat, Elishiba. I'll need strength for the journey."

"All right. But we don't have much." Elishiba quickly pulled together what food there was, put it into a leather satchel, and handed it to him. "How long will you be gone?"

"How can I know, woman? I have no idea what I'm doing. All I know is that I have to go." He hesitated, then said, "I'll be back as soon as I can."

"Be careful. Oh, be careful."

Aaron nodded, patted her shoulder awkwardly, then turned and left their hut. Elishiba moved to the door and watched him walk away, but he was swallowed up almost immediately by the darkness. Fear gripped her, and she stood there for a long time wishing she knew how to pray. She had been exposed so much to the gods of Egypt that the unseen God of the Hebrews, having no form and known only by the aural legends of the elders, seemed vague and powerless. She stood trembling in the darkness, then turned and went back inside, her heart heavy with fear.

Night was coming on, and Aaron, footsore and weary almost to death, stopped and took a deep breath. He was absolutely exhausted. For several days he had made his way toward the mountains, most of the time calling himself a fool. He had encountered other travelers in caravans, who had given him food and water. Without those provisions, he would surely have died. He had not been patient with other men's dreams and visions, and now here he was headed out into the dangerous wilderness on no more authority than a vague dream he'd had!

Finally he came to the mountain many called "The Mountain of God," although no one quite knew why it had that name. He knew he could go no farther, for the dark would soon swallow him. He had reached a tiny creek, no more than a few feet across, but the water was cold and pure. Quickly he gathered sticks and built a small fire. A tree had fallen and there was plenty of dried wood. He took the last of the meat he had, stuck it on a sharp stick, and heated it over the fire. When it was hot, he began to eat it slowly and thought, *That's all the food. How will I eat tomorrow?*

He sat by his fire, miserable and frightened, as the darkness closed in. He trembled at the sounds of wild animals and drew his cloak around him. Strangely, he was not sleepy, although his body was completely exhausted.

After sitting for a long time, he finally grew sleepy. He lay down, wrapping himself in his cloak, still wondering what he would eat the next day.

As he was drifting off to sleep he heard twigs snapping and rocks tumbling nearby and sat up abruptly, his heart pounding in fear. Stifling a cry, he peered into the murky darkness. There was a sliver of moon giving light, and the shadows of the bushes and the spindly trees of the desert seemed to grow monstrous to his frightened imagination.

He gasped when a huge form suddenly appeared to his right. Scrambling to his feet, he fumbled to pick up his staff. He held it like a weapon. *Is it a bear or a lion?* But as he saw it more clearly, he could make out that it was a man—and a big man, at that. Thoughts of bandits and robbers, murderous hill people, came to him, and he cried out in an unsteady voice, "Stay right where you are! Don't come any closer!"

The form did stop, and then Aaron was shocked and at the same time gladdened to hear his name called.

"Aaron, is that you?".

"Moses!" Aaron dropped the staff and moved forward.

Moses emerged from the darkness, and the moonlight made a silvery track on his face. He reached out and embraced Aaron, and the two men clung to each other. "What brought you out here, Aaron?" he asked.

"I . . ." Aaron choked, unable to answer. He found it difficult to tell Moses that he was here because of a dream. Finding the courage, he explained, "I had a dream, and a voice told me to come to the wilderness."

"That was God talking to you. The God of Abraham is speaking to men."

Aaron was shaken by the meeting and yet filled with a sudden burst of joy such as he had never felt. "You must come home with me, Moses!"

Moses laughed deeply. "The truth is, I am on my way. I have much to tell you. Stoke up the fire. I have some food with me."

Aaron at once began building up the fire, and the two men sat down.

"Tell me everything," Aaron said. "Everything that's happened since you left . . ."

"Go before Pharaoh? But, Moses, that . . . that can *never* be! He would have us killed, thrown to the crocodiles!"

Aaron had listened breathlessly as Moses recounted the story of his sojourn in the land of Midian. He had been enthralled as Moses related how God had spoken to him out of the burning bush, but when Moses repeated the commission that God laid upon him to go before Pharaoh and demand the emancipation of the entire nation of Israel, Aaron's heart froze. "Surely God cannot have meant that!"

"I think God always means what He says," Moses said, smiling slightly. "But we won't be killed."

"How can you know that?"

"God would not give us this task just to be killed." He leaned forward, and for the first time Aaron saw the eyes of Moses blazing, filled with a light such as he had never seen in the eyes of any man. "It is the time of the Redemption, Aaron. God is going to deliver His people from the Egyptians."

Far into the night Moses spoke about what God was going to do, and finally he said, "I have been remiss in not telling you about my family. My wife and sons left Midian with me, but Zipporah was not happy over my reasons for going to Egypt. She could not accept that God had spoken to me, and the more we talked about it on the way, the angrier she got."

"What happened?" Aaron asked gently.

"She and my two sons refused to go any farther and they returned to Midian."

"I am so sorry, brother," Aaron said, laying his hand on Moses' arm.

"It is probably for the best," Moses said with a sigh. "What I am about to do may be very dangerous. I am praying that God will be with her and that someday she may understand."

Both men sat quietly for a moment, then Moses said, "What about our family, Aaron? Are Father and Mother well?"

"Our parents are gone. Father died fourteen years ago and mother, three."

Moses sighed. It hurt him to think of never seeing his parents again, but he had been gone a long time. "What about Miriam?"

"She's alive."

"Does she have a family?"

She never married, but she adopted a son. Do you remember her friend Illa? She married Uri, the son of Hur in the tribe of Judah."

"Yes, I remember him."

"They had a son named Bezalel. Both parents died, and Miriam took the child to raise. She loves him dearly, but he's no good, Moses."

"How old is he?"

"Almost seventeen."

"Well, he still has time to improve." He reached over and grasped Aaron's shoulder with a strong hand. "I'm glad to see you, brother."

"And I you, Moses."

"We'll sleep for a time, then start back at dawn."

Aaron nodded; then as he lay down, he muttered, "There's going to be trouble in all this, Moses. I don't know how the elders will take it."

"They'll be glad that God is beginning to move among His people."

"I hope so. But they are stubborn. You know that."

"So is God," Moses said firmly, then closed his eyes and went to sleep.

———————

Bezalel had been asleep, but he woke suddenly at a touch, and when he saw a huge stranger leaning over him, fear leaped into his throat. He thought at first, in the dim light, that it was Laaman coming to finish the job of killing him. But the huge man said, "I am Moses, the brother of Miriam and Aaron. I take it you are Bezalel."

"Yes," Bezalel said, struggling to sit up. There was not so much pain now, and he got to his feet, staring at the huge man. He had heard so much about this brother of Miriam and Aaron, but Moses had been gone for so many years he had become almost a mythical figure. The Egyptians had forbidden anyone to speak his name, but the Hebrews had long memories. Now Bezalel said, "You've come back, Uncle."

"Yes. Where is Miriam?"

"She has gone to help a sick woman."

Moses studied Bezalel and said, "Your uncle Aaron has told me about you."

Bezalel felt his face grow warm. He could not think of a single thing to say. Moses put his hand on the young man's shoulder. "Be good to Miriam. Aaron tells me she loves you very much, and he himself loves you. Now I am back, and I will care for you too."

A warmth came over Bezalel at Moses' words. Something about this man inspired trust, and somehow he knew he would follow him to the death if need be.

"Aaron has gone to his family," Moses said. "Do you have anything to eat?"

"Yes," Bezalel said. "Sit down, sir. Let me fix something."

While Moses sat down on a small rug on the ground, Bezalel hurriedly put together a meal and placed it before him. Moses had not finished eating when Miriam came in. He quickly stood to greet her. Her cheeks flushed and her eyes opened wide.

"Moses!" she cried, throwing herself into his arms. "You've come back, just as I told everyone you would!"

Moses held her tightly. "Sister, I have missed you so."

Miriam was shocked by Moses. He was so much older now—but, then, they all were. Other than his age, though, something was different about him. He was stronger, more powerful, and his eyes seemed to look directly into her heart. She whispered, "Why have you come home?"

"It's the time of the Redemption, my sister. Our people must be free, and the God of our fathers has chosen me to lead them out of their bondage."

Overcome by joy, Miriam could not speak. "Moses, God raised you up for this hour. I knew it from the time I put you in your little basket in the Nile and Princess Kali pulled you out of the water. You will be the Redeemer of our people."

"No, the Almighty will be the Redeemer of our people."

"Yes, brother, you are right. But He will use you," Miriam said, and her heart was filled with pride and joy at the return of Moses.

CHAPTER

10

The elders of Israel had assembled themselves secretly to meet with Moses. Having been gone for forty years, he barely recognized the older men, and now there were several young men he had never laid eyes on. He did recognize Korah and his sons, and also Dathan and Abiram. He knew these two as overseers of the Hebrews, appointed by the Egyptians to get the most work out of the Hebrew slaves.

Moses said almost nothing at the meeting. When he and Aaron had been invited to come in, he had felt every eye fixed upon him, and was even more aware of the doubts of the assembly. He stood quietly while Aaron repeated his testimony of how God had appeared to him in the wilderness in the mountains of Horeb. Aaron spoke well and related how God had told Moses to assemble the elders of Israel and tell them that it was time for the Redemption.

"God has told my brother," Aaron said with bold confidence, "that He will lead us out of the land of Egypt to a land that flows with milk and honey. He has commanded my brother to go to Pharaoh and demand that we be released to go into the desert for a distance of three days to sacrifice to our God."

Aaron spoke at great length, and all of the elders were absolutely silent. For the most part their eyes were fixed on Moses, not on Aaron, and after Aaron finished and sat down, this silence continued. At last Korah spoke up. Though he was now an old man, he was still the leader of the elders and still the most powerful. Moses remembered him well as a headstrong, domineering man. Korah stared straight at Moses and demanded, "How are we to know that the voice you heard was the voice of the God of Abraham? It may have been an evil spirit. Did he tell you his name, Moses?"

For the first time Moses spoke up. "Sir, I did ask Him His name, and He told me to say when I would come to stand before the elders that I AM had sent me. He said that He was the God of Abraham and Isaac and Jacob and the great I AM. He said that was His name."

Moses hesitated, then went on, "I did not come to this place willingly. I asked God to select a more suitable man, one worthy of such a task, but God said that I should come before you. He also said that He would harden Pharaoh's heart."

"What does that mean?" Korah demanded.

"I am not sure. I am not sure of very much, but I do know that God intends to demand an accounting for every injustice and every hardship that the Egyptians have laid upon our people."

The elders began to stir. They whispered among themselves, and Moses could do nothing else but stand before them.

Finally, Dathan said, "It is not enough, Moses. We must have a sign that God has spoken to you. Any man can make a mistake about things like that."

Moses was ready for this request, and now he threw his rod upon the ground. It turned into a hideous serpent, raising itself up and flicking its tongue at the assemblage. The elders cried out in fear, but then Moses reached down and picked up the snake by the tail and it became a rod again.

"The God of Abraham is with us again," one of the elders cried out. "It is the time of the Redemption."

Moses' heart grew warm as he saw that the assembly was convinced, but then Korah spoke up, his face stolid and stubborn. "The magicians of Pharaoh can do tricks like this. It will not get us free. You must have more than signs like this."

Moses' anger began to stir, and for the first time Korah and the elders saw the fury reflected in his eyes. "Do not speak of signs. I speak of the power of the God of Abraham! All things are possible with God!"

"You are no speaker. You have told us that yourself. How can you expect to influence Pharaoh?"

"That is the question I asked of God, but He said that Aaron will speak for me."

A crafty look came into Korah's eye. He glanced around at the assembly of elders and said loudly, "My counsel is that Moses and Aaron go alone before Pharaoh."

A murmur of assent went through the crowd, and Moses knew that it was Korah's way of keeping clear of personal danger. He nodded and said quietly, "My brother and I will go stand before Pharaoh."

"Then we will wait and see what happens," Korah said, smiling. "This meeting is over."

"O mighty Pharaoh, two representatives from the Hebrew slaves request audience."

Pharaoh Amunhotep II was half reclining on a couch listening as musicians played soft, gentle music. He frowned and said, "What do they want?"

"They will not say, Pharaoh, but they insist on an audience."

"Probably want some more time off from their work to tend their own gardens," Pharaoh muttered. He was accustomed to such requests. "Send them in. They'll be a nuisance if I don't speak to them personally."

Pharaoh sat up, pulled his linen robe around him, and prepared to receive the Hebrews. Amunhotep was not the pharaoh that Moses had known, for Amunhotep's father, Seti I, had died while Moses was living in Midian; neither was Egypt the same as it was. It was battered on all sides by rebellions, so Egypt was now more concerned with survival than expanding its territories.

Pharaoh Amunhotep, like his deteriorating kingdom, was not impressive. Years of rebellions had drained him so that the body which had once been young and strong was now weak and feeble. He wore the double crown of Egypt on his head to represent both kingdoms, as the law required, and when the two Hebrew men were ushered in, he waited until they bowed. "What is it you want?" he demanded.

Aaron began to speak, and Moses remained silent. "O mighty Pharaoh, you well know the history of the land. You will remember that our people did not come as captives but voluntarily at the invitation of Pharaoh himself and his servant Joseph. When they came, they brought with them their own God and refused to worship the gods of Egypt." Pharaoh listened idly, not particularly interested. He had heard of Joseph, but he was not interested in twists of ancient history.

"I know that," he said impatiently. "What is your request?"

"The Lord, the God of Israel," Aaron said boldly, his voice steady, "has revealed himself to us. He has commanded us to appear before you, Mighty Pharaoh, and to say, 'Let my people go, so that they may hold a festival to me in the desert.'"

Anger shot through Pharaoh. He was a proud man, and the very mention of an alien god was heresy to him. He cried out in a voice tight with fury, "Who is the Lord, that I should obey him and let Israel go? I do not know the Lord and I will not let Israel go."

Aaron and Moses did not flinch. Aaron said firmly, "The God of the Hebrews has met with us. Now let us take a three-day journey into the desert to offer sacrifices to the Lord our God, or he may strike us with plagues or with the sword."

Furious, the pharaoh jumped to his feet and shouted, "Moses and Aaron, why are you taking the people away from their labor? Get back to your work!"

Pharaoh dismissed the pair and as soon as they had left, he cried out, "Bring me the head taskmaster for the Hebrews." He waited impatiently until the head taskmaster came, then gave these orders: "You are no longer to supply the people with straw for making bricks; let them go and gather their own straw. But require them to make the same number of bricks as before; don't reduce the quota. They are lazy; that is why they are crying out, 'Let us go and sacrifice to our God.' Make the work harder for the men so that they keep working and pay no attention to lies."

Pharaoh's command brought a terrible hardship to the Hebrews. The straw had always been collected in the grain fields and brought to the mud pits. Now that this system was stopped, the Hebrews had to go into the fields themselves and gather straw as best they could. Desperate to gather enough straw, the oldest men and women, and even the youngest children had to help. The Hebrew overseers argued with the Egyptians: "We cannot squeeze more out of the Hebrew laborers."

"If you don't, Pharaoh will punish you."

"We cannot do it. It is impossible."

The following days and weeks were a nightmare for the Hebrew laborers in the mud pit. The Hebrew overseers were stripped naked and beaten terribly for not driving the slaves hard enough, but they showed some degree of heroism in that they refused to surrender, insisting to the last that the pharaoh had asked for the impossible. They were whipped daily, and finally the highest Hebrew officials—Korah, Dathan, and Abiram—obtained an audience with Pharaoh.

Korah cried out, "O mighty Pharaoh, why have you treated your servants this way? Your servants are given no straw, yet we are told, 'Make bricks!' Your servants are being beaten, but the fault is with your own people."

Pharaoh said loudly, "Lazy, that's what you are—lazy! That is why you keep saying, 'Let us go and sacrifice to the Lord.'" Now get to work. You will not be given any straw, yet you must produce your full quota of bricks."

The elders wasted no time in making their feelings known to Moses and Aaron. They summoned the brothers before the council, and words of bitterness poured from their lips. "May the Lord look upon you and judge you!" Korah screamed. "You have made us a stench to Pharaoh and his servants and have put a sword in their hand to kill us."

Moses was silent, and he turned at once and left. He found a quiet place and began to call out to God. "O Lord, why have you brought trouble upon this people? Is this why you sent me? Ever since I went to Pharaoh to speak in your name, he has brought trouble upon this people, and you have not rescued your people at all."

And then the same voice that Moses had heard speaking from the burning bush said, *"Now you will see what I will do to Pharaoh: Because of my mighty hand he will let them go; because of my mighty hand he will drive them out of his country. I am the Lord. I appeared to Abraham, to Isaac and to Jacob as God Almighty, but by my name the Lord I did not make myself known to them. I also established my covenant with them to give them the land of Canaan, where they lived as aliens. Moreover, I have heard the groaning of the Israelites, whom the Egyptians are enslaving, and I have remembered my covenant.*

"Therefore, say to the Israelites: 'I am the Lord, and I will bring you out from under the yoke of the Egyptians. I will free you from being slaves to them, and I will redeem you with an outstretched arm and with mighty acts of judgment. I will take you as my own people, and I will be your God. Then you will know that I am the Lord your God, who brought you out from under the yoke of the Egyptians. And I will bring you to the land I swore with uplifted hand to give to Abraham, to Isaac and to Jacob. I will give it to you as a possession. I am the Lord.'

"See, I have made you like God to Pharaoh, and your brother Aaron will be your prophet. You are to say everything I command you, and your brother Aaron is to tell Pharaoh to let the Israelites go out of his country. But I will harden Pharaoh's heart, and though I multiply my miraculous signs and wonders in Egypt, he will not listen to you. Then I will lay my hand on Egypt and with mighty acts of judgment I will bring out my divisions, my people the Israelites. And the Egyptians will know that I am the Lord when I stretch out my hand against Egypt and bring the Israelites out of it."

Moses' heart had been brought low by the afflictions that had fallen on his people, yet now as God spoke, he suddenly realized that wonderful things lay ahead for his people, whom he loved dearly, and Moses knew that the time of the Redemption had come. He cried out for joy, "O Lord, mighty is your name and your will shall be done...!"

———

Rishef spoke abruptly to his slave Bezalel. He had sent for the young man and now stared at him. "Well, are you over your beating?" A sly smile crossed his lips. "You did not know that I knew the details of your foolishness?"

"I am ashamed, master," Bezalel said, his head bowed. He was humiliated that his Egyptian master would hear of such things, but there was no defense he could make.

"I hope you learned a lesson."

"Oh, indeed I have, master."

"Very well. I'll say no more about it. I have a new task for you."

"Yes, master?"

"The high priest, Jafari, requires your services. He has heard of your work. I must say he is very impressed."

"I am pleased to hear it, sire."

"You will go to the high priest and follow his commands exactly. Stay as long as you are required, then return here."

"Yes, master."

"And another thing. I've heard of this nonsense about the Hebrew slaves wanting to be set free. What do you know about that?"

"Nothing, sire." Actually, Bezalel knew a great deal about it, for the Hebrews had spoken of little else. He himself had been spared the arduous labor of gathering straw and mixing mud, but many of his kinsmen were almost dead of fatigue. It would not do, however, to speak of such things to Rishef.

"Good," Rishef replied. "See that it stays that way. Slaves should know their place."

"Of course, master. I will go at once to the high priest."

———

As Bezalel met with the high priest, he was frightened by the coldness of Jafari's gray eyes. They looked like stone.

"So you are Bezalel. I have seen your work in the home of Rishef. You do very good work indeed."

"Thank you, sir."

"Do well here, and I will see that you are rewarded."

"What is it you wish of me, O master?"

"I want you to make a golden statue of the goddess Hathor, the wife of Horus."

For some reason the commandment stirred an unpleasantness in Bezalel. He was not particularly committed to the God of his ancestors, but the many gods of Egypt were frightening to him. He could not see the sense of bowing down to a piece of clay molded into a statue, or of gold either, for that matter. But there was no chance for him to refuse. He was at the mercy of Jafari, as was every other man and woman and child in Egypt. The high priest was second only to Pharaoh in power.

"I will do my best, master."

"Good. Zara, take this young man to the workshop."

"Yes, at once."

A young woman came forward and motioned for Bezalel to follow her. He followed her out of the room and down a long corridor. She gave him a frank look, then said, "You are one of the Hebrews, aren't you?"

"Yes, mistress."

"My name is Zara."

Bezalel wondered about the woman. Was she a wife to Jafari, or could high priests even have wives? Was she simply a concubine, as he knew many of the priests had?

They made many turns, but finally they arrived at a large area that was obviously used for all sorts of work. Zara turned to him. "This is where you will labor. Let me know what materials you need, and I will get them for you."

"Yes, mistress."

Zara was studying him carefully. Suddenly a smile turned the corners of her full lips up. She came closer and looked up into his face, then leaned against him. "Not all of the Hebrews are as handsome as you," she whispered. She saw confusion in his face, then laughed. She reached up, put her hand on his cheek, and whispered, "I will be interested in your work, so I will be back often." She laughed at his expression, then turned, saying, "Come. I'll show you to your quarters."

As Bezalel followed the woman, he felt a premonition. *She's like a fruit ripe for the taking, but a man would be a fool to tamper with the wife or concubine of the high priest of Egypt!* He made up his mind then and there not to have anything to do with her. But when she turned and smiled at him again, he felt his resolution slipping away.

CHAPTER

11

Miriam stood over her brothers, listening as they talked. She had brought them an unimpressive meal of boiled barley and hard, crusty bread. Now she stood waiting, and finally Moses looked up and saw her. "What's troubling you, sister?"

"It's Bezalel," Miriam said quickly.

"Has he been in another fight?"

"No, but . . ."

When Aaron saw that Miriam could not finish, he spoke up, for he and Miriam had talked about this before. "He's headed down the wrong path, Moses," he said almost harshly. "In the first place, the high priest has him making idols."

"Of the Egyptian gods?"

"Yes. That's sin enough. But there's also a woman involved."

"A woman? What woman?"

"Her name is Zara. She's one of the prostitutes that the high priest keeps. Disgraceful."

Moses was troubled. He knew how much his sister loved this young man, and Moses himself had seen something in him that was worth saving. "Surely he's not sleeping with her."

"No!" Miriam spoke up quickly in Bezalel's defense. "But she's after him all the time. We've got to get him out of that place."

"That will be hard to do," Aaron said. "The high priest has brought him there, and from what I hear, he's very pleased with his work."

"We can't leave him there when God takes us out of Egypt."

"No. We must take him with us."

Aaron nervously drummed his fingers on the table. "What do we do now, Moses? The people hate us because they have to find their own straw. I don't know how we can do anything else."

Moses turned to Aaron, and his eyes seemed to burn. "It's time to move on."

"Move on? Move on how?"

"It is time to show the pharaoh the power of our God."

"The pharaoh will never give in!"

"No, he will not," Moses said at once. "God has told me He will harden Pharaoh's heart. As I have told you, He is going to send plagues upon Egypt, and before each plague, we must tell Pharaoh exactly what is happening. He must understand these plagues are not natural but are a punishment upon Egypt for what they have done to our people for four hundred years. Come. We will begin this morning!"

As far as Aaron was concerned, the second audience with the pharaoh had been a total failure. He had, in fact, been astonished when the pharaoh had even admitted them. He had not been so surprised, however, when the pharaoh merely laughed after he had listened to their demands to let their people go. "This god of yours has no power," he scoffed. "Show us a sign if he is the great I AM."

Aaron had glanced at Moses, and Moses nodded. Aaron threw the staff of Moses onto the floor, and it sprang to life as the hissing serpent he had seen before. Aaron drew back, frightened by the reptile, but Moses did not even glance at the snake. He was watching Pharaoh's face.

"Is this a sign from your god?" Pharaoh scoffed. "Magicians!" he called out, and a group of men who had been watching from the edge of the room swiftly stepped forward.

"O Mighty One, we can do such things as this." The speaker was the chief magician, named Jambres. He nodded to the other magicians, and they immediately began a wild dance, chanting to their gods. They surrounded the serpent that had been Moses' staff, and from somewhere small snakes began to appear. To Aaron it appeared that they had been concealed in the robes of the magicians. He saw with astonishment, however, that the large serpent, which had been the staff of Moses, darted out and swallowed one of the magicians' snakes. He then moved on to others, and all the magicians shouted, afraid of the monstrous serpent that was swallowing up every snake they could produce.

Aaron glanced at Pharaoh and saw that his face was pale, but anger flared in his eyes, and he shouted, "I will have no more tricks! Leave at once!"

"Come, brother," Moses said. "We will see Pharaoh later."

As soon as they were outside, Aaron looked at the staff of Moses. "The God of Abraham is powerful."

"Those magicians are nothing but tricksters. They have no real power," Moses said.

"What shall we do now, brother?"

"We will seek God. That is what we must always do."

———————

Whenever Moses was uncertain about what to do, he would find a quiet place by himself to seek God. After their encounter with Pharaoh he was gone for hours. Aaron waited all day and part of the night. Finally he went to bed, and when he awoke the next morning, Moses was sitting in the doorway. Coming off of his sleeping mat, Aaron rubbed his eyes. "You have been gone all night."

"God has been instructing me."

"What did He say?"

"He said that you and I are to go to the River Nile and speak to Pharaoh when he goes for his daily visit there. We must command him to let our people go. He will not do so, however, for God has told me that He will harden Pharaoh's heart."

"Then what will we do?"

"Then, according to God's command, I will strike the river with my staff, and the water of the Nile will be changed into blood, and the fish that are in the river will die, and the river will stink, and the Egyptians will not be able to drink its water. Come. Let us go."

———————

Pharaoh rode in his throne chair, carried by his powerful guards, for his morning trip to the river. He was accompanied by an armed guard and his oldest son, who walked before him. A choir sang a hymn of praise to Ra, the god of the sun.

Just as they reached the river, Pharaoh was startled by a shout. He straightened up in his throne chair and glanced around to see Moses and Aaron. The pharaoh's brow knitted, and anger touched his eyes. He had no time to speak, however, for Moses immediately cried out, "The Lord, the God of the Hebrews, has sent me to say to you: Let my people go, so that they may worship me in the desert. But until now you have not listened. This is what the Lord says: By this you will know that I am the Lord: With the staff that is in my hand I will strike the water of the Nile, and it will be changed to blood. The fish in the Nile will die, and the river will stink."

Pharaoh cried out in an incoherent rage, and Moses immediately turned to his brother and said, "Aaron, take your staff and stretch out your hand over the waters of Egypt."

Aaron did as Moses commanded. He lifted the staff above his head and brought it down forcefully on the water of the Nile, and in the blink of an eye the river began to behave as it never had before. Huge ripples appeared, and the surface of the water was broken by what appeared to be the thrashing of many fish. The color of the water changed to a dull red at first, which became brighter by the second. Fish broke out on the surface, their bodies bloated and swollen as if they had been smashed by a mighty hand. An unbearable odor arose from the river, and Pharaoh, whose eyes were wide with horror, screamed, "Away, away! Take me back to the palace!"

His guards carried the throne chair as quickly as they could back to the palace, and no sooner were they through the front gate than Pharaoh frantically summoned the magicians. He met them in his throne room and told them what had happened.

"Be calm, O Mighty One," Jambres, the head magician, said in his most soothing voice. "There is nothing to fear. We can do the same." He immediately sent for two clay vessels and water, and taking them, he poured water from one to the other. The water in the second became red, and he held it up to the pharaoh to examine. "Behold."

Pharaoh took the vessel, smelled it, and then flung it at Jambres's head. "It's nothing but colored water! I tell you the river has turned into actual blood and the fish are dead!" Pharaoh screamed at the magicians, who scattered in disarray. The mighty ruler then flung himself down on his throne and found, to his disgust, that he was trembling. "This cannot be," he muttered over and over. Then raising his head, he stood to his full height and shook his fist toward the ceiling. "This god of the Hebrews cannot defeat me! I am the son of Ra. *I* am god!"

All that day the Egyptian people wept and cried out to Pharaoh, for the river was filled with rotting fish and no fresh water could be found anywhere in it. They immediately began to dig wells for water, but for seven days the river remained so foul it made the whole land stink.

Pharaoh paced back and forth in his throne room. What was he to do? His wise men and magicians were useless. He could concede defeat and let the Hebrews go. . . . No! His insides raged at such thoughts! From that moment Pharaoh saw the struggle against the Hebrews as a struggle for his very life. If this god of the Hebrews should defeat him, the people would see that there was nothing divine in him. They would know that the great Pharaoh Amunhotep II was a mere man—a pretender upon the divine throne of Egypt. Everything that had been said about him would be seen as the lie that it was. He was not going to concede defeat that easily.

"I will die before I give in! I *will* defeat him!" Pharaoh panted as he shook his fist toward heaven. "I am the son of Ra, the god of Egypt! I will not let this god of slaves defeat me!"

At the end of the week, the Lord spoke to Moses again, telling him to repeat the commandment to Pharaoh to let the Hebrews go, then to say to him, *"If you refuse to let them go, I will plague your whole country with frogs. The Nile will teem with frogs. They will come up into your palace and your bedroom and onto your bed, into the houses of your officials and on your people, and into your ovens and kneading troughs."*

Moses strode into Pharaoh's throne room and delivered the message. Pharaoh refused point blank, and Moses could feel the pharaoh's glaring eyes on his back as he left. Before he made it to the outer gate, he saw swarms of frogs pouring into the outer court. The plague had begun. There had always been numerous frogs around the Nile River, but now they appeared to multiply instantly and one could not take a step without landing on one. They were ugly, monstrous things, and they filled the houses of Egypt, invading their food supplies and getting into their beds. The palace was not exempt, becoming a chaos of noisy, smelly amphibians.

Finally Pharaoh sent for Moses and Aaron. They stood quietly before the ruler, who glared at them while madly shooing frogs off his lap. "All right," he growled. "Pray to the Lord to take the frogs away from me and my people, and I will let your people go to offer sacrifices to the Lord."

Moses calmly said to the pharaoh, "I leave to you the honor of setting the time for me to pray for you and your officials and your people that you and your houses may be rid of the frogs, except for those that remain in the Nile."

"Tomorrow," Pharaoh said.

"It will be as you say, so that you may know there is no one like the Lord our God. The frogs will leave you and your houses, your officials and your people; they will remain only in the Nile," Moses replied.

God did exactly as Moses had promised the pharaoh, and the frogs died by the thousands—in all the houses and villages and out in the fields. The stench from the rotting frogs was unbearable, and the Egyptian taskmasters drove the Hebrew slaves to gather them into heaps and burn them.

Once the frogs were finally gone, Pharaoh stood at the wide window in his throne room and looked over the land, smiling. His land was clean again! He could see his mighty building projects going on all over the great city, and he thought of his promise to Moses to let the Hebrews go.

"Never ... never will I let them go," he uttered to himself, the rage in his heart burning at the very thought of losing the workers that were building his city and his great tombs and monuments. While Pharaoh's heart grew colder and colder the more he thought about it, Moses and Aaron were waiting patiently outside the throne room.

Aaron had some hope that Pharaoh would keep his word to let the people go, and he said to his brother, "I am optimistic that these two plagues have proven to Pharaoh that he cannot fight the Lord of Creation. I believe today he will set our people free."

Moses shook his head sadly, for he had heard the word of the Lord. "No, my brother, as hard as it may be to believe, he will not let them go," he said to Aaron. "He will harden his heart time and time again, and God will send more plagues, until they destroy the land of Egypt."

Indeed it happened as Moses said. A series of plagues, each more terrible than the last, fell on Egypt, and not a single inhabitant of the land could escape the horror of them. At first the wise men and counselors to Pharaoh insisted they were but natural disasters. They persuaded their king that they would survive, as Egypt had survived for millennia, and that he, Pharaoh Amunhotep II, would prove his divinity and be remembered for all eternity. As each plague occurred, however, the counselors gradually relented, one by one.

When the third plague—of gnats—struck Egypt, the head magician, Jambres, was already losing his faith in the gods of Egypt. It did not escape his attention that each plague was targeting one of their gods. The very creatures they worshiped in their temples were turning on them one by one. The challenge from this god of the Hebrews could not be any clearer. When the gnats covered Egypt, he gathered his magicians and tried to produce gnats using their secret arts, but they could not make one single gnat. Quietly the magicians told Jambres, "We are afraid! This god has power we cannot duplicate." And Jambres went to Pharaoh and said, "My Lord, this is the finger of God. You cannot fight this."

But Pharaoh's heart was like granite, and he would not heed Jambres's pleas. He lied to Moses. Over and over he promised he would let the people go, and over and over he took back his promise. After the gnats came flies, covering the people and animals and leaving open sores on the horses and oxen and livestock of the Egyptians. But in this case, and for the remainder of the plagues, God protected the Hebrews, making the land of Goshen, where they lived, a haven from the effects of the plague. In this way, the Hebrews and Pharaoh both knew that God was singling them out, making a clear distinction between His people and Pharaoh's people.

Following the biting flies came a plague on livestock. After that came a plague of boils, and when the magicians attempted to duplicate this, they were stricken by terrible boils themselves. But, still, the pharaoh's heart remained hard, and he refused to let the people go.

"Will you let the land be utterly destroyed?" Pharaoh's chief counselor cried. "Let these slaves go!"

"No, no, no!" Pharaoh shouted. "*I* am god, and the god of these worthless slaves will not defeat me!"

———

And so the plagues continued. A terrible hail pounded the land, crushing all the crops and trees in the fields. After the hail came great swarms of locusts, blackening the sky and consuming what crops were left after the hail. The Egyptians' lives became more and more miserable as it seemed their whole world was covered by these hideous swarms.

But Pharaoh's heart remained hard, so God sent a terrifying darkness over the land, a darkness so thick one could almost feel it. As horrible as all the plagues had been to the Egyptians, it was the plague of darkness that frightened them the most. It was a direct challenge to their chief god, Ammon-ra, who, to the Egyptians, was the source of all light. According to their belief, Pharaoh was his son. The darkness was so great that no light at all existed in the land. People groped about like blind men in utter terror that the light might not ever return.

Even the pharaoh was paralyzed by it, staying in his chambers and holding himself, rocking back and forth like a small child. This son of Ammon-ra was helpless in the face of such total darkness. For three days Egypt remained in darkness until Pharaoh could stand the cries of his people no longer.

"Go, worship the Lord. Even your women and children may go with you; only leave your flocks and herds behind."

"Our livestock too must go with us," Moses replied. "Not a hoof is to be left behind. Until we get there we will not know what animals are required to worship the Lord."

"Get out of my sight!" Pharaoh bellowed at Moses. "Make sure you do not appear before me again! The day you see my face you will die!"

Moses was silent for a moment, then said in a voice like distant, rumbling thunder, "Just as you say. I will never appear before you again."

Then he and Aaron turned and left the pharaoh's throne room for the last time. As they exited the palace, Aaron turned to look at his brother and saw that Moses' face was set like flint. "What more dreadful thing can be done, brother?" Aaron asked. "It appears the pharaoh will never relent."

Moses looked at Aaron with great sadness in his eyes, but with a smoldering fire behind them that his brother had come to recognize as the Spirit of God in him. Boldly, with no shred of doubt, he declared, "One more plague shall come upon the land, Aaron, and after this last plague, Pharaoh will know that the God of Abraham is the God of all the earth. *Then* he will let God's people go!"

CHAPTER

12

While the Egyptians, from the most humble peasant to Pharaoh himself, felt as if they had been buried alive in a tomb of darkness, the Hebrews were enjoying the brightness of the noonday sun in their humble abodes in the land of Goshen. Unable to work during the plague, they enjoyed their first extended time off of their lives. They visited one another, shared meals, and began to believe that their deliverance was finally upon them.

It was during this period of relaxation that Aaron thought a great deal about the future of his people. He had often thought about the necessity of a priesthood for the Hebrews, a special group of men that would intercede for the people with God, and show them how to live their lives. Now it seemed to him that the day for creating such an institution had finally come.

Aaron was a pragmatic man—more so than his brother, whose thoughts were so focused on God that he never seemed to consider the practical, everyday needs of people. At least in Aaron's opinion. So he was troubled by the cost of creating such an institution for such a large number of people, and he wondered how this might be accomplished, as poor as they were. Aaron was familiar with the priesthood of the Egyptians, whose ceremonies, vestments, and temples were filled with gold and silver idols and decorations of all kinds, so he began to ponder. "We have nothing. How could we have a priesthood?"

A partial answer to his question came when, after the darkness had filled the Egyptians with terror, they began to show a different spirit toward the Hebrews. Where they had once treated them with contempt or, at best, indifference, now they began to transfer their fear of Moses to the entire race of slaves. Aaron seized on this as a door of opportunity. He was well acquainted with the wealth of the Egyptians, and he felt it was time to make provision for the days that were coming. He noticed how the Egyptians were now speaking quite respectfully of the great festival for which the Hebrews were preparing to journey into the wilderness. From this observation came Aaron's idea. He explained it to no one, but in his own mind his reasoning went something like this: *The Egyptians have kept our people slaves. They have reaped all the rewards of our labors for four hundred years. They owe us for our labor. We have created the wealth of Egypt, and now at least part of that wealth belongs to us. Now is the time to take it.*

As Aaron thought on these things, he realized that it would never do to take the wealth of Egypt by force. Instead he began to whisper advice among the people so that the Hebrews themselves began approaching the Egyptians. Aaron led the way by presenting himself to the house of Macu, a wealthy Egyptian with whom he had become friends, and bowed before him. "Oh, master," he said, "you have heard of the great celebration that our people want to make."

Macu began to quake. His gardens and fields and much of his home had been stripped bare by the succession of plagues, and now he greatly feared the Hebrews. "Yes, Aaron, I have heard."

Aaron spread his hands apart in a futile gesture and shrugged. "But we have nothing to take with us. We are so poor. How shall we celebrate?"

"Oh, let me help you with that, Aaron," Macu quickly offered. "What is it you need?"

Aaron did not hesitate. "We are just slaves and barely have any clothes. Can we worship our God in rags? If we could just borrow some of your rich-looking clothes and perhaps a jewel or two . . . a ring for my wife's nose, perhaps. And possibly you could spare some of your cattle for us to sacrifice to our God. . . ."

"Of course, of course," Macu said gladly. "I will see to all of it. It is my great privilege."

When Aaron arrived at the slave camp later, he drew quite a crowd as he made his way toward home, his arms piled high with rich garments and gifts of gold and leading three fat cows. The news quickly spread all over the land, and the Egyptians found themselves facing the Hebrews, who asked to "borrow" things for the great festival.

It would never have happened without the encouragement of the plagues, but the Egyptians began plundering their own houses to give the Hebrews their personal possessions——golden rings and ornaments, richly sewn silk, furniture set with ivory, and household goods of all kinds.

When Moses got wind of what was going on, he was of a mind at first to put a stop to it. But then he considered that there was certainly some justice here. For hundreds of years the slaves had worked for no wages, so he prayed about what to do and received God's answer. He appeared before the elders and said, "God has spoken to me and here is what you are to tell the people: Let every man gather from the Egyptians articles of silver and gold and clothing." The Egyptians gave no objections, and the Hebrew slaves found themselves acquiring a portion of the great wealth of Egypt.

The high priest, Jafari, was a shrewd businessman as well as being adept in knowing how to worship Egypt's thousands of gods. As a businessman, he owned much property and many possessions. When he saw what was happening in Egypt, he sent for Bezalel and told him, "I understand that your people are going to celebrate a great feast to your god."

"That is true, sire," Bezalel said. He had no idea whether it was true or not, but he would never disagree with the high priest. He himself could not see how the Hebrews could ever get out of Egypt.

"I also understand," Jafari said, his eyes almost closing, "that our people have been providing you Hebrews with a few of the comforts and things you will need for sacrificing to your god."

"It is as you say, master."

"I would not want to be left behind in such a practice. After all, we must be understanding of other gods as well. Come. I will show you what I wish to do for your people."

Jafari led Bezalel out into a special room that was piled high with gold and silver ornaments and precious artifacts. "All of this is for your people. I hope your god will accept it."

"I am sure He will, master," Bezalel said, his eyes wide and hardly able to breathe at the sight before him.

"Shall I have this loaded onto a cart for you to take to your leaders?" Jafari asked.

"That would be most kind of you, sir."

Jafari's servants immediately brought a cart and began loading the rich collection onto it while Bezalel waited.

The high priest smiled benignly. "Come back as soon as the festival is over, Bezalel. I think we can do a little better for you in the future."

"That is most kind," Bezalel said with a servile bow. He could hardly wait to get away, but he did not want to appear ungrateful to his master.

As soon as the cart was loaded, he brought it directly to the home of Aaron. Moses and Miriam were with him, and Bezalel cried out, "Look, Mother! Look, Uncles! See what the high priest has given us!"

Moses, Aaron, and Miriam all stared at the cart, Aaron and Miriam in joyful awe, but Moses appearing indifferent.

"How did you convince him to give you all this, Bezalel?" Miriam asked.

"He was afraid. I could see it in his eyes. He tried to hide it, but he was quaking with fear." Bezalel was enthusiastic about this amazing turn of events. He had never before in his life paid much attention to the God of Abraham, but he was learning more and more about this God who could send plagues, the likes of which Egypt had never seen or heard of, and who could make the proud Egyptians quake before their own slaves! He also knew and greatly appreciated the value of gold and silver. "Look at all this," he cried. "Think of all the wonderful things I can make!"

"Gold is only yellow metal," Moses said with a smile. "It is like butter, only you cannot spread it on bread."

Bezalel stared at the great man. He could not understand him, but he agreed with him at once. "Yes, sire . . . but it *is* good to have it, isn't it?"

"Indeed it is," Aaron said. "You have done well." It was one of the first positive things Aaron had ever said to Bezalel, and the young man beamed at his praise.

"Our people will be leaving Egypt soon, Bezalel," Moses said to the boy. "What are *you* going to do?"

The question caught Bezalel off guard. "Why, Uncle . . . I don't know."

"You must not stay here," Miriam spoke up. "You must come with your people."

Bezalel felt her arm around his shoulders, and he looked at her, then at Moses. "Well, of course I will go with my people, Mother."

Moses nodded his approval. "Come. It is time to give the people instructions about what is going to happen."

Moses directed the elders to gather where he could meet with them all at once. He now stood on a small rise, addressing the assembly that had grown significantly since they had first met with him. Moses had insisted that all of the twelve tribes be represented, and he had added to their number Caleb, the son of Jephunneh, and Joshua, the son of Nun. As he stood before them, he could not help comparing the present meeting to his first meeting with the elders. Then he had seen nothing but doubt and fear. Now most of their faces were filled with hope. Of course, some of the older members, especially Korah and those closest to him, still appeared doubtful, but Moses paid no attention to this.

"Listen carefully to my instructions, my brothers!" Moses began. "We know what God has done for us here in the land of Egypt, so that our Redemption is upon us! Now we must do exactly as He says in order to accomplish His plans."

The elders looked at one another and nodded their heads. Most of them no longer doubted the power of their God to deliver them, and they were ready and anxious to take this next step.

"Tell the whole community of Israel," Moses proclaimed, "that on the tenth day of this month each man is to take a lamb for his family, one for each household. If any household is too small for a whole lamb, they must share one with their nearest neighbor, having taken into account the number of people there are. You are to determine the amount of lambs needed in accordance with what each person will eat. The animals you choose must be year-old males without defect, and you may take them from the sheep or the goats. Take care of them until the fourteenth day of the month, when all the people of the community of Israel must slaughter them at twilight. Then they are to take some of the blood and put it on the sides and tops of the doorframes of the houses where they eat the lambs. That same night they are to eat the meat roasted over the fire, along with bitter herbs, and bread made without yeast. Do not eat the meat raw or cooked in water, but roast it over the fire—head, legs and inner parts. Do not leave any of it till morning; if some is left till morning, you must burn it. This is how you are to eat it: with your cloak tucked into your belt, your sandals on your feet and your staff in your hand. Eat it in haste; it is the Lord's Passover."

Moses paused and a murmur ran round the assembly of elders as they took in this information. Then Moses continued, quoting the very words of God to His people:

"'On that same night I will pass through Egypt and strike down every firstborn—both men and animals—and I will bring judgment on all the gods of Egypt. I am the Lord. The blood will be a sign for you on the houses where you are; and when I see the blood, I will pass over you. No destructive plague will touch you when I strike Egypt.'"

The elders stood in shocked silence at this pronouncement of doom upon the Egyptians. When they had had sufficient time to take in these harsh words of God and the promise of their own deliverance, Moses gave more specific instructions for the departure of the children of Israel. When he finally dismissed the elders, they immediately scattered to tell each of their tribes to begin making their preparations.

When the night of liberation came, everyone knew they would be leaving Egypt, and they loaded their bundles on donkeys and on their backs. On the fourteenth day of the month, the people rushed around to get ready while the Egyptians watched in fear and in awe from a distance.

During that day every family killed its sheep and, with a bundle of hyssop, sprinkled the blood over the entrance of their dwelling. They roasted the sheep whole and ate it hastily. They kneaded flour with water and packed it in linen cloths and then stood ready—gathered inside their homes as Moses had commanded them, watching to see what the God of Abraham would do next.

In the midst of these preparations, Caleb suddenly realized that Bezalel was still at Jafari's home. He hurried there to bring him back, and he found Bezalel working as if nothing were going on.

"You foolish boy," he said. "Come with me!"

"What is it, Caleb?"

"Don't ask questions. Just come."

"But my things—!"

"Leave your things!" He dragged Bezalel out, explaining what was very shortly going to happen. The two rushed through the city and to the slave camp, getting to Caleb's home just as darkness was beginning to fall. Caleb shoved Bezalel inside, stepped in himself, and closed the door. He saw his family's faces filled with fear as they were illuminated by the candle. "Now," Caleb said with a grim smile, "we will see what the God of Abraham and Isaac and Jacob will do to the Egyptians."

They sat quietly, everyone afraid to speak. Outside they heard the croaking of frogs and the humming of insects and palm trees swaying against the house in the breeze.

Then came a complete silence. It was as if everything outside of the room had died. Caleb's wife came to him, and he put his arm around her and murmured, "Do not be afraid. It is our God who has come."

Bezalel sat hunched up with his back against a wall and whispered, "I hear something." No one in the small room could tell what it was. Perhaps it sounded like the rushing of waves against the shores of the Great Sea, or of huge flocks of birds passing overhead, or the rumble of distant thunder. To Bezalel it sounded like deep and tragic music, such as he had only imagined.

On and on the sound went, and Bezalel, along with the family of Caleb, sat like statues. Finally Bezalel, whose ears were sharper than most, whispered, "What is that?"

"I hear nothing," Caleb said.

But the sound grew stronger, and Caleb's wife said, "It is the sound of women's voices crying with grief." She started for the door, but Caleb grabbed her back. "No! Stay inside," he ordered.

That was the longest night Bezalel had ever endured! The distant screams grew more frantic, and everyone tried to ignore what they meant. Bezalel was not a young man given to fear, but he knew that what was happening had to be God's doing.

When daylight began seeping in under and around the door, Caleb went to it and cracked it open. He heard a powerful voice crying out, "Come out, O children of Abraham, children of the Most High God! It is the day of liberation!"

"It's Moses!" Caleb cried, his eyes flashing. "Come on."

Bezalel hurried outside with the others, and then he saw many Egyptians in the Hebrew slave camp, their faces swollen with weeping. Even one of the Egyptian workers in Jafari's household was there, his clothes torn and his face ashen.

"What has happened?" Bezalel asked him, and the man wailed, "Your God has killed us! Leave our place! There is not a house in Egypt where the oldest child has not been taken."

Another cried out, "The pharaoh's own son was found dead in his bed!"

A great clamor arose from the Egyptians. "Leave us before all of Egypt is dead!"

Then Moses appeared, seeming to tower above the people around him. His eyes flashed, and his voice rolled like thunder. "Come. It is the day of Redemption. Come, O people of God."

And then the procession began. Men, women, and children poured out of their small homes. They loaded their burdens on the backs of donkeys and on their own backs. The rising sun struck the golden and silver plates and bowls and gifts they had borrowed from the Egyptians as the whole city of slaves began moving forward, raising great clouds of dust.

Bezalel took the huge bundle that Caleb had handed him and joined the crowd. He noticed as the Hebrews left that they were being joined by slaves who were not Hebrews, who were anxious to flee Egypt too. Bezalel had no idea where he was going, but when he saw Moses, the giant of God leading the way, he knew he could not stay in Egypt.

"Will all be well, Master Caleb?"

Caleb laughed. "Redemption is what we have, and that is always well. Come, Bezalel, the new life awaits us. We are no longer slaves but free men!"

Moses was moving forward when he felt a touch. He turned quickly and found Miriam and Aaron behind him. "It's the Redemption!" Miriam cried.

Moses lifted his hands toward heaven. "Yes," he said, his voice trembling, "the God of Abraham has delivered His people."

PART THREE

DAY OF REDEMPTION

CHAPTER

13

The disorganized mob that flowed out of Goshen seemed to be nothing but a mass of confusion. It slowly moved forward amidst the bleating of sheep, the lowing of oxen, and the babble of hundreds of thousands of voices.

The number seemed to grow larger as they left, for the Hebrews themselves were joined by many slaves captured from other nations who had heard what the God of the Hebrews was doing and were determined to be a part of it. Along with the Hebrews were Ethiopians, Canaanites, and many Asiatic people. Many of them were dark skinned, and there was much murmuring among the Hebrews over this.

"Moses, look at them!" Aaron protested. "They're not of our people. Tell them to return to Egypt."

But Moses shook his head, for he had already been instructed by the Lord God. There was no doubt in his mind about the purpose for the Exodus. He was not merely taking the people out for a three-day festival in the wilderness, but was leading them toward a land that would be theirs—a land where the Hebrews would not be slaves but would be a holy people separated unto the Lord. He said briefly, "No, Aaron, those that go with us are of us. The Lord has told me there will be only one law for our people and one law for any strangers who join our people." Aaron could not protest God's word, so he remained silent.

During the journey out of Goshen, until they reached the edge of the wilderness, Moses went over and over the task that lay before him. He alone of all the multitude was aware of the tremendous thing God was doing. He was calling to himself a people that would be His own. They would be different from all other people, but while Moses exalted in this, he also understood that to bring a people from bondage to freedom would mean a new spirit would have to be in them. They would have to be introduced to the laws of God and taught how to handle their new freedom.

For this reason God directed Moses not to follow the shortest route to the Land of Promise, for this way went through the land of the Philistines. The Hebrews, who had barely tasted freedom, still thought like slaves, and when faced with the warlike Philistines, they would turn tail and flee back to their bondage in Egypt.

Without saying a word to Aaron or anyone else, Moses led the people toward the great Red Sea. He knew how dangerous this would be, but there was no other way.

During this trek into the wilderness, the people acted as if they were celebrating a holiday. They were singing and shouting, and there was plenty to eat. They had brought large supplies of vegetables, honey, and other provisions with them. The mass of travelers raised immense clouds of dust, hiding much of the procession from view. During the day a pillar of dust and smoke swirling together arose to go before them, and at night the dust cloud turned red with an inner fire, burning throughout the dark night to lead them on their journey.

Although their destination was clear in the mind of Moses, it was not so clear to the elders of Israel. They began muttering to themselves about where they were going, and soon Korah called the elders together for a conference. Korah was no doubt the most influential man among the Hebrew people, and when he spoke, the elders listened respectfully.

"It is time," Korah announced solemnly, his small eyes gleaming craftily, "that we demand from Moses how he intends to lead us to this land he speaks of."

Dathan nodded at once. "You are right, Korah. We are wandering in a place that is fraught with danger, and who knows what lies ahead of us?"

Abiram, who, along with Dathan, had been one of the task-masters set over the Hebrew slaves by the Egyptians, was quick to join in. He twisted his short, muscular body and a customary shifty look touched his eyes. "Right," he said. "Very true. Very true indeed! We must call this man to account."

A murmur went around, and soon all of the elders were swayed. Korah nodded with satisfaction. "How does he intend to take this multitude across the Sea of Reeds? Why, it would take hundreds of ships for such a feat!"

"Yes. Very true," Jacob said. He was one of the followers of Korah, and he was always anxious to show his loyalty. "Pharaoh agreed to let us go for a three-day festival, but he must know by now that Moses has no intention of bringing the people back."

"He knows," Korah said, "that Moses has from the beginning planned to form a nation, and that he would make himself the king of the Hebrew people. Pharaoh cannot be treated like this. He will follow us and kill us all."

Fear fell upon the elders and it soon spread to the people. "The pharaoh will bring his army," the whisper began. "We will all be slaughtered. This Moses has led us to our deaths!"

———

Although Pharaoh had not heard the murmuring and complaints of Korah and his followers, he was indeed angry and determined that he would have his revenge upon Moses. The Exodus had struck at the very heart of his claim to be a god. He, the great pharaoh of Egypt, had been defeated by a mere shepherd! It must not be!

Added to Pharaoh's disgrace and humiliation was his grief over the death of his beloved son. It had been settled in his mind that his son would sit upon the throne of Egypt, and now, even while the funeral preparations were being made, an intense fury was burning within Pharaoh. He had sent out spies at once to follow the slaves, and from all reports it was clear that they had no intention of coming back to Egypt.

"Where is he taking them?" Pharaoh wondered aloud as he paced back and forth. "My spies tell me he is about to reach the

Red Sea. Why has he led them to a dead end? His God may be powerful, but He is not powerful enough to pick up thousands of slaves and carry them across the water on wings."

The high priest of Ammon-ra, Jafari, had suffered a loss of prestige too. He was a shrewd, crafty man and well understood that the people had carefully watched the duel between the God of the Hebrews, and Ammon-ra, the chief god of Egypt. Now Jafari clearly understood that something must be done to regain his lost reputation.

He decided to plead with the pharaoh. "O Mighty Pharaoh," he said, "this Moses is a mere man. We cannot allow him to make a mockery of you and your divinity. We must send the army and bring the slaves back again."

Pharaoh stared at Jafari, then asked, "But what about the plagues? Will their God not start again to reek his vengeance on Egypt?"

"It will not be so, Pharaoh. The plagues were nothing but nat-ural phenomena. When the fish in the river died, it was natural there should be more flies and frogs. It is not the work of a god at all."

Pharaoh listened intently as Jafari urged him, saying, "The gods of Egypt are not dead. You must act at once. You are, after all, the son of Ammon-ra. Send for them. You will find them helpless—backed up against the Red Sea—and you can bring them back."

Pharaoh was persuaded by his high priest and decided on his course of action. "Call the army together. Assemble the chariots. We will run these ragtag followers of Moses and his God down!"

"Good. They will be gathered there close to the sea. They can-not flee any farther. We have them trapped!" Jafari exclaimed. This victory over your enemies will prove to all of your people that you are indeed a god!"

"See to it!" Pharaoh cried, and as soon as Jafari left, he also left the palace and went to the quarters of Princess Kali. During his reign, he had come to trust this daughter of his predecessor. She was only a woman and yet he knew she had more intelligence than most men—certainly more than his advisors.

When he entered her apartment, he saw that she was lying on

a couch, her face pale and lined. His heart smote him when he realized she was not far from death. He softened his voice as he approached and said, "How is it with you, Princess Kali?"

"It is well with me, sire."

"You do not look at all as if you are recovering."

"I am going to be with God."

The simple declaration from the woman struck a chill in the pharaoh. "God?" he said. "Which god? Ammon-ra?"

Kali's voice was frail and weak, but her eyes were alive. She did not even lift her hand but turned her face toward Pharaoh. "I have prayed much to the gods of Egypt all of my life, and they have never spoken to me. But now I have prayed to the God of Moses. They call Him the great I AM, and He has spoken."

"You saw this God? But He has no form."

"I saw nothing," Kali whispered. "But He came into my heart. It was like a warm sun coming into a cold room or like a light coming into a dark room. Suddenly my heart knew that all that Moses has said about this God is true."

"Impossible! It cannot be! You are losing your mind!" the pharaoh shouted. He began to tremble and said, "You are not well. I will send the physicians and the priest."

"Send no priest. I need no physicians," Kali murmured.

"What about our gods?"

"They are not gods at all, sire. The God of the Hebrews," Kali faintly whispered, "He is the only God." She smiled then, and Pharaoh was frightened, for he himself was afraid of death. He saw that she had no such fear. There was a peace on her face, the light of joy in her eyes, and she lifted her hand now and said, "The God of the Hebrews, He is the only God...."

Pharaoh turned and fled from the apartment as if pursued by demons. He was trembling, for he believed strongly in the wisdom of Princess Kali, but when he related what had happened to Jafari, the high priest had said soothingly, "She is a very old woman, sire. You know that people lose their minds when they are old and almost ready to cross to the underworld. The princess is confused, but you must not weaken in your resolve."

"No," Pharaoh said, straightening himself up, "we will defeat

Moses, and the princess will know then that the god of the Hebrews is no god at all. Is the army ready?"

"It is assembling."

"I will personally lead them into the battle," Pharaoh said loudly, as if to bolster his own fears. "Come. We must make a sacrifice to the gods before the battle!"

Oholiab uttered a shrill cry and leaped toward Bezalel, grabbing hold of him. Bezalel stumbled and nearly fell. "Let go of me, Oholiab!" he snapped. "What's the matter with you?"

"I thought I heard the sound of Pharaoh's chariots," Oholiab said, his naturally high-pitched voice was even more shrill than usual. He was a small young man, the same age as Bezalel, but different in every respect. He was as homely as mud and skinny and thin as a stick. Three things about his life defined and controlled him: one was his gift of crafting things of metal and wood. In this he was second only to Bezalel among all of the Hebrews. The second was a distinct negative: His life was controlled by fear. He was afraid of practically everything! A spider or a snake could send him screaming, and just the thought of Pharaoh's army made him turn ashen. The third thing that defined his personality was his misconception about his prowess with women. Despite his being undersized, homely, and afraid of his own shadow, he was convinced that women loved him. Experience never seemed to teach him anything, and even as he clung to Bezalel's arm, he turned to watch a beautiful young Hebrew woman walk by. "Look at her. Isn't she a beauty?"

Bezalel could not help laughing. "Not a beauty you're ever likely to talk to."

"Oh, I don't know. I have a way with women, you know."

"I know your way with women." He looked back over his shoulder and squinted through the dust raised by the pilgrimage of the slaves. "You're right about Pharaoh, but I don't hear him yet."

Oholiab tugged at Bezalel's sleeve. "You'd better listen to me, Bezalel."

"I have listened to you ever since we left Goshen. I'm tired of listening to you."

"We'd better go back. It's the only safe thing to do. After all, we don't know what lies up ahead of us except the sea. We'll all drown if we try to get across that. I can't swim and it's full of beasts."

Bezalel listened for a time, then shoved his friend away. "Go chase after that girl," he said. "I think she gave you a certain look."

Instantly Oholiab forgot the terrors of the sea ahead and the army of Pharaoh behind. "You really think so?" he said. He spit on his hand and smoothed his hair back with the flat of his palm. "Well, you're probably right. I'd better go talk to her."

Bezalel grinned as his small friend scurried off in pursuit of the young woman. He was well accustomed to Oholiab's fantasies. They were amusing, and he was a good fellow, clever with his hands and a good assistant.

Suddenly Bezalel saw Caleb striding along toward the head of the line. They were both of the tribe of Judah, and there was no one, even Moses, that Bezalel admired more than Caleb. He hurried forward, and when he caught up with the tall, older man he said, "It looks bad to me."

Caleb turned and looked at Bezalel with his steely, gray eyes. "What looks bad to you?"

"Why, it's obvious we don't know where we're going."

"Moses is the man God has chosen as our leader. We will follow him wherever he goes."

"Oh, come on, Caleb. You know he's only a man."

"He's the man God has chosen."

"But when we get to the sea what will we do?"

Caleb snorted impatiently. "It's not what we're going to do. It's what our Lord God will do." His face grew fixed, and his lips drew together in a pale line. He was a stern man full of faith, and now he snapped, "If necessary, our God will bear us in His hands!"

"Why, I thought He didn't have hands," Bezalel said, "that He didn't have a form."

Suddenly Bezalel found himself on the ground. It happened so quickly he did not know how he got there. His face was burning, and his head was ringing. He had not even seen the blow coming. Caleb reached down and jerked him to his feet. "A man of Judah will not speak lightly of the Lord God!" he said. He shook Bezalel until the lad's head spun and then loosed him so abruptly Bezalel nearly fell to the ground.

"What was that all about?"

Bezalel turned to see Miriam who had come to see what was happening. She was bearing a heavy basket on her shoulder and leading a nanny goat with a young one following, trying to nurse.

"It was nothing, Mother."

"Caleb doesn't strike men for nothing. What did you say?"

Bezalel knew that there was no way he could hide anything from Miriam. "Well, I simply said I didn't think we were going to be able to get across the sea."

"He wouldn't slap you for that. What else did you say?" She soon had the whole story out of him and then said, "I ought to slap you myself. What's the matter with you, Bezalel?"

"Nothing. I'm all right."

"No, you're not. You have such a gift." Miriam's face grew sad, and she reached out and touched his face with her free hand. "You could do so much, but instead of that you just wander around. I've heard it said that sailors can follow a star. That's how they get across the sea, but you don't have a star. You don't have anything to guide you. You're like a man with nothing on the inside." She turned and walked away, her back bent. Bezalel watched her go and felt terrible. "I didn't mean it," he whispered aloud. He trudged along after Miriam, and gloom seemed to encircle him.

———————

"He's coming! Pharaoh is coming with his army! There are hundreds of chariots!"

The people in the rear had seen the Egyptian army, and indeed Pharaoh had a mighty host of six hundred chosen chariots with captains over every one of them. They had overtaken the Hebrews who were encamped by the sea beside Pi Hahiroth.

Panic spread at once among the entire multitude. Their cries rang out, and Moses was trapped in the middle of a group of screaming people. One of them shouted, "Was it because there were no graves in Egypt that you brought us to the desert to die? What have you done to us by bringing us out of Egypt?"

Korah was standing close enough to hear, and he said, "Didn't we say to you in Egypt, 'Leave us alone; let us serve the Egyptians'? It would have been better for us to serve the Egyptians than to die in the desert!"

Moses suddenly flung his way through the crowd, shoving people aside until he came to stand upon a slight mound. His voice was like a trumpet as he cried out, "Do not be afraid. Stand firm and you will see the deliverance the Lord will bring you today. The Egyptians you see today you will never see again. The Lord will fight for you; you need only to be still."

The shouting of the people softened, and Moses prayed desperately, "O God, show your power. Deliver your people."

Instantly Moses heard in his heart the voice that he had heard speak out of the burning bush. As clearly as he had ever heard anything, the Lord said to him, *"Why are you crying out to me? Tell the Israelites to move on. Raise your staff and stretch out your hand over the sea to divide the water so that the Israelites can go through the sea on dry ground. I will harden the hearts of the Egyptians so that they will go in after them. And I will gain glory through Pharaoh and all his army, through his chariots and his horsemen. The Egyptians will know that I am the Lord when I gain glory through Pharaoh, his chariots and his horsemen."*

Even as God spoke, the cloud of dust raised by the army of Pharaoh grew thicker. But somehow the mighty army did not reach the Hebrews. From Pharaoh's vantage point, a darkness seemed to fall on the Hebrews so that they were no longer visible, but the Hebrews were, in fact, not in darkness.

Moses lifted up his staff as God had commanded and instantly the sound of a moaning wind filled the ears of the frightened Hebrews. They stood there trembling, all except Moses and a few like Caleb and Joshua. Even as they watched, they saw the water of the Red Sea become agitated, and suddenly it began to roll back. It moved until there were two walls that led directly through the sea.

Moses turned and cried out, "Children of the Living God, the

Lord has made the way. Go now through the midst of the sea."

At first no one moved, but then one man advanced, holding his wife by one hand and his young son by the other. He cried out with exaltation on his face, "The God of our fathers is here! Come, this is the day of Redemption!"

As soon as the multitude closest to the sea saw this man go through with his wife and child, a glad cry arose and they began to follow. Soon the dry path between the two walls of water was filled with people. Bezalel was stunned. He could look through the wall of water and see fish moving inside of it.

As for Moses, his heart was rejoicing, for the God who had spoken to him out of the burning bush had delivered him. While Pharaoh's men groped in the darkness, the children of Abraham moved through the depths of the sea.

When the Hebrews had all reached the other side, Pharaoh and his army could once again see them. "Look, there they are!" Pharaoh cried out.

"Yes, Mighty Pharaoh," his chief general cried. "Shall we go after them?"

Pharaoh stared at the path through the sea and pointed. "Look! Ra has made a way for us to pass through so that we may overtake his enemies. Forward!"

Moses watched and saw the Egyptians pursuing, and the Lord said to him, *"Stretch out your hand over the sea so that the waters may flow back again over the Egyptians and their chariots and horsemen."*

And Moses stretched forth his hand, and instantly the sea began to join itself together. The mountains of water collapsed and fell back, swallowing up the pharaoh and his army.

Pharaoh saw death as the waters closed and knew that the Hebrew God had won. He threw himself to the floor of the chariot and cried out for mercy, but it was too late, for the sea had come to claim him.

The Hebrews watched as Pharaoh and his army were swallowed up, and Moses and the people began singing a joyful song to the Lord. Miriam led the women in dance and song, and as they danced on the shores of the sea, the people feared the Lord and believed Him and Moses, His servant.

CHAPTER
14

Many found it strange that Moses had chosen Joshua, the son of Nun, to be always at his right hand. Not a little jealousy ensued among the Hebrews as a result of Moses' choice, for Joshua was a young man that few people noticed, but Moses had seen in him a quality that he had found in no one else. He mentioned this to Miriam, saying, "I've not found so much faith in any of our people. He never doubts the Lord God."

Joshua was probably more surprised than anyone that he was chosen for such an honorable position. He was a tough man of no more than average height, but was built like an oak and possessed an absolute fearlessness.

After the waters closed in upon Pharaoh and his army, and the people were celebrating their deliverance, Joshua did not join in the singing. He felt almost envious as he watched the dancers and singers who lifted up their voices in an explosive cry of praise to their God. But he himself was not a singing man.

What interested Joshua most was what they could salvage from the destruction of Pharaoh and the soldiers of Egypt. He begged Moses to let them stay by the shores of the Red Sea until the bodies of the Egyptians washed up, and they could take their weapons and armor.

Moses agreed, and the people gave shouts of joy as it happened just as Joshua said it would. In addition to the armor and weapons they found gold and silver treasure, for it was customary for the chariot captains to carry precious-metal images of their gods to help them in battle. They also found rich clothing, such as the silk tunics the soldiers wore under their armor. But Joshua and the young men who gathered themselves around him cared little for this. What they sought and found were the quivers full of arrows suspended on the bodies of the soldiers and anything else in the way of weaponry.

Finally Moses gave the command to go forward, and the pillar of cloud began to move down the Suez arm of the Red Sea and directly into the Desert of Shur. Moses, of course, knew that this would be so, for God had told him when speaking out of the burning bush that after the people were delivered they would serve Him on Mount Sinai.

The people were ecstatic over their deliverance. There was still plenty of food in the packs on their backs and in the carts that they pulled, and every night the camp was filled with singing and rejoicing. Moses was in a continual state of excitement, seeing the hand of God at work. Many Hebrew children were safely born, and the people marveled to see this miracle occur many times. Moses was also aware of the foreigners who had joined them and who had come to be called the "mixed multitude." He himself had no doubt that this was God's will.

When he spoke to Joshua about it, the young man remarked that some of them had gone back to Egypt, but many had passed through the sea with them.

Moses was as adamant as he had been when he spoke to Aaron. "Those who have thrown in their lot with the children of Abraham, no matter what their nationality, shall live under the one law with us."

Joshua nodded solemnly. He accepted whatever Moses said without question. He did wonder about one thing, though. "Sooner or later we are going to run out of food, my lord Moses. What then?"

Moses had thought about this. "How much is left?"

"Some are already out of food. Quite a few of the people have a good supply—mostly vegetables, eggs, and honey. There's a little hunger in the camp but not much." Joshua hesitated, then said,

"What I'm most worried about is water. We can do without food for a time, but not without water. There's already some complaining against you."

Moses did not reply, but all that day and late into that night he pondered the situation. The lack of water had become the most pressing issue for the people, for they had consumed what they had brought and had not found any more in the desert.

He waited for the word of God to come to Him, begging God to speak so that he might know how to act. He had led an army at one time and knew well how much thought and effort went into providing for a multitude of men through a hard journey. He remembered clearly how months of preparation had been necessary for such a journey, and now here he was with barely any preparation at all!

"Oh, God, I cannot do this alone! Please speak to my heart. Tell me what to do."

God was totally silent on this question, but Moses did not complain. He was confident that whatever happened, God would come through, and late at night he would cry out his praises to God.

———

"Moses, we have found water!"

Moses' heart leaped at his sister's cry, and he looked up to see her running toward him, her face radiant.

"Water!" Moses said, leaping to his feet. "I knew God would provide."

Aaron suddenly appeared, his face long and filled with tension. "Come quickly, brother. There's trouble."

"Trouble? I thought we found water."

As Moses followed Aaron and Miriam out of his tent through the crowd of people, he trembled at how the people had been crying for water for days. Their animals had been crying piteously out of dried mouths.

Finally he reached the edge of the crowd, and he heard his name being called, "Moses . . . Moses, what shall we drink?"

Moses moved quickly to where the water had been found, and

he saw several wells. Korah was there, dipping a gold cup into the water. He took a gulp of it, then spat it out, and thrust the cup at Moses, scowling. "Drink it, Moses! This is not fit for animals. What will you do to feed this multitude?"

Moses took the cup and tasted it; then he too spat it on the parched ground. The water was undrinkable! He stood there while the cries of the people went on about him, but in his heart he too was crying out to God. As the noise of the crowd seemed to fade away, there came an impulse from inside his spirit. "Is this you speaking, O God?"

There was no answer, but Moses suddenly knew what to do. He looked around and saw a laurel tree, and with one swift motion he leaped toward it. He pulled off a few of the laurel twigs and thrust them into the well. There was an immediate stirring of the water, and Moses commanded Joshua, "Put the laurel leaves into all the wells."

Joshua leaped to obey, and as soon as it was done, Moses, without even tasting the water himself, knew that God had worked another miracle. "Now, take and drink. God has provided, as He always will."

Cries of doubt were soon transformed into cries of joy. Like any good shepherd, Moses stood back and waited until everyone else had drunk. Finally Joshua brought him a cup and his face was alight with joy as he said, "Taste, master. It's the best water I've ever had. Almost like wine."

Moses took the cup that Joshua handed him and drank from it. When he lowered it, he smiled and put his hand on the young man's shoulder. "That which God provides is always good, Joshua."

As the three men came to stand before him, Moses felt a great weariness descend upon him. Korah, Dathan, and Abiram, the self-constituted spokesmen for the rest of the assembly, stood before Moses with a resolute stance. Korah said, "We have to talk to you, Moses."

"What is it this time, Korah?" Moses knew that the assembly would have to be reorganized as soon as they had met with God at

Sinai. The tribes would all have to be represented, not just a few powerful men who had found their place by devious means. He prepared his mind to listen, although he knew that whatever they had to say to him would not be good.

"We have come to ask what you intend to do," Korah said. "We can't go on like this forever."

"Why can't we?"

"Why, it's obvious!" Korah said with astonishment. "We move from disaster to disaster."

"God has always provided, hasn't He?"

"Well, yes, up till now, but we can't live day by day waiting for God to give us a miracle."

Moses smiled. "Why not?" he asked gently. "You think it's hard for the Lord to perform a miracle?"

"That's not the problem, Moses, and you know it!" Dathan said hotly.

Korah agreed, nodding vigorously. "We left Egypt prepared only for a three-day festival, and now who knows how long we may be in this wilderness?"

"You knew all the time we weren't going back to Egypt. I made that clear," Moses said mildly.

Korah was angered by the meekness of Moses. "How are you going to provide for all the needs of the people?"

"I have no intention of providing for the needs of the people."

"You see," Abiram cried. "I told you! He has no plan at all."

"It is the Lord our God who will provide for our needs. He will send water. He will provide food. He is the God of all power. Have you forgotten already how He delivered us from bondage in Egypt? He is all-sufficient."

"Well enough to talk like that, but we must be practical!" Korah snapped, his eyes sharp and hard as stone. "We have the right to know what you intend to do."

"God has given me a promise," Moses said calmly, "that He would take us out of Egypt and bring us to a land flowing with milk and honey. He has promised me that we would be His holy people. He has given us the pillar of cloud by day and the pillar of fire by night, and we will follow it faithfully."

"Until we die," Korah said. "When we leave these wells, who knows where the next water will be?"

"It will be wherever God leads us. He will not let His people starve or die of thirst."

The three knew they were dismissed when Moses turned abruptly away.

"As soon as the people grow thirsty again," Korah muttered to his two cohorts, "then we will see what this fellow will do."

The worry of water running out was in the minds of many people, but God led the people to Elim, only a half-day's march ahead from Marah, where the water had been bitter. There, they were ecstatic to find twelve springs of fresh, pure, sweet water and a beautiful oasis of green growing things and palm trees.

Aaron was almost crying with joy as the people drank and enjoyed the greenery in the middle of the burning desert.

"Let us stay here, Moses. This is a good place."

"This is not the land that our God has promised us," Moses said.

"But we are here, and we could have a good life."

"No. We could not have a good life here, because we would not be obedient to God."

Aaron angrily waved at the burning desert that lay outside of the oasis. "We do not know what lies out there."

"No, but God knows, and He is also able to supply all our needs in the wilderness, my dear brother."

Moses left Aaron, knowing he had not pacified him. He listened to the people singing and the happy voices as they enjoyed the fresh water and soothing beauty of the oasis, but he knew they would soon turn angry when they had to move on into hardship.

Moses walked as far away from the camp as he could, until the babble of voices grew dim. There, he threw himself down on his face and began to pray.

"Almighty God, I cannot bear the weight of this people. Only you are strong enough for that, but I beg you, God, speak to me. Let me know that I am in your will."

Moses prayed until he grew faint, but there was not a single word from God.

Finally he got up and stretched out his arms toward heaven. "I have not heard your voice, almighty Lord, but even if you never speak to me again, I will still love you!"

As Moses made his way back toward the camp, he found himself filled with amazement. *How is it that I love God? I have never heard of people loving God before. The Egyptians are terrified of their gods. If you asked one of them to love Ammon-ra, they'd think you were crazy.*

He looked up into the endless blue sky and an indescribable joy filled him. "I love you, O my God, and I always will. If we all die in the desert, I will love you anyway. I pray that your people will learn to love you like this."

As Moses hurried back to the camp, he was filled with joy, yet he knew that his people were still slaves at heart, that they had neither his courage nor his confidence in the God he had heard speaking to him from a burning bush. Again he cried out in prayer. "God, speak to them and help them to love you as I love you!"

CHAPTER

15

"I knew it was a mistake to leave Elim. We should have stayed there. There was plenty of water and feed for the cattle."

Bezalel glanced over at Oholiab, who was trudging along beside him. They were out looking for a spring and a little grass for the cattle of Aaron and Miriam.

"You sound like the mixed multitude, Oholiab—always complaining."

"Well, I have a right to complain. We had everything we wanted there in Elim, and we should have stayed."

"Aaron says that Moses forbade it."

"Moses is always forbidding something," Oholiab said grumpily. "He's a great forbidder."

"If you can't do anything but complain, go somewhere else."

"Go where? I can't go back to Egypt. We've been traipsing around for a month now in this desert, and you've got to admit, Bezalel, it doesn't look good."

Although Bezalel never complained in front of Aaron and Miriam, he felt pretty much the same way that his friend did. During the past several days, the Hebrews had consumed every bit of the food they had brought with them out of Egypt. All was gone now, including the honey, the wine, and the cakes. Some, he knew, had already in desperation begun killing their flocks. This Moses had strictly forbidden, knowing that the flocks were the only source of nourishment for their small children.

The two young men trudged along and finally found a bit of grass that had been missed by other herdsmen.

"We'd better get back and bring our flocks over here before someone else finds it," Bezalel said.

"Why don't you go do that? I have business."

"You're not still chasing after that girl from the tribe of Dan, are you?"

"I'm not chasing her," Oholiab said with indignation. "She's chasing *me.*"

"All right. Go on. I'll take care of this."

"I'll see if she has a sister for you."

"Never mind that. Just go."

Bezalel trudged along under the burning sun. He was weary to the point of exhaustion. The land of milk and honey seemed very far away, and the greatest desire of Bezalel's heart was to return to Egypt. Yet he knew there was nothing for him there. The pharaoh was dead, and in all probability the nation was in an uproar. He was well aware that the enemies of Egypt knew that the army had been decimated and would very likely be surging over the borders to take advantage of Egypt's weakness. The new pharaoh would have his hands full.

"Well," Bezalel said, "sooner or later we're going to have to turn back. We're all going to starve out here in this desolate place!"

Moses' heart was heavily burdened by the plight of his people. He saw himself as the shepherd of the flock, and in desperation he had prayed day after day and night after night for God to give him clear direction. God did not speak directly to Moses, but the pillar of cloud and fire continued to move before the people, leading the way. There was nothing for them to do but wearily pick up their belongings each day and follow the cloud.

All night long Moses tried to pray, but he could hear the people crying, "Give us food, Moses!" At first Moses had been indignant. "Who am I that I could provide food for this multitude? Don't they know that it's the Lord who is the provider, not me?" But his indignation soon passed, and he realized more every day that turning a nation of slaves into a nation of free men and women was not a task that could be accomplished in a month.

Late one afternoon Aaron came rushing into Moses' tent, crying out, "Moses, you've got to do something!"

"Do what?" Moses asked wearily. "What can I do?"

"The people are getting restless. I'm . . ." Aaron hesitated. "I'm really afraid of what they might do."

"What can they do—kill us?"

Aaron swallowed hard. "I think you're going to have to talk to them."

"All right, I will."

Moses rose from his knees, and as soon as he exited his small tent, the cries and the shouting went up. He could hear the weeping of the women and the angry shouts of the men, and soon he found himself surrounded by the people. One tall, rangy individual planted himself in front of Moses and said loudly, "If only we had died by the Lord's hand in Egypt! There we sat around pots of meat and ate all the food we wanted, but you have brought us out into this desert to starve this entire assembly to death."

Moses said at once, "It was not I who brought you out of the land of Egypt. It was the Lord God. Have you forgotten His miracles? The parting of the Red Sea? He who brought you out from that bondage will not allow you to die now."

"But we're starving," a woman cried out, tears running down her face. "My baby has nothing to eat. How is God going to feed us in the desert?"

In desperation Moses pleaded with them. "We must believe in God. I do not know how He is going to care for us, but I know that He loves us, and He *will* provide."

"When? When will He feed us? I need food now!" The cry went up from the back of the crowd and others took it up.

Moses held up his hands and said wearily, "I will go pray, but the Lord knows even before I pray that you are hungry. He always knows of His peoples' troubles, but He will give an answer."

Moses turned and trudged wearily back to his tent. He heard the murmuring of the people and was aware that they were only a razor's edge away from total revolt.

Entering his tent, he fell on his face, so agitated that he could not even formulate words. His cry was simply, "Help, O God, help!"

Almost at once the voice that he had grown to love spoke to him: *"I will rain down bread from heaven for you. The people are to go out each day and gather enough for that day. In this way I will test them and see whether they will follow my instructions. On the sixth day they are to prepare what they bring in, and that is to be twice as much as they gather on the other days."*

With joy bubbling over in his heart and tears running down his cheeks, Moses leaped to his feet. He dashed out of the tent and began to shout, "Hear, O people, the Lord God has spoken! In the evening you will know that it was the Lord who brought you out of Egypt, and in the morning you will see the glory of the Lord, because He has heard your grumbling against Him. Who are we, that you should grumble against us? You will know that it was the Lord when He gives you meat to eat in the evening and all the bread you want in the morning, because He has heard your grumbling against Him. Who are we? You are not grumbling against us, but against the Lord."

"Do you really think, Mother, that God will feed all these people?"

Miriam turned to look at Bezalel, who was sitting beside her in front of their tent. They were both aware of the strange silence that had fallen upon the people. It was eerie and unnatural. There was no sound of voices, of arguments, of complaining. There was not even the sound of the children shouting in play. All was still, and Miriam noted that almost every person she could see had their head turned upward toward heaven.

"Yes. I believe it shall be as my brother says. God is going to feed us."

Bezalel shook his head slightly but said nothing. What kind of miracle could feed hundreds of thousands of people? He had never counted them, but he knew they appeared to be as numerous as the sands on the shore.

"If the food doesn't come," he said, "I'm afraid of what will happen to Moses. The people are desperate."

"The food will come," Miriam said boldly. She turned again to face him and took his hand. "I would that you were a believer in our God, my son. Without that belief, you are nothing."

Bezalel could not answer, for he felt the weight of her argument. He was ashamed but could not think of an answer. He looked away, unable to meet her eyes and suddenly said, "Listen, do you hear that?"

Darkness had almost fallen, and Miriam's hearing was not as keen as Bezalel's. "Hear what?"

Bezalel did not speak for a moment. "It's . . . it's the twittering of birds. Many birds!" He leaped to his feet and said, "Look, Mother! That's not a cloud up there. Those are birds!"

Indeed, that which appeared to be a cloud was nothing less than an enormous flock of birds. A cry went up from the people everywhere, and almost at once several birds plopped down at the feet of Bezalel. He leaped forward, grabbed one that made no attempt to escape, wrung its neck, and tossed it to Miriam. "Clean it, Mother, while I get some more!" he cried. "Look at them all!"

The camp was filled with quail that had apparently been driven to them by an enormous wind. It required no effort to catch them. They simply fell to the ground, and all that a person had to do was pick them up and wring their necks.

Soon small fires began to dot the darkness, and the sound of happy voices rang out in the night. Bezalel had saved enough wood to get a fire started, and he roasted the small birds on sticks held over the fire. He, along with Miriam and Aaron, ate like starved wolves.

"Nothing ever tasted so good!" Miriam said, wiping her mouth with her sleeve. "You see, Bezalel, it is as the Lord promised Moses. We have meat to eat."

"Yes, we do," Bezalel said, swallowing a huge morsel and reaching out for another bird to roast. "But what about bread? We don't have ovens. How can we bake bread?"

"You're such a doubter," Aaron said, shaking his head with disdain. "Did you ever see birds come up like this, asking to be killed?

It's all God's doing, my boy. It's all of God!"

"Yes, and the bread will come," Miriam said. "You will see. God said it would be here in the morning, and when we get up, there will be bread!"

Bezalel stuffed himself with roasted quail and slept like a dead man. He awoke to the sound of people shouting. He came up off of his mat and bolted from the tent. Everywhere people were bending over and saying, "Manna?" which meant, "What is it?" Bezalel looked down at the ground and saw that it was covered with small white particles.

He reached down, picked up a few, and rolled them around in his palm. "What is this, Mother?" he asked.

"It is the bread from heaven. God has sent it. Taste it, my son, taste it."

Bezalel picked up a handful of morsels and tasted them. They were rather brittle, but in his mouth they became moist. "Why, they're sweet like honey cakes!" he exclaimed.

"I'm going to fry some in oil," Miriam said and immediately began stirring up the fire.

The coming of the bread from heaven, or "manna" as it came to be called, was an obvious miracle to all. Moses walked through the camp, shouting, "Listen to me! God has given me commands concerning this bread from heaven. Everyone shall gather enough for one day only. No one is to leave any of it until the morning."

And so they gathered the manna quickly, putting it in pots and in jars and eating it as they went. The sun came out, and the crystals seemed to melt, and there were doubters, of course, who said, "It will not be there in the morning." But Moses assured them, "It will be on the ground every day except on the seventh day. On the sixth day, let each of you gather enough for two days."

Suddenly Moses fell on his knees in front of all the people. "I thank you, O merciful God, that you have fed your people with bread and meat. I thank you for the day of rest that you have ordained. I thank you for your love and concern for your people."

The manna fell every day, but there were some who tried to

store up enough for several days. This was unsuccessful, however. On the second day the stored manna was filled with worms and stank.

This was not true on the sixth day, however. They gathered twice as much, according to the commands of Moses, and what was left over on the seventh day was good and sweet and pure. Everyone was happy for the time being, and Aaron said to Moses, "Now the people have seen God's hand. They will never doubt again!"

Moses stared at Aaron and said nothing, but in his own heart he knew that their trials were not yet over.

CHAPTER

16

Miriam was frying up a meal of manna in sweet oil. It gave off a fragrant odor, and she said to Aaron, "Come, brother, let us eat."

Aaron, who had been standing at the door of the tent looking out on the camp, turned, walked toward her, and sat down. He took the earthen dish she handed him. When she sat down, the two of them bowed their heads and Aaron said a quick prayer. "Thank you, our God, for feeding us with bread from heaven."

They both began to eat, and Miriam said, "You look worried, Aaron. What's wrong?"

"Oh, it's nothing."

"Come, I know you better than that. What is it?"

"There are so many problems. Who knows how far it is to the land of milk and honey."

"It doesn't matter," Miriam said. "God will get us there safely."

While the two ate, Aaron shared with Miriam the problems of the travel. It was a monumental task to move hundreds of thousands of people, including small children and infants, along with herds and flocks, and of course, Moses had to bear the brunt of all the complaining. Just finding water and grazing land to keep the cattle alive was daylong work for the herdsmen.

"What's Bezalel doing? Why isn't he here?" Aaron asked.

"He's out with his friends." Miriam took another bite from the dish before her, and her brow furrowed. "I'm worried about him."

"Why? What's wrong with him?"

"Nothing specific. It's just that ... well, he doesn't have any faith in the Lord."

"Most of the people don't have a true faith," Aaron said gloomily.

"Why, Aaron, how can you say that?"

"It's true enough," Aaron said, shaking his head vigorously. "They are not looking to the Lord. They are looking to Moses and me to solve all their problems."

"That's natural enough. People need leaders."

Aaron did not answer. He was given to worry, and many sleepless nights had caused him to grow thin and gaunt. "I think Bezalel needs firmer discipline."

"I'm going to ask Caleb to talk to him."

"That would be a good idea. He likes Caleb and respects him. Everybody does, of course. I advise you to do it at once."

"Your kinsman Caleb wants to see you, Bezalel."

Bezalel, who had been sitting beside a small fire, looked up with alarm. "What does he want, Mother?"

"He just wants to talk to you."

"Have I done something wrong?"

Seeing the alarm on Bezalel's face, Miriam smiled. "No, not at all. But he's a man you should pay heed to. He's well respected by our people. Go to him now, before he goes to sleep."

Bezalel got to his feet and made his way to the part of the camp occupied by the tribe of Judah. He found Caleb tending his injured sheep, putting ointment on a gash that the sheep had incurred on its journey.

"What's wrong with the sheep, Caleb?"

"Got a bad cut here, but she'll be all right." Caleb gave the sheep a final dab with the paddle, loosed her, then wiped his hands on a piece of cloth. "Sit down. I want to talk to you."

Bezalel sat on the ground, glancing uneasily at Caleb's family, who were staying away to give them plenty of space. "Have I done something wrong?" he asked Caleb.

"I'm sure you have," Caleb said, grinning playfully. "You want to tell me about it, that secret thing nobody saw you do?"

Bezalel laughed shakily. He knew Caleb was teasing him, and this was a good sign. "There's not much trouble a fellow can get into out here in this desert."

"Yes, there is. A man can get into trouble anywhere." Caleb sat down facing Bezalel. He studied the young man silently and was quiet for so long that Bezalel grew even more nervous.

Bezalel tried to still his shaking hands, then finally stammered, "What . . . what did you want to talk about?"

"About the tribe of Judah," Caleb said. "Your tribe, Bezalel."

"What about it?"

"I want to refresh your memory about an event that happened a long time ago. You've heard it from the teachers and the elders, but young fellows like you tend to forget such things, so I'm going to repeat a bit of history for you."

"I'm listening, and I promise I won't forget."

"Good! Now, you will remember our ancestor Jacob had twelve sons. Each son became the leader of his own tribe. When Jacob lay dying, he gave prophecies concerning each of his sons. I'm afraid some of them were pretty rough. He proclaimed that his oldest son, Reuben, was unstable as water because he had sinned with his own father's concubine. He also cut off Simeon and Levi, saying that they were cruel individuals. He pretty much went down the list, but do you remember what he said to his son Judah?"

"I . . . I can't quite remember it, not exactly. . . ."

"I'm going to quote it for you, and I want you to memorize it."

"Yes, of course."

"He said, 'Judah, your brothers will praise you; your hand will be on the neck of your enemies; your father's sons will bow down to you.'"

"You mean all the other tribes?"

"Just listen, memorize it and think on it. He went on to say, 'The scepter will not depart from Judah, nor the ruler's staff from between his feet, until Shiloh comes, and the obedience of the nations is his.'"

When Caleb fell silent, Bezalel thought hard, then said, "Who is Shiloh?"

"No man knows, not even the wisest of the elders. We do know that when He comes, He will bring everything we need. He will be the Great Redeemer of the sons of Israel and indeed for the whole world."

"Then Judah is the most important tribe of all?"

Caleb grinned frostily. "Don't get swollen up with pride, now. That would be fatal."

"But we are the ones who will bring forth Shiloh."

"Yes, and that's why I wanted to talk to you and show you something."

Caleb reached up and pulled at a leather thong that was under his tunic. A gold medallion flashed in the sunlight as he pulled it out. Bezalel leaned forward to look more closely at it.

"Look at it well, Bezalel. Hold it in your hand."

Bezalel took the round gold medallion and said, "There's a lion on this side and it's beautifully crafted," he said with admiration.

"Turn it over. Look at the other side."

Bezalel turned it over. "Why, it's a lamb," he said. "The lion and the lamb. What does it mean, Caleb?"

"No one really knows. In his final prophecy, Jacob described Judah as a lion's cub, but we do not know what it means."

"Where did you get this?"

"This medallion is very old. It was given to Noah by his grandfather and with the admonition that God would tell him whom to pass it to before he died. And so it has come down through our history. A member of the tribe of Judah always possesses it, and one day before I die, I will pass it along."

"Pass it to whom?"

"Didn't you hear what I said, Bezalel? God will tell me when the time comes. We are the lions of the tribe of Judah. God is going to do His miraculous work through our people. That's why it's important, Bezalel, that you be a man of honor, a man of faith . . . which right now you are not."

"I do the best I can, Caleb."

"No, you don't," Caleb said sternly. He held the medallion up to look at it, then rubbed it with his thumb and forefinger. "The man who gets this will be the man of God's choice. My father gave it to me years ago. It has come down through our line, and one day Shiloh will come through our line as well."

The two men sat talking for a long time. Caleb spoke intently about the responsibility of being a member of the tribe of Judah while Bezalel listened, astonished by what he was hearing.

Finally Caleb said, "Do not be a burden to Miriam and Aaron. God has put a great gift in your hands. You are able to craft beautiful things out of silver and gold. I don't know how that will be used, but God will use you if you will be obedient to Him."

When Bezalel said nothing, Caleb moved his shoulders impatiently. "Go now. I will be watching you."

"Yes, Caleb. I will try to do my best to be a man you can trust."

As Bezalel walked back toward his tent, he looked up and saw the stars overhead. They looked like tiny flickering sparks spread across the ebony sky. Their number seemed immense, but he remembered another prophecy he had heard from one of the elders that the descendants of Abraham would be as numerous as the stars. Now, looking up at the glittering heavens, he was struck with awe, and for the first time in his life he began to feel that there was more to life than pleasure.

———————

As Moses had feared, the people were not satisfied for long with God's provision of food. The manna that came down each morning nourished them well for the day, but as they continued their trek through the barren land to Rephidim, they found themselves in an even more arid desert. There was no water to be found, and Moses began to hear the pitiful cries of the children and the bleating of the sheep.

It came as no surprise to Moses that the elders appeared before him, demanding what must be done. Moses had heard the rumor going through the camp that God had decided to remove Moses from his leadership role, but he paid no heed to that.

Korah, chief of the elders, was the first to speak. "What will you do, Moses? The people thirst and the animals are dying. Give us water to drink."

Other voices rose in anger, and Joshua rushed to Moses' aid, bringing his small band of warriors, all well armed with the swords and knives of the Egyptians. Joshua moved closer, his eyes fixed on the elders, ready to defend his leader.

"Why do you quarrel with me?" Moses asked the elders sadly. "Why do you put the Lord to the test?"

"We believe the cries of our people. Do you have no care for them?" Korah demanded.

Moses had no answer for him. Heavily he said, "I will pray that God will provide water."

Returning to his tent, he began to pray. He shut out the sound of the angry voices just outside the tent, and for a long time he lay facedown, begging God to speak. Finally the voice of the Lord came to him clearly: *"Walk on ahead of the people. Take with you some of the elders of Israel and take in your hand the staff with which you struck the Nile, and go. I will stand there before you by the rock at Horeb. Strike the rock, and water will come out of it for the people to drink."*

As Moses exited from the tent, his eyes were flashing, and he cried out, "Our God, the God of Abraham and Isaac and Jacob, will now feed Israel." He lifted the staff high and walked toward a wall of rock that was the first of an uplifted series of rocks, and in one quick motion, he struck the rock with all of his might.

Stunned silence fell over the people, and then someone cried out, "The Lord—He has sent water!"

The people watched with astonishment and joy as water flowed from the rock, forming a pool as the stream gushed out like a mighty torrent.

Moses cried out, "This place shall be called Massah and Meribah, because of your quarreling and your testing of the Lord!"

The people were ashamed at his words, but their thirst drove them to the water. The animals, scenting the water, rushed toward the growing stream as it splashed on its downward course over the rocky ground.

Moses stood back, with Aaron beside him. The two men were

silent, and finally Moses said wearily, "Will they never believe God?"

"You must be patient, my brother," Aaron said. "They are a weak people, but they will become stronger."

"They will have to," Moses said. "We have a long way to go in our journey for the Lord."

CHAPTER

17

One of the rare blessings Moses experienced was to spend time with old Hadar, the most ancient of the elders of Israel. Hadar was feeble and had to be carried every step of their journey, but he was held in such high regard among the people that no one minded the inconvenience. Bezalel had made a cart that the old man was placed in each morning when the procession started. He had built it of some fine wood and metal that had been brought from Egypt, and it was drawn by a pair of milk-white oxen.

Moses had spoken to the old man many times since they had left Egypt, and one late afternoon he found himself so weary with the weight of responsibility, he felt he could no longer bear it. He sought out Hadar's family, who welcomed him warmly. They were flattered by the great leader's interest in their family member and seated him close to the old man in the tent where Hadar slept. Moses thanked them and greeted Hadar courteously. "How is it with you, my father?"

"It is well. And you, my son, are you well?"

"Yes. Very well indeed."

Hadar's body was frail, but his eyes were still sharp and his mind was keen, except for those times when he drifted off into a deep sleep. He had always come back from these spells, and now as the two men sat quietly, Hadar said, "You're burdened with many trials, Moses."

"Yes, it is hard, but God will give me strength." He hesitated, then added, "But I am troubled about the land that we must pass through."

"Why does that trouble you?"

"I have been in this land before. It is called Paran, and it has always been inhabited by a strange and violent people."

"Which people?"

"The people of Amalek."

"Ah yes, indeed. The descendants of Esau. They were named after one of his grandsons."

"Yes. When I first came to the land of Midian, I was sitting at a spring waiting to learn the will of God. I was exhausted and tired and filled with defeat. A group of young women came to the well, and while they were attempting to water their sheep, a number of these Amalekites began to assault the young women. I drove them off. One of the women I defended," he said, "was Zipporah, a daughter of Jethro, and she became my wife."

"Do you think the Amalekites will give *us* trouble?"

"They give trouble to everyone who crosses their land."

The two men sat silently, and finally the older man said, "These people should welcome us. After all, we come from the same line."

"Indeed we do. But the Amalekites are a powerful people. They have occupied these lands for years, and I must make it clear that we are not coming to take their lands or even to live in them."

"You speak of Edom and Moab."

"Yes. God's promise to our people makes allowances for these, but the Amalekites have not become shepherds, as have most of Jacob's descendants. They have become brigands, bandits, and robbers of the worst kind."

Hadar thought for a time and finally nodded. "I remember my own father talking of these people. They are blasphemers, and they sacrifice their own children to their idols. They care nothing for family life."

"That's true," Moses said. "And when a man grows old, his family simply kills him."

"The situation does appear grim, my son."

"They are known for their cruelty," Moses went on. "I fear that we will not be able to pass through their land in peace."

What Moses and Hadar had said concerning Amalek was true. They had become the worst of the desert tribes, murdering and killing any strangers who passed through their land. They had heard of the deliverance of the children of Jacob from Egypt. They had also heard of the rich bounty of gold and silver, the weapons, and all the treasures that they had carried away with them. Their leaders at once made plans to attack and take such treasures for themselves.

The Amalekites were fierce, but seeing the huge number of Hebrews they were up against, they went to some of the neighboring tribesmen to entice them to join them. One of the warriors they approached was Magon, ruler of a large tribe. Magon simply stared at the leaders of Amalek. "Have you not heard what their god did to Pharaoh and to Egypt? You are fools to think of attacking them. Let them go. The Lord, their god, is strong."

"What is the Lord to us?" Lotan, the Amalekite chief, sneered. He left the camp and drew his subordinates about him. "We will go greet them. We will be crafty as wolves."

This strategy was put into play almost at once. Lotan and a group of his underchiefs came to the camp and greeted them as if they were allies. "Are we not all of one people?" Lotan said, spreading his hands wide. "Is not Abraham the forefather of us all?"

Moses watched the savage figure carefully. "That is true," he said. "And we will pass through your lands with your permission. We will disturb nothing."

"Of course, of course," Lotan said expansively. "Perhaps we can do some trading."

Moses agreed and the trading began at once. The people of Amalek had fresh food, which they traded for some of the treasures brought out of Egypt. This activity gave Lotan and his men a chance to spy out the Hebrew defenses, and they determined that the Hebrews had no army and few weapons. So as soon as the Israelites reached the low-lying hills, he cried to his warriors, "We have them now! We will attack as they go through the passes."

"We will have them all!" they rejoined.

"Kill all the men but save the best of the women," Lotan ordered. "We will keep their children for slaves!"

———————

Moses had not been deceived in the least by Lotan, the Amalekite chief. He called Joshua to his tent, and when the young man stood before him, he said, "You must be the captain of our army, Joshua."

Joshua blinked with surprise. "Me? I am but a young man. There are older—"

"God has told me that you are the man who will lead our men into battle. You have already begun. I have watched you select strong men. I've watched you practice with weapons. Take these men and form as good an army as you can to fight the Amalekites. You will be in the lead."

Joshua was troubled by this. "But I'm not worthy."

"None of us are worthy, Joshua. God will give you the strength you need. Here is the plan. You lead the soldiers as they fight the battle. Tomorrow I will stand on top of the hill with the staff of God in my hand and my hands held high. I will pray, and you will be victorious."

"Perhaps God will deliver us miraculously," Joshua offered. "He is able."

"Certainly He is able, but in this case we must prove that we are willing servants."

Joshua had no fear now, but he expressed some of his thoughts aloud. "The warriors of Amalek are armed with bows and arrows and spears. They can hide behind rocks and cut us down."

"That is true, and because you are thinking this through, it proves that you are a worthy general for the army of God. Here is what we will do. You must divide the army into two parts. Put those who have bows and arrows in the front, but take the rest of the army, the men bearing only swords or knives or clubs, around to the back, along the flanks of Amalek."

"And then what, master?"

"Sooner or later, Amalek will charge at those few men they see. They will come out of the hills and will leave the protection of the rocks. When they do, that will be the signal for you and those who have hidden themselves to hit them hard. They will be caught between two forces, and the Lord will destroy them by our hands."

The battle went exactly as Moses had foretold. Bezalel had been one of those armed only with a sword. He and his friend Oholiab were led by Joshua far off to the flanks. They crept and crawled and kept themselves hidden. As they approached, Oholiab said, "I hear the sound of battle."

"Yes, I hear it too," Bezalel whispered. "Come. Don't fall behind."

"I don't care for this kind of thing," Oholiab said. "I'd rather be working, making a fine necklace."

"Be quiet, Oholiab! We've got to defeat these monsters. If we don't, they'll kill us all."

The two, along with the other members of Joshua's force, finally came to the brink of a small bluff. Looking down, they could see the battle plainly. They lay there all afternoon, and Bezalel noticed something on the hill across the valley. "Look, Oholiab, as long as Moses holds his hand and the staff of God high, our forces win. But when his arms grow tired, the men of Amalek win."

Finally they saw two men come stand beside Moses. One was Aaron and the other was Hur. They held Moses' arms up, and even as they did so, Joshua stood to his feet, his eyes flashing. "Look, the men of Amalek are coming out of the hills to attack our forces. Now, you soldiers of the Lord, strike!"

Bezalel rose and joined the force that swarmed down the bluff. They hit the flank and the rear of the enemy band like a battering ram. Bezalel was no Joshua, but he struck until his arm grew weary.

The cry of victory sounded, and the Amalekites began to flee.

"After them!" Joshua shouted. "Let none of them live!"

Bezalel was one of the best runners among the Israelites, so he was in the band of those who pursued the Amalekites.

In his battle rage, he spotted a savage-looking Amalekite who was attacking a woman. She was trying to shield a young girl in her arms. Bezalel yelled as he leaped forward, but he was too late. The sword of the warrior descended, and the woman fell dead. The Amalekite raised his sword to strike the young girl too, but Bezalel was there first. He struck a mighty blow that caught the man in the throat. Scarlet blood exploded in a gush, covering the girl, who was huddled on the ground. Bezalel turned to her and said, "Are you all right?"

The girl could not answer. She was covered with dirt and the Amalekite's blood was on her face. Bezalel had nothing to clean her with. He looked up and saw that the Amalekites were escaping; then he looked down and saw that the girl was pale and clinging to the dead form of her mother.

"Is this your mother, child?"

"Yes. She's dead, and I have no one now."

"Where is your father?"

"He's dead too."

Even though Bezalel was usually quite selfish, the sight of the girl touched him. "What is your name?" he said.

"Shani."

"Do you have other relatives among the people of Israel?"

"No. No one."

"Which tribe do you belong to?"

"I . . . no tribe."

By that Bezalel understood that she was one of the mixed multitudes. Her parents had probably been slaves in Egypt who had joined themselves to the Israelites when they had been delivered.

Bezalel stood for a moment, uncertain what to do, and finally he said, "Come with me."

"But my mother," the girl wailed.

"I will come back and bury her, but now you must come."

The girl looked up with enormous green eyes. Bezalel had never seen eyes of that color in anyone. She was thin—her arms were nothing but sticks—and she was trembling. He pulled off his upper garment and began to wipe the blood off her face. "Here," he said, "you'll be all right. I'll see to it."

"I have no one," Shani whispered.

Bezalel took her hand and said, "Come along. I'll take you to my mother, Miriam. She will help you."

———————

"What are you going to do with the girl?" Miriam demanded. "Why did you bring her here?"

Bezalel was tired of answering Miriam's questions. He had brought Shani to the tent and had drawn Miriam aside, whispering about the death of the girl's mother. Now he said, "What was I to do—leave her there?"

Miriam cast a glance at the girl, who was huddled on the ground, sitting with her head between her knees and her hands covering her head.

"She's an unhealthy-looking child."

"Yes, she is, but I couldn't leave her out there, and I've got to go back and bury her mother. I promised the girl."

"Let me talk to her."

Bezalel moved to one side and listened as Miriam went over and spoke to the girl. "What is your name, child?"

"Shani."

"We must find you a place to stay. Your mother must have had friends."

"No, no friends."

"No relatives, not even an aunt or an uncle or a cousin?"

"We had no one. Just each other."

The plaintive answer touched Miriam, who had a kind heart toward the unfortunate. "Well, let's get you cleaned up. But I'll find you something to eat first. Are you hungry?"

"No. I want my mother."

Miriam reached over and put her arms around the girl. She was silent for a moment as she considered the situation. "I will be your mother, child."

The girl was silent. When she lifted her tearstained face, she said, "You will?"

"Yes. And Bezalel here—he's the one who saved you—he'll be your father."

"He's too young to be my father."

174 ♦ GILBERT MORRIS

"Well," Miriam smiled, "he can be your brother, then."

Bezalel stepped forward and put his hand on the girl's shoulder. "It'll be all right, Shani. I'll take care of you."

"You've never taken care of anyone but yourself, Bezalel," Miriam scoffed.

"Well, she'll be no trouble, will you, Shani?"

"No . . . no trouble."

"After all," Bezalel said with a careless shrug, "how much trouble can one girl be?"

CHAPTER
18

Shani awoke from a terrible nightmare, screaming and trembling like a leaf in the wind. But suddenly she felt strong arms go around her, and she was being held close to someone.

"Now, little lamb, don't be afraid. I won't let anything harm you."

Sobbing and choking, Shani clung to the man who held her, for she recognized his voice. It was the man who had killed the warrior who had cut her mother down. She held to him fiercely, and he gently smoothed her hair.

"Now then, little one, you've had a bad dream, but everything's all right now."

"Mother—!"

"Just be still, and I'm going to tell you a story." The voice was soothing and warm, and as Bezalel began to tell her a story about two little rabbits that had lost their way but had each other, Shani began to quiet down. She still clung tightly to Bezalel, and when he had finished his story, she whimpered, "Please . . . please don't leave me!"

"I won't leave you, little lamb. Don't worry."

The smell of food cooking touched her senses, and Shani suddenly awoke, realizing she was ravenous. For a moment she lay there confused, fragments of her nightmare continuing to play in her mind. She tried to wake up fully, to quell the horrible images of the battle in which her mother was killed. She then remembered the man who had come to her and held her and told her a story. She looked around for him—but instead of the man, she saw a woman squatting before a small fire just outside the tent.

Shani sat up and coughed, and the woman turned to her and smiled. "I see you had a good sleep. Are you hungry?"

"Yes."

"Well, you can come and help me make breakfast. Do you know how to make cakes?"

Shani was struggling with the memories of the battle and the death of her mother, but the woman's face was kind and she was smiling. "Yes, I do."

"Do you remember my name? It's Miriam. And I know your name. It's Shani."

Shani got off of the sleeping mat and came out to stand before the fire. She took the knife the woman handed her. "Try not to let the cakes burn."

"I won't." The girl knelt down and watched the cakes intently.

As Miriam got up and went over to a bag, she shot a glance at the child to estimate her age—eleven, maybe?—then opened the bag and pulled out a garment. "Here," she said. "You can put this on."

Shani turned and stared at the beautiful blue embroidered garment with enormous eyes. "For me?"

"Yes. It belonged to the daughter of a woman I used to know." Miriam did not add that the child had died. She thought it might disturb the girl. She watched while Shani dropped the rag of a garment she was wearing and started to pull the new dress over her head. Miriam flinched at how thin and birdlike the girl appeared. She looked half starved.

When she got the dress on, Miriam smiled. "See? It just fits. Here. I have a bit of leather you can use for a belt. Let me help you with it." She tied the leather around the girl's waist and said, "Now, you look so nice. You finish the cakes, and I'll find that bit of honey I've been saving."

The cakes were soon done, and Miriam came out with a small

jar of honey. She spread the honey on the cakes and watched the girl eat them like a starving wolf cub. Miriam was careful to see that she got the biggest part of the breakfast. As the girl ate, she studied her carefully.

Shani was young but on the verge of womanhood. Miriam guessed she might be closer to twelve. She still had the body of a child, however, and was gawky and thin and as dirty as a child could be. Her hair was caked with dirt and looked as if it had never been washed. Her face was smudged with dirt, as were her hands, but on her unexposed skin where she had stayed clean, Miriam noticed she had a beautiful complexion of a light almond color. In her present state she was not a pretty child, however. Her eyes seemed too large for her thin face, her cheeks sunken from hunger.

"How old are you, Shani?"

"Don't know."

"Have you become a woman yet?" When the girl only stared at her without a light of understanding, Miriam asked, "Have you started bleeding every month?"

"Bleeding? No."

"Well, we'll talk about that later, then. Now, if you're finished, you can go with me to get water from the stream. While we're there"—she reached out and touched Shani's hair—"I'll give you a bath." When the girl turned to look at her with surprise, Miriam said, "You'll feel much better with that dirt washed off of you." She noted the strange green eyes of the girl and also that, beneath the dirt, the girl's brown hair had a prominent reddish color that she had rarely seen. She almost asked the girl if her hair and eyes were the color of her mother's, but it was too soon to speak of her mother, so she simply rose and said, "Come along."

Shani stood up and looked around the small tent. "Where is he?"

"Who?"

"The man who brought me here."

"Oh, you mean Bezalel. He's gone to repair a wagon for a man."

"Is he your husband?"

Miriam laughed. "No indeed, child. He's my son."

"Will he be back?"

"Of course he will." Miriam saw relief wash through the girl, and for a moment she was troubled. She thought, *I'll have to talk to Bezalel. The poor child has put her trust in him—and he's never been responsible for anyone. I'll have to warn him he must be careful with her feelings.*

The smoke from a small, portable forge rose and blew into Bezalel's eyes. He could not see, and his eyes burned like fire. He quickly stepped back from the forge, and his heel came down on something soft. He heard a small, muffled cry, and turning, he saw Shani hopping around on one foot while holding the other with a look of anguish.

"Shani, I didn't even know you were here," he said. "You shouldn't sneak up on me like that."

"I'm . . . I'm sorry." Tears came to the girl's eyes, and her lips trembled.

Bezalel sighed and put his tools down. He came over and stood over her. "Don't cry. Let me see your foot." He picked up her foot to examine it and noted that she was as limber and loose as a piece of rope. She was all legs and arms, and he had never seen such enormous eyes—but now they were filled with tears from the pain he had caused her. "Don't cry, Shani. It'll be all right. Does Miriam know you're here?"

"No."

"She'll be worried about you, Shani. You shouldn't run off from her."

The girl did not answer. She simply stood there staring at him, and Bezalel thought back over the last few weeks. Ever since he had brought Shani home from the battle with the Amalekites, she had been clinging to him. Every night her nightmares returned, and he was the one who went to her to comfort her by telling stories until she went back to sleep.

She had become quite a pest, for now she followed him everywhere he went. She acted frightened whenever he was out of her sight. Miriam was good to her, and Aaron was also, in his own way, but it was Bezalel whom she sought out and clung to. He tried sneaking off at times, but even when he was successful, he would look up from whatever he was doing to find her watching him from far off.

He remembered as he studied the girl how he had complained to Miriam about Shani's chasing after him. "I can't go anywhere without her being right there. When I try to sneak off without her, she finds me. It's aggravating."

Miriam had replied sternly, "You were the one who saved her life, son. She's transferred her trust to you."

"Well, I can't have a child following me around."

Miriam had reached up and grabbed Bezalel's black glossy hair and shook him, her eyes angry. "When you save someone's life, son, you have a responsibility."

"I thought it was the other way around."

"No, it's not. You've always been selfish, Bezalel, but this time I'm going to see to it that you do the right thing. You be good to that child or I'll make it hard for you." She saw the hurt in his eyes at her threat, and she said more gently, "I've heard you comforting her and telling her stories when she has awful dreams. That's a very good thing."

"Will she always have those dreams?"

"I hope not, but for now she's lost everything, and she's terribly afraid. You're all she has to cling to. She's afraid she'll lose you too. I know it's troublesome." She had released his hair, and now she put her hand on his cheek. "I want you to show her extra special attention. Talk to her. Play games with her. Take her with you sometimes when you go to fix something."

"All right, Mother," Bezalel sighed. "I will do as you say." He grinned crookedly. "But I'm afraid I don't make a very good father."

In the days following his talk with Miriam, Bezalel had done his best to follow her advice. He went to extra trouble to pay more attention to the emaciated little girl. He found time to play games with her and quickly discovered she had a very quick mind. He talked with her and cautiously tried to find out about her life. But she didn't respond to that. He suspected she had had a very hard life and seemed reluctant to speak of her family. She continued to have bad dreams, although they occurred less often. He still went to her each time it happened, and she would cling to him and whisper, "Please, Bezalel, tell me a story." During the day, he made it a point to invite her to go with him whenever he went to get water or to repair something that was broken, and when he did this, he saw that she was happy.

———————

About a week after he stepped on Shani's foot at the forge, Bezalel was returning from a hunting trip. Having managed to kill three coneys, he was looking forward to a stout, well-seasoned soup—the way his mother made it. He was surprised to see Shani sitting beside a small scrubby bush, her legs drawn up, encircled by her arms and her face hidden. He saw her shoulders shaking, and he quickly went to her and said, "Well, now, Shani, look what I've got. Three nice, juicy, plump rabbits. We'll have a good supper tonight."

When Shani looked up and saw the rabbits, she tried to smile, but he saw tears running down her cheeks.

"What's the matter, Shani?" Putting the bow and quiver down along with the dead coneys, he laid his hand on her thin shoulder. "What's the matter?"

"Nothing."

"Come on, now. You can tell me. Something's wrong."

"They . . . they won't play with me."

"The other children? They won't play with you?"

"No."

"Why not?"

"They don't like me."

"Oh, that can't be true. Who wouldn't like you?"

Shani turned her tearstained face up to him, and her mouth twisted as she tried to stop crying. "They say I'm not a Hebrew. Why don't they like me, Bezalel?"

"Oh, children just don't have much sense sometimes. They're stupid not to like a sweet little lamb like you. That's what you are, my little lamb."

Shani smiled shyly up at him, pleased with the name.

"Is that all that's wrong, a bunch of stupid children who don't have sense enough to like a nice girl like you?"

"I . . . I'm worried that you'll leave me."

This was a recurring theme for the child, and Bezalel knew it was a very real fear. "That will never happen," he said. He put his arm around her and leaned forward and whispered, "Did I ever tell you the story of the lion and the mouse?"

"No, Bezalel, tell it."

Bezalel started making up a wild story about a mouse and a lion. He had no idea where the story was going, but he saw that as he spoke her eyes grew warm, and several times he made her laugh.

Suddenly he broke off when he saw a small party arriving, obviously travelers from some distance. "I wonder who they are?"

Shani tugged at his garment. "Never mind them. Tell the rest of the story, Bezalel. . . ."

Moses could hardly keep his eyes open. He had been sitting for hours, with only a short break for some food and water at midday. It had become his custom to sit and listen to the arguments and charges brought by various members of the Hebrew tribes. Sometimes they were important, such as a man charging another with incest, but often times it was minor things, such as the one he was now listening to. One of the Hebrew wives felt she had been insulted by the wife of a prominent elder. Moses tried desperately to keep his mind on the issue, but he could not. Finally he was aware that Joshua had come and knelt beside him.

"Master," Joshua whispered in his ear, "your family is here."

Moses started. "My family?"

"Yes. Your father-in-law, your wife, and your two sons."

Moses scrambled to his feet and said quickly, "I will hear this tomorrow. I must leave now." He turned and followed after Joshua, who led him through the crowd. "When did they get here?"

"They just arrived," Joshua said. "They've come all the way from Midian."

Moses could not help but feel guilty pangs that Zipporah had felt it necessary to return to Midian during their trip to Eygpt. She had accused him of being a worthless husband and father, since he never paid any attention to his family.

Moses saw his father-in-law, Jethro, standing and talking to Aaron and went to him. He bowed and then put his arms around the older man. They embraced, and Moses said, "I am glad to see you, Jethro."

"And I you," Jethro said. His words were not harsh, but his eyes were heavy with concern. "I have brought your family, my son."

"I see." Moses went to Zipporah and put his arm around her. "I am glad to see you, my dear."

But she did not return his affection, and Moses quickly removed his arm and smiled at his sons. "It is good to see you both."

His sons bowed slightly and greeted him.

Moses quickly threw himself into the business of finding them a place to stay. "Joshua," he said, "we must have a good meal tonight to welcome my family."

"Of course, master."

Moses shot a quick glance at Zipporah and saw no kindness in her gaze. He made himself smile and said, "We will have a good meal, and then I will tell you everything I've been doing."

———

Moses took a great deal of time after the meal that evening to explain to Jethro and his family all that had happened since their return to Midian. He made the story as long as possible, for he was aware that sooner or later he would have to speak directly to Zipporah. When the meal ended, he waited until Jethro and his sons had left together and then said, "I hope you are well, Zipporah."

"I'm very well."

"I have thought of you a great deal."

"No you haven't." The words were harsh and cold, and Zipporah went at once to the heart of what was burning in her eyes. "We never should have married."

"Don't talk like that."

It was as if Zipporah had not heard him. "I thought you'd join with my father and become a priest of Midian as he is, but you did not care enough for me or your sons to stay. All you think about is this band of slaves. You took the first chance you could to run away and leave us."

Moses tried as gently as he could to explain how leaving Midian was not his choice. "The God of my fathers has spoken to me. I have to be obedient. I am truly sorry that I have failed you, Zipporah."

When she sat staring coldly at him, he went on in desperation, "We have been married a long time, Zipporah, and our sons are grown. Can't you see that my job now is to care for all of these people, hundreds of thousands of them?" She neither moved nor blinked but kept staring at him in obvious anger, and he added quickly, "I would have been happy to have you with me, Zipporah, but you chose to go back to Midian. I will always provide for you, but I must obey the voice of my God."

Zipporah said coldly, "I knew it would be useless to come here, but my father insisted. You are no husband to me!" She turned and left the tent.

Moses stood there grieved and agitated, but though he tried desperately, he could not think of any way to be the kind of husband she wanted him to be. She wanted a husband who could be available at all times, who could listen to her and stay close by. Moses knew he could never be that kind of man. God had called him out to lead the new nation of Israel, which was being birthed. He was the one God had chosen, and it grieved him that Zipporah and his sons had to suffer for it—even as he himself suffered.

"I'm worried about Moses," Miriam said to Aaron later that day. "He's disturbed about what he's done to his family."

"Well, he shouldn't be," Aaron said. "Zipporah will just have to take Moses as he is." Aaron shrugged and said, "God has called him to be more than just a husband. She will have to learn to accept that. My wife understands what God has called me to."

Miriam shook her head. "Zipporah is not likely to ever accept that. Your wife is a far different kind of woman than Zipporah. She's meek and mild and will do exactly as you say, but Zipporah has some of that Midianite streak in her. She's a strong, stubborn woman, and she'll never accept second place—not even to God!"

CHAPTER

19

Three months after the Hebrews left Egypt, they came to the wilderness of Sinai. A remarkable plan had been forming in Moses' mind to put into writing the history of the Hebrews and of the world, so he called for specially treated lambskins to write on, and had ink made from a fluid extracted from a fish found in the streams along the way. As a young prince in Egypt, he had studied Egyptian history recorded on stone and clay tablets, but such a method would not work for a traveling people.

Moses had listened to the elders carefully and was impressed at how their recitations of Hebrew history never changed. Word for word they were always the same, and he incorporated these verbal accounts into the work. He began his chronicle with the time of creation, and moved on to the beginnings and growth of the Hebrew nation, through the histories of Abraham, Isaac, Jacob, and particularly of Joseph.

As he meticulously recorded each word, he was also careful to submit the book to the elders from time to time for their scrutiny, for every word had to be true. He included the bad as well as the good. He was well aware that God was in the making of the book, for not all of it came from the elders and their oral history. Much of it was placed in his mind by God himself.

While Moses worked on this extraordinary project, he also thought about the worship of the Hebrew people. Should this new nation have a priesthood? he wondered. Other peoples had priesthoods, but they were so polluted by sinful practices that he could barely conceive of an honorable priesthood. It troubled him deeply to think of the worship of the Hebrews falling into such error. He had raised an altar after winning the victory over Amalek, but he had not slain a sacrifice on it, for God had not told him to do so. He continually sought God for wisdom, and as they approached the mountains, he prayed even more ardently. Faith came into his heart that God would tell him all that he must do to bring the people of the Lord into a covenant relationship with their God.

The camp lay a half-day's journey from the mountains. Moses left early in the morning, and soon he saw the mountains of Horeb ahead of him. As he made his way toward the mountain where he had encountered the flaming bush, he kept praying to God to show him how to lead His people. He lifted his voice and cried out, "O God, instruct me. I am weak and frail and have no wisdom. Tell me what to say to your people."

God's voice came to him as clearly as it had from the burning bush, ringing through the craggy peaks and valleys of Sinai like the tolling of a mighty bell: *"This is what you are to say to the house of Jacob and what you are to tell the people of Israel: 'You yourselves have seen what I did to Egypt, and how I carried you on eagles' wings and brought you to myself. Now if you obey me fully and keep my covenant, then out of all nations you will be my treasured possession. Although the whole earth is mine, you will be for me a kingdom of priests and a holy nation.' These are the words you are to speak to the Israelites."*

With tears running down his cheeks, Moses heard the voice of God, then turned at once back toward the camp. He was filled with joy, and when he had called the people together to hear the words of God, he challenged them to listen and obey. "Will you submit to the law that God will give you to be His holy people according to His desire?"

And the people cried out, the elders shouting the loudest, "We will do everything the Lord has said."

Moses went back to God with their response and received

detailed instructions for how the people were to prepare themselves to meet with God. They were to wash themselves and their clothes and meet at the base of the mountain but go no farther. And then on the third day the Lord would descend on the mountains and speak directly to His people.

———————

Moses led the people of Israel to Mount Sinai, and they camped for the night near the base of it. The men and older boys he directed to one side of the mountain, the women with the little ones to the other. As they found their places, Moses watched them and was struck at the great changes that had come over the people in the three months since leaving Egypt. They no longer had the ashen gray complexion of slaves, but their faces were firm and bronzed. Black curly beards adorned the faces of the men, and the women had dressed themselves in the rich garments they had brought from Egypt and had ornamented themselves with earrings, nose rings, and neckbands.

The people remained quiet and expectant while the heavens opened with a display of frightening intensity. A massive dark cloud descended on the mountain; lightning pierced the cloud on all sides, and thunder rolled down the mountain and through the valleys, causing the mountain to shake. The people were so terrified, many thought they would die. Out of the dark cloud sounded a voice like a trumpet as the people stood trembling and staring upward. Mount Sinai seemed to be on fire, and many could not even bear to look at it. The trumpet voice sounded long and grew louder, and finally the Lord himself came down on Mount Sinai and called Moses to the top of the mountain.

Leaving the people to wait for him, Moses climbed to the summit, and there God told him: *"Go down and warn the people so they do not force their way through to see the Lord and many of them perish. . . . Go down and bring Aaron up with you."*

So Moses went down to speak to the people. The lightning and thunder stopped, and an intense silence enveloped the waiting tribes of Israel. In the midst of this silence, the voice of God was heard like a mighty trumpet, solemnly giving His people the laws they were to obey: *"I am the Lord your God, who brought you out of Egypt, out of the land of slavery. You shall have no other gods before me. You shall not make for yourself an idol in the form of anything in heaven above or on the earth beneath or in the waters below.... You shall not misuse the name of the Lord your God.... Remember the Sabbath day by keeping it holy.... Honor your father and your mother.... You shall not murder. You shall not commit adultery. You shall not steal. You shall not give false testimony against your neighbor. You shall not covet your neighbor's house ... your neighbor's wife ... or anything that belongs to your neighbor."*

After God had spoken His commandments, the lightning returned, and the people fell on their faces, not daring to look on the flaming mountain.

The people backed away from the mountain and kept their distance, begging Moses, "Speak to us yourself and we will listen. But do not have God speak to us or we will die."

Moses told them, "Do not be afraid. God has come to test you, so that the fear of God will be with you to keep you from sinning."

Then Moses went back up the mountain, and the people watched as he disappeared into the thick darkness at the summit to talk with God. There he received many more laws from God, which he was instructed to write down. After a time he descended from the summit and stood on a high rock, calling out to the people, "You have heard the commandments that God has spoken to you. Will you accept them?"

And with a single voice, it seemed, the children of Abraham cried out, "We will do everything the Lord has said; we will obey."

———

The next morning Moses led the people in offering their sacrifices to God as a promise to obey all that He had instructed them. They built an altar on which to sacrifice and burn their offering of oxen. Moses first sprinkled the altar with the blood of the slain animals, then sprinkled the blood on the people, saying, "This is the blood of the covenant that the Lord has made with you in accordance with all these words."

After this Moses, Aaron, and two of Aaron's sons, Nadab and Abihu, along with seventy of the elders of Israel, went up the mountain together, and they saw the God of Israel. Under His feet was something like a pavement made of sapphire, clear as the sky itself. But God did not raise His hand against these leaders of the Israelites; they saw God and they ate and drank.

The Lord then told Moses, *"Come up to me on the mountain and stay here, and I will give you the tablets of stone, with the law and commands I have written for their instruction."*

Moses told Joshua to come with him, then turned to the elders and said, "Wait here for us until we come back to you. Aaron and Hur are with you, and anyone involved in a dispute can go to them."

Moses and Joshua set off back up to the summit, disappearing into the cloud, and the people watched, wondering when Moses would return.

CHAPTER
20

No one expected Moses to be gone for so long. Days went by, then weeks, and still he did not return. The people grew frightened and began to weep, believing that he would never come back. They cried to Aaron, "Moses is gone! He is dead. God has killed him." Others wailed in grief and fear, "Who will help us? Who will defeat our enemies? Joshua is with Moses, and he is dead too."

A peculiar thing during this time was that the Hebrews seemed to have forgotten the miracle of the manna. It continued to fall from the sky daily, but they came to regard it as simply a natural thing. They took the bread and ate it, no longer giving any thought to the fact that no people had ever been fed in this manner before.

As the days wore on and Moses still did not appear, Nadab, the oldest son of Aaron, became a spokesman for the people's grievances. "We must do something, Father," he complained to Aaron. "The people are unhappy. No one knows what to do. What will become of us without a leader?"

Abihu, Nadab's brother, chimed in, "Yes, and why did he take Joshua, a man from the tribe of Ephraim, and not you, Father? Were you not called by God to help Moses lead the people?"

Aaron listened in anguish and total confusion. He tried to defend himself, but he was overwhelmed by his sons' words.

"The people are looking for a leader, Father," Nadab insisted. "They want a god they can see but one that does not frighten them so much. They're bringing their gold and silver to Korah now to melt down, and he will set up a form of worship they will like."

"Yes," Abihu said, nodding vigorously, "and who knows whether Moses will ever come back with His commandments or not? The people are saying that all God does is give difficult commandments the people cannot possibly keep. Go out and listen to them."

Aaron did listen day after day, and the people's cries became louder. "Where is Moses? Why isn't he here?"

Some of them went to Korah, urging him to be the leader, but Korah was shrewd and knew that if Moses came back he would be angry at anyone who usurped his position. He refused, saying, "Go to Aaron. Go to others. Not me."

Weeks passed and still Moses did not return. Finally the Hebrew people succumbed to the most shameful event in their history. During their long enslavement in Egypt, they had been exposed to the gods of the Egyptians and to the gods of other heathen nations. They were well aware of Ashtoreth and the god Moloch. Calf worship was particularly strong in this cult, and the people began to cry out for a god they could see. They finally came to Aaron, screaming, "Come, make us gods who will go before us. As for this fellow Moses who brought us up out of Egypt, we don't know what has happened to him."

Nadab and Abihu grabbed their father by the arms and said, "Quick, we must do what the people say. We must make them a golden calf."

Stunned, Aaron licked his lips with uncertainty, but his sons urged him, and he finally cried out, "Take off the gold earrings that your wives, your sons and your daughters are wearing, and bring them to me." So the people brought him their gold jewelry from Egypt, and he took the massive pile of ornaments and melted it down. He asked Bezalel to fashion the gold into a calf, and the young man considered it, but then refused. So Aaron himself created a golden calf and presented it to the people, saying, "This is your god, O Israel, who brought you up out of Egypt."

When Miriam heard what was happening, she ran to Aaron, weeping and wailing for him to stop, but she was held back by Nadab and Abihu from going to her brother. Bezalel also tried to stop them, and fought with Aaron's sons to come to their senses and let his mother go. "We cannot do this thing! Remember what we promised God!" Bezalel's heart had been gradually changing as he had spent time in the wilderness, watching God's deliverance and provision for His people. Now he could not abide this terrible abomination against the God who had made himself known to them all.

But Aaron ignored Miriam's and Bezalel's protests, crying out to the people, "Tomorrow there will be a festival to the Lord."

He built an altar before the golden calf, and the next day the people rose early and eagerly brought their animals to offer burnt sacrifices to their new god. They spent the day, and far into the night, eating and drinking and indulging in all manner of revelry.

That night in the desert, below the very mountain where God himself spoke to the people, the demons were loosed from their captivity to play among the Hebrews, encouraging them in all the abominations of the heathen worship from which they'd been delivered.

Finally, at the height of the festivities, Miriam ran through the camp, crying, "Hebrews, listen to me! Remember the holy covenant that you swore to the Lord to keep. Have nothing to do with this idol. The Lord is your God."

"Out of the way, old woman," one of the men said with a laugh, shoving her roughly to the ground.

She lay there weeping, and Bezalel came to her and helped her to her feet. "Come, Mother," he said sadly. "There is nothing we can do here."

———

For several weeks Joshua had been camping on the side of Mount Sinai, just below the summit, awaiting Moses' return. He heard a sound and looked to see Moses finally descending from the peak after his long sojourn with God. Joshua was shocked to see him. His white hair shone as brightly as the sun, and he wore a mantle that blazed like silver in the sunlight. In his hands he carried two stone tablets, which flickered in fiery letters that spelled out the commandments from God.

Joshua was afraid to even speak to Moses. He had waited for forty days and nights, hunting for his food and drinking from a spring. He wondered what Moses had done for food all this time.

Joshua could not interpret the stern look on Moses' face. He did not know what God had just told him: *"Go down, because your people, whom you brought up out of Egypt, have become corrupt. They have been quick to turn away from what I commanded them and have made themselves an idol cast in the shape of a calf. They have bowed down to it and sacrificed to it and have said, 'This is your god, O Israel, who brought you up out of Egypt.'"*

Joshua followed Moses as they made their way down to the stony plateau at the base of the mountain. Joshua heard the shouting and tumult of the people and said to Moses, "There is the sound of war in the camp."

"No," Moses replied. "It is not the sound of victory; it is not the sound of defeat. It is the sound of singing that I hear."

As they came to the rim of the plateau, Joshua saw thousands of people below in a frenzy, dancing wildly around a glittering calf. He threw a worried glance at Moses, who stood silently without speaking. Then suddenly Moses lifted the two tablets above his head and flung them down the slope. The tablets shattered into fragments, and Moses ran down the hill toward the camp, leaving Joshua behind.

As Moses entered the camp, flinging right and left with his mighty arms to make a path through the crowd, panic struck the idolaters. They drew back while Moses took hold of the golden calf and threw it on the stony ground, breaking it to pieces. He cast the pieces into the fire that burned on the altar. He did not say a word as the people fearfully watched him. He took the blackened pieces out of the fire and ground them into a powder, which he carried in a basin to a pool of water nearby formed by a stream flowing down the mountain. He poured the powder in the water and commanded the elders to make all the people drink the water.

The people cried out in fear, but Moses did not listen. He found Aaron and shouted at him, "What did these people do to you, that you led them into such great sin?"

Aaron stuttered, his face pale as parchment. "Do not be angry, my lord," he stammered. "You know how prone these people are to evil. They said to me, 'Make us gods who will go before us.'"

Moses glanced around at the people running wild, and his anger toward his brother burned within him that Aaron would have let them get so out of control and become a laughingstock to their enemies. He stood at the entrance to the camp and declared, "Whoever is for the Lord, come to me."

The sons of Levi quickly rallied around him. So Moses said to them, "Each man strap a sword to his side. Go back and forth through the camp from one end to the other, each killing his brother and friend and neighbor."

The men of the tribe of Levi carried out Moses' order, and immediately began slaying people right and left throughout the camp. When three thousand lay dead or dying, Moses finally called a halt to the massacre. Wails of sorrow and grief rose up all night from the camp of Israel.

Moses went to his tent and stayed there, listening to the sounds of grief and wailing from the camp throughout the night. He cried out to God in despair, and God spoke to him that night.

The next morning he spoke to the people, who stood before him, shaken and wan. "You have sinned a great sin," Moses said. "But now I will go up to the Lord; perhaps I can make atonement for your sin."

Moses went back to the Lord and prayed again. "Oh, what a great sin these people have committed! They have made themselves gods of gold. But now, please forgive their sin—but if not, then blot me out of the book you have written."

The Lord replied to Moses, *"Whoever has sinned against me I will blot out of my book. Now go, lead the people to the place I spoke of, and my angel will go before you. However, when the time comes for me to punish, I will punish them for their sin."*

Moses bowed on his face before God and wept, for he knew that the people whom he loved so much were a long way from being the people of God.

Moses went a distance from the camp to a special tent of meeting he had set up, where people could go to inquire of the Lord.

196 ❖ GILBERT MORRIS

There Moses met with God face-to-face while the entrance to the tent was guarded by a pillar of cloud from God. This day he met with God to seek His assurance. How could he possibly continue to lead these people, he wondered, when they would not listen to him?

God did assure him, saying, *"My Presence will go with you, and I will give you rest."*

"Show me your glory, Lord!" Moses pleaded.

And God said to him, *"I will cause all my goodness to pass in front of you, and I will proclaim my name, the Lord, in your presence. I will have mercy on whom I will have mercy, and I will have compassion on whom I will have compassion. But you cannot see my face, for no one may see me and live. . . .*

"Be ready in the morning," the Lord continued, *"and then come up on Mount Sinai. Present yourself to me there on top of the mountain. No one is to come with you or be seen anywhere on the mountain; not even the flocks and herds may graze in front of the mountain."*

Moses bowed his head and worshiped.

———————

Moses looked out over the desert that lay at his feet as he climbed toward the top of Mount Sinai. He turned back to look up the mountain and saw a cloud descend and wrap itself around the summit. The Lord passed before him as Moses stood still, waiting for God's further direction. First the Lord commanded Moses to chisel new tablets of stone. And after they were completed, the Lord wrote on them the commandments that were on the first tablets.

Then the voice of God proclaimed, *"The Lord, the Lord, the compassionate and gracious God, slow to anger, abounding in love and faithfulness, maintaining love to thousands, and forgiving wickedness, rebellion and sin. Yet he does not leave the guilty unpunished; he punishes the children and their children for the sin of the fathers to the third and fourth generation."*

Moses bowed his head and made a covenant with his God, knowing that God would forgive His people. But he also realized that the way to the promised land of milk and honey was going to be much longer than he had ever imagined.

PART FOUR

THE JOURNEY TO
CANAAN

CHAPTER
21

"Miriam, what's wrong with Bezalel?" Shani asked one day.

Miriam looked up from the goatskins filled with milk that were attached to two small saplings. She swung them back and forth, making butter, and kept up the rhythm while studying the young girl's face. "I didn't know anything was wrong with him."

"He's so quiet, and he doesn't tell me stories very much anymore."

Miriam continued the rhythm, pushing the goatskin with one hand. With the other she tucked a loose curl up under the scarf she wore. She wanted to put the girl off, for she was always full of questions, but she felt this was too important to ignore. Ever since Bezalel had saved her from death, she had clung to him closely, which both troubled and pleased Miriam.

Finally she answered, "He's troubled about himself, Shani."

"Why?"

"Because he thinks he's not a good man."

Shani's oddly colored green eyes shone with anger. "He is *too* a good man!"

"I didn't say he wasn't. I said he doesn't *think* he is."

"Why would he think that? He's good to me."

Miriam laughed, reached over, and pulled the girl closer. She still seemed to be nothing but skin and bones, but Miriam knew that soon she would grow out of her awkwardness, blossom and fill out, and one day be a tall and beautiful woman. "He's worried about that golden calf that nearly brought us all to disaster."

"Why's he worried about that?"

"Well . . . Aaron was wrong to build that idol, but at first he asked Bezalel to make it."

"But he didn't do it."

"No, he didn't, but he *almost* did, and that's what's been bothering him, I think."

Shani's face assumed a stubborn set. "You can't blame yourself for something you *almost* did. It's what you *do* that matters."

"Well, our people have very strong feelings about idols. The father of all of us, Abraham, was once an idolater. He lived in a land called Ur of the Chaldees, but when the Lord spoke to him, he gave up his idols to follow the one God. Even though Abraham showed us the truth we are to follow, our people have always had a weakness about turning back to idols whenever things get bad."

Shani listened as Miriam spoke at length concerning the history of the Hebrews and their struggle against idolatry.

When Miriam finally stopped talking, Shani said, "I'm going to tell him that he hasn't done anything wrong."

"No, don't bother him, Shani. Some things a person just has to work out alone. What he's trying to find out," she said, her face growing sober and troubled, "is what kind of a man he's going to be. And God will help him to make the right choices!"

Bezalel had wandered away from the camp. He had taken his bow and a quiver of arrows with him on the off chance of seeing a deer or a coney that he might bring back for the pot. So far he had seen nothing except one bear that he was rather glad was far off in the distance. It occurred to him that he might pursue the beast and bring him down, but bears were bad business, especially a wounded one. Bezalel knew he was not the greatest archer in the world. *If Joshua or Caleb had been with me, we would have taken that beast,* he thought.

He shrugged his shoulders and headed eastward, his eyes on the far-distant mountains. The sky looked brittle enough to scratch with a stone, and there was not a single cloud in it except for the cloud that continually hung over the camp. It was a daily miracle to Bezalel that a cloud would lead such a multitude of people to their destination. He glanced at it now and saw the towering column rising high into the sky. It was stirred slightly by the wind but immediately resumed its shape.

As Bezalel walked along, he tried to push bad thoughts out of his mind—-thoughts that had troubled him ever since the incident of the golden calf. He could not understand why he was so shaken. He had, after all, made many idols for his Egyptian master. That had not troubled him in the least. He had known that no matter what the Egyptians said, the idols he made had nothing to do with human existence. He could not understand how anyone could be so stupid as to think that something a man made with his hands could control his life. He had laughed secretly with Oholiab behind the backs of the Egyptians, the two of them seeing a ridiculous situation in all of it.

Bezalel grew thirsty and started hunting for a spring or a little pool of water trapped in a rock. He finally found a tiny spring no bigger than his hand. He lay on his stomach and drank from it, finding it deliciously cool.

He rolled over on his back and lay with his eyes half closed, trying to put aside the memory of how he had almost agreed to Aaron's request to make the golden calf. A shiver ran over him, and he remembered the fear that had touched him and how confused he had felt. He could not understand how Aaron could do such a thing! And then, of course, he remembered the terrible and depraved behavior of the people as they worshiped the idol, and the wrath of Moses and the massacre of so many by the tribe of Levi.

I could have been one of them! Bezalel thought, realizing that he had come very close to death.

For a long time he lay there and had almost dozed off when something touched his shoulder and brought him out of his half-sleep with a start. His first thought was that the bear had found him, and he let out a cry and leaped to his feet. But when he whirled, he saw Shani standing there looking up at him.

"Don't sneak up on a man like that, Shani! You scared me to death!"

"I'm sorry," she said. "I thought maybe you might want some company."

Bezalel could not help grinning. "You always think I want your company." He sat down and drew his feet up under him, and Shani sat down beside him. "How did you find me out here?"

"I saw you take your bow and arrow, and I've been following you," she said simply.

Bezalel could only shake his head. "Why don't you go play with the other children?"

"No, I don't want to."

"Well, it can't be much fun for you sitting out here with me in the desert."

"I don't like to see you sad."

Surprised, Bezalel turned to face the girl. As always he was rather shocked by her enormous green eyes. They were well-shaped, and one day, he reasoned, they would be the eyes of an attractive woman. He studied her, thinking of how she clung to him like a burr, and said, "I'm not sad."

"Yes, you are. I can tell. Besides, Miriam told me why you're sad."

"Didn't she have anything to do but talk about me?"

Shani reached out and took his hand and held it. She stroked the back of it with one of hers and said, "You cut your hand on something."

"It was a chisel. What did she tell you?"

"She said you were sad because you almost did a bad thing." She looked up and nodded confidently. "You shouldn't be sad about that. You didn't make that gold calf."

"I almost did."

"But you didn't. You're not a bad man. You're the best man in all of Israel."

Bezalel suddenly laughed. He reached out with his free hand and tousled her auburn hair. It was clean now, thanks to Miriam, and reached down her back almost to her waist. "I'm not the best man in Israel, Shani."

"You could be if you wanted to be. You could be anything you want to be, Bezalel."

Bezalel was touched by the child's faith in him. He put his arm around her and hugged her and left it there. She sagged against him, and he said, "I wish I were as good a man as you think I am."

As for Shani, she was content. He was holding her, and she was leaning against him, and no matter what he said, he *was* the best man in all of Israel!

———

Bezalel could not forget Shani's words: *"You could be anything you want to be."* She had spoken them without thought, but he knew that her faith in him was as boundless as the sky above. It pleased him, yet troubled him at the same time. Again and again he seemed to hear her small voice, saying, *"You could be anything you want to be."*

For days he would go for long walks in the desert, trying to forget the golden calf incident, but it would not go away from him. He could not sleep well at night, and his work was poorly executed so that Oholiab said more than once, "What's the matter with you, Bezalel? You can't do anything right these days."

"Nothing's wrong with me."

"Sure there is," Oholiab said. "Any time you make a mess like you just have with this job, something's wrong with you. What you need is a woman. You want me to find you one?"

This caused Bezalel to laugh, because Oholiab could not even find a woman for himself. Yet he was still convinced that he was the desire of the young women of the tribe. "No, thanks, Oholiab. Someday I'll find one of my own."

Almost every evening, when the sun had set and the desert air was growing cool, Bezalel would wander off to be alone. It took some doing to escape Shani's notice, but he managed to do it one evening as the sun was going down. He had come back to the very spring where he had taken a drink and where Shani had uttered the words that still haunted him. He stood beside the spring, thoughtful and troubled, wishing he could do something to erase the memory.

A sound caught his ear, and he whirled quickly to find a man standing there watching him. Bezalel had never seen him before, and he nodded. "Hello. I didn't know anyone was here."

"I thought I might talk with you," the man said.

Bezalel stared at him. He did not look exactly like a Hebrew. His eyes were a bright grayish color and very intent. He was smoothly shaven, which was unusual for Hebrews or for any of the other tribesmen. His age was indeterminate. He seemed neither young nor old, but there was something in his strange eyes that troubled Bezalel. "I don't know you, do I?"

"We've never spoken, Bezalel."

"You know my name?"

"Yes, I do, and I know your trouble. I'd like to help you."

Bezalel instantly grew suspicious. "I'm not troubled, and I don't do business with people I don't know."

The visitor smiled suddenly, his teeth showing very white against his bronze skin. "You're not being very honest."

"What are you talking about?"

"You *are* troubled—more so than you've ever been in your life. It doesn't take a very wise man to see that in your expression."

Bezalel could not think of a reply for a moment. He did not trust strangers and knew many of the wild desert tribes still lingered on the outskirts of the Hebrew camp. "I'm no more troubled than anyone else."

"Sometimes it helps to share what's on your mind and your heart with someone else."

"With you?"

"Well, since I'm here, I'd be glad to listen."

Bezalel was tempted. There was something about the stranger that attracted him. He had a light smile on his lips, and there was a quality about him that made Bezalel feel he was trustworthy. Having been a slave, Bezalel had learned not to trust anyone, but without knowing why, he had an impulse to open his heart to this man. "Well, to tell the truth, I *have* been a little upset."

"About what?"

And then it all came out. Without understanding why he was trusting a total stranger, Bezalel told the whole story about the golden calf. When he got to his part of it, he said haltingly and with effort, "Aaron asked me to make the calf, and ... well ... I almost did."

"Why didn't you, Bezalel?"

"Because it was *wrong*! I knew it was wrong and Aaron knew it was wrong. So did Miriam."

"So you almost made the idol?"

"Yes. It would have been a challenge. I like to make new things."

"Yes, you make very beautiful things, but you didn't do it."

"No, I didn't, but I'm ashamed that I was even tempted to do such a thing!"

"You can't dwell on that. You chose not to and that's what's important."

"I don't know why I'm telling you all this," Bezalel said with a shrug. "There's nothing you can do about it. But ever since it happened, I've been wondering what kind of a man I am and what kind of a man I'll turn out to be."

"You'll turn out to be the kind of man you choose to be."

Bezalel smiled. "I have a young friend who has said about the same thing."

"Yes. She said you could be anything you wanted to be."

Bezalel grew stiff and stared at the man now in fear. "How could you know that? We were alone."

"You're never alone, Bezalel," the stranger said.

"What do you mean?"

"I mean that the eyes of the Lord run to and fro throughout the whole earth to show himself strong in those whose hearts are perfect toward him."

"My heart's not perfect."

"Not yet."

Bezalel felt strangely light-headed. "I don't know how you know all these things, but if you know that, you must know I've always been totally selfish."

"You saved the life of Shani, and you've been a friend to her. That was not selfish."

"Well, she believes I'm a good man, but there's no goodness in me."

The wind ruffled the stranger's hair. There was almost a glow to it, and he seemed ageless. There was not a single line in his face.

His voice was soft, but Bezalel had the impression that if the man were to call out loudly, he could shake the mountains.

"All goodness comes from God," the visitor said. "No man's good of himself."

Bezalel looked down at the ground and thought about this. When he looked up, the stranger was watching him closely. "But how does a man get this goodness?"

"The same way that a thirsty man gets water. How do you get water, Bezalel? You have to go find a spring. Then you drink from that spring."

"Water's easier to find than goodness. How do you find it, sir?"

"You seek for it, and I think that's what you've been doing ever since the calf incident. When you find it, you let it flow into your body. The same as a thirsty man takes water into his body, a man thirsty for God takes God into his soul. You seek and you will find, for He is looking for those who seek Him."

"What you said about God looking for perfect hearts—I could never have a perfect heart. I'm not a good man."

"Ah, but you have a great longing for goodness. I can see that in you, and God will fill you, for as I have said, He looks for those whose hearts are hungry."

Bezalel suddenly felt very strange—as if he wanted to cry—and he dropped his head so that the man would not see his expression. For a long time he stood there, struggling to think of some way to answer the strange man's remark, and finally, when he looked up—the man was gone!

Bezalel turned all around, wildly looking in every direction. He saw nothing on the horizon anywhere. Instantly Bezalel knew he had been speaking with one who was more than a man!

"O God," he cried, falling to his knees. He put his forehead on the earth and wept, knowing now that he'd been in the presence of God, and he began to pray for forgiveness. Finally, when he had wept as much as a man can weep, something entered his spirit. It was like an unheard voice—unheard at least by the ears—but his heart knew that it was the God of Abraham, saying: *I will put my goodness in you, and you will serve me and love me.*

Miriam looked up as soon as Bezalel entered the tent. She started to greet him, but then cut off her words and rose quickly to her feet. "What is it, Bezalel? Why do you look so strange?"

Bezalel had no idea that he looked strange, that his face was alight and his eyes were bright. He came over and put his hands on Miriam's shoulders and whispered, "I've found the Lord."

"Tell me," Miriam said. "Tell me all about it."

"I want to hear too," Shani said. She pulled at his sleeve, and when he sat down, with Miriam on one side and Shani on the other, he repeated the essence of his experience. "He looked just like a man, but he knew things about me that no man could have known." He turned to Shani and said, "He knew that you told me I could be any kind of man I wanted to be."

"Do you think he was an angel?"

"I think he was God's messenger," Bezalel said thoughtfully.

Miriam was overjoyed. She hugged Bezalel hard and cried out, "Now we will see how God will use you, my son!"

"You see! I told you, you could be a good man!" Shani cried, her green eyes glowing with pure pleasure.

CHAPTER

22

The way was steep as Moses made his way upward along the lower heights of Mount Sinai. As he ascended, he was impressed, as always, by the terrain. Leaving the desert behind and coming among the trees that grew at the higher altitude was always a pleasure. He inhaled deeply, enjoying the sharp odors of the vegetation, so different from the scrubby plants of the desert. Finally he passed into a grove of trees that were growing more thickly than was usual. Moses stopped and put his hand on one of the trunks, then rapped it with his knuckles. Pulling out his knife, he began to cut into the side and was astounded at the hardness of the wood. He was accustomed to the soft fibers of the trees in Egypt, but this wood was so hard it was almost like bronze.

Replacing his knife, he continued his journey. He was almost to the crest of a rise when a desert ram appeared. The animal stopped and looked Moses directly in the eye, then went bounding away.

A thought came to Moses' mind that was not of himself: *"The woods of these trees will be used for the framework of the tabernacle and the tent itself will be made of ram skins."*

Moses, by this time, was accustomed to God's coming to him in different ways. Since the time God had spoken audibly out of the burning bush, there had been many visitations. Sometimes God came to Moses during sleep and gave him counsel in dreams. Sometimes in the midst of a busy day, a sudden thought would occur that Moses had learned to recognize as the voice of the Lord.

He breathed a sigh of relief at this message, for now one of the biggest problems of building the new tent of meeting God wanted was resolved. The framework and the skins would be easy to obtain right here in this area. Finally reaching the summit, Moses took a deep breath and looked out. He looked toward the Red Sea in one direction and the Promised Land in the other. One represented slavery and the other freedom. Moses bowed down, and as he did, he cried out, "O mighty and gracious God, our people have sinned against you, but I pray that you will forgive them."

Again the voice that Moses heard was not an audible one. It was like a breeze that went through his entire body, but the words were familiar. *"The Lord, the compassionate and gracious God, is slow to anger, abounding in love and faithfulness, maintaining love to thousands, and forgiving wickedness, rebellion and sin."*

For a long time Moses stood there as God poured himself into his servant, and finally the Lord's voice said: *"I am making a covenant with you. Before all your people I will do wonders never before done in any nation in all the world."*

The Lord then gave Moses detailed instructions on how to build a new tent of meeting, a tabernacle or sanctuary, to which the people would come to offer their sacrifices to atone for their sins and to worship God. Concerning the building of the tent and its furniture, God said, *"See, I have chosen Bezalel son of Uri, the son of Hur, of the tribe of Judah, and I have filled him with the Spirit of God, with skill, ability and knowledge in all kinds of crafts—to make artistic designs for work in gold, silver and bronze, to cut and set stones, to work in wood, and to engage in all kinds of craftsmanship. Moreover, I have appointed Oholiab, son of Ahisamach, of the tribe of Dan, to help him. Also I have given skill to all the craftsmen to make everything I have commanded you: the Tent of Meeting, the ark of the Testimony with the atonement cover on it, and all the other furnishings of the tent. . . . They are to make them just as I commanded you."*

Shani was secretly watching Bezalel as he stood by a small fire, talking with a young woman who was cooking over it. A flash of jealousy went through her as she saw Bezalel smile and laugh at something the young woman said.

Finally Bezalel turned and moved away, leaving the young woman to her cooking. Shani ran and caught up with him, and before he could even say hello, she blurted out, "You can't marry that woman!"

"What!" Bezalel said, surprised and shaking his head. "Do you have to watch me all the time?"

"You can't marry her, Bezalel," Shani insisted. "Her eyes are too close together."

"What are you talking about? She has beautiful eyes."

"They're too close together. Anybody with eyes close together is selfish. You can't marry her."

Bezalel reached out and grabbed Shani. He lifted her off the ground and swung her around, as he often did, and when he put her down, he asked, "Why do you worry so much about the woman I might marry?"

"Because you've got to marry *me*."

Bezalel's teeth flashed and he laughed. He reached out and tousled her hair, and she shoved his hand away angrily. "By the time you get old enough to marry, I'll be an old man!" He started to say something else but turned to see Caleb approaching quickly. "Hello, Caleb."

"Moses is back. He wants to see you."

"To see me? What for?"

"I have no idea, but I wouldn't keep him waiting."

"All right. You run along, Shani."

Caleb watched the young girl reluctantly walk away, and he shook his head. "That girl follows you like a puppy."

"Well, she is a pest, but somebody has to look out for her."

Caleb shrugged. "Moses is different. You'll see."

Indeed, Moses *was* different. As Bezalel entered his tent and bowed low before the leader of the Hebrews, there was a glow about Moses' face that silenced Bezalel. He did not know what to say in the presence of this man, so he waited for Moses to speak.

"Hello, my son."

"Lord Moses, I am glad you have returned."

"Sit down. We have many things to say." Bezalel sat down, and Moses looked at him carefully. "I have a word from God concerning you."

"Me?" Bezalel was shocked. "What is it, my lord?"

"The Lord has told me that He will use you to build the tabernacle and the things that go in it. You will build the tabernacle, the ark of testimony, the mercy seat. You will make the table and the furniture and the pure candlestick."

As Moses continued to name off the tasks that Bezalel would do, the young man was stunned. He waited until Moses had finished and said, "I am unworthy, master, to do such things."

"We are all unworthy, but God has put something in your hands, and now He has filled you with His Spirit. Has something happened recently? Have you heard from God?"

At once Bezalel related his meeting with the stranger out in the desert, and Moses listened carefully. "That is good! Now we must begin to collect the materials for the tabernacle. It must be very light in weight, for we will be moving often, and it must be taken down every time we move. We will begin today." He leaned forward and put his large hand on Bezalel's shoulder, and a smile touched his lips. "I am glad to have you, for I know God will use you mightily."

———————

Moses stood before all of the people with a veil over his face. They had gathered together knowing that God had spoken to their leader, and now Moses cried out, "This is what the Lord has commanded: From what you have, take an offering for the Lord. Everyone who is willing is to bring to the Lord an offering of gold, silver and bronze; blue, purple and scarlet yarn and fine linen; goat hair; ram skins dyed red and hides of sea cows; acacia wood; olive oil for the light; spices for the anointing oil and for the fragrant incense; and onyx stones and other gems to be mounted on the ephod and breastpiece."

A glad cry went up from the people, and they began at once stripping rings from their fingers and earrings from their ears. Baskets were put in front of Moses, and they were soon overflowing with gifts for the altar.

"I have never seen the people give like this," Aaron whispered to Miriam.

"No. It is a new time. God is speaking, brother! We will see His hand in this new tabernacle!"

———

The offering was but the beginning. Moses dispatched crews to cut down the trees on Sinai's slopes. He sent hunters to catch rams and fishermen to the shores of the Red Sea to catch huge sea cows—the skins of both animals would furnish the outermost covering of the tabernacle.

Sinai was rich in the ore of rare metals, and soon the Hebrews were digging mines to obtain the ore needed to make the metal objects for the tabernacle. Bezalel was in charge of this process, and along with Oholiab, began smelting the ore. Finally Bezalel went to Moses and said, "It is enough. We have plenty, lord Moses. I have never seen such ardor for God!"

Moses' face still glowed. "Yes, my son, it is good. How different from the days of slavery. Now as free men and women we will build the house of God together."

———

Days passed, then weeks, and finally months. The time rolled by so quickly that the people almost lost track of it. There was so much to do! But there were many hands to do it. Spinners and weavers made the coverings for the framework. Carpenters and laborers built the frame of the tabernacle. And all was done with joy.

As for Bezalel, during this long period he worked constantly with Moses. Moses would describe one of the articles that needed to be in the tabernacle, and Bezalel would begin to create it. From time to time Moses would come look at his work and make corrections. "No. I did not see it like this," he would say, and Bezalel would rework the object until it matched God's specific instructions.

The most sacred object of all was the ark. This was the cabinet that would contain the tablets on which God had inscribed the Ten Commandments. Bezalel carved out the body of the ark from a single block of wood. He carefully lined it with the finest gold. This part was simple, but somehow Moses could not describe clearly the covering for the ark. It was the most complicated of all the articles, calling for the crafting of two cherubim. Moses was concerned that the people might see the figures on the cover as idols. He wanted nothing that would lead the people into idolatry.

Finally, after many efforts, Bezalel made the cover of the ark with two gold cherubim facing each other, their wings bent over. Between the faces of the cherubim would be the glory of God, which Moses called *shekinah*.

Throughout the long period that the tabernacle was being built, Shani had come into her time as a woman and had grown taller. She was still slender, but her figure had begun to take shape. Although no one knew her exact age, she had the look of a young woman who was old enough now to be married, according to the Hebrew customs. Her face had filled out, and there was a beauty in her light green eyes that many of the younger men had begun to notice. But Bezalel did not notice. To him, Shani knew, she was still the frightened child he had rescued from the vicious soldier's sword.

As the celebration for the completion of the ark grew near, Shani grew more determined that she would make Bezalel look at her not as a child but as a woman. She had worked for months on a special dark green garment of a finely woven cloth she had obtained from one of the wealthier families in exchange for doing some work for them. She had worked for weeks to get enough to make herself a dress, and now she was finished!

She could hear the sounds of laughing and men shouting outside, for the celebration was going to be the biggest thing that had ever happened in the life of Israel. Stripping out of her simple everyday dress, she slipped on the green garment. She had traded some wild-bird eggs she had found for the material to make a belt with a silver buckle. Miriam had given Shani a pair of her earrings, which she fastened in her ears. She stood up and tried to look down at herself but could not see much. Still she knew she was a woman and no longer the child that Bezalel still thought of.

"He'll notice me today," she whispered sturdily. "I'll make him notice me."

Leaving the tent, Shani was plunged at once into a whirlwind of activities. The framework of the tent for the tabernacle was up, and the final adjustments were being made to the coverings. She stood for a moment and looked at it. It had become a familiar sight to all of the Hebrews now, but it still was impressive. It was a simple rectangular structure surrounded by a fence made of curtains with an entrance at one end. No one could enter the tent itself except Aaron and the sons of Levi, whom God had appointed as the priests of the Hebrew people.

After some difficulty, Shani finally found Bezalel. He had a crew working hard, and he was covered with sweat. She came up to him and said, "Bezalel—"

Bezalel turned and said, "Not now, Shani. Can't you see I'm busy?" He turned again and hurried away, shouting commands.

Shani stood there, her shoulders slumping. "He didn't even see me," she cried, tears spilling down her cheeks. She turned and walked away. All of the shouting and celebration meant nothing to her. *I'll never be anything to him,* she thought. *He'll never see me as anything but a dirty, frightened child.*

Finally the sanctuary of God, the tabernacle, was completed and the dedication began. Moses had counseled with the priests, especially with Aaron, spending much time with them, and finally he led Aaron forth, along with his sons Nadab and Abihu, in a ceremony of washing with water. As they approached the new sanctuary, the cloud covered the tabernacle and the glory of the Lord filled it. Moses was not able to enter the tabernacle himself; only the priests and Aaron, the high priest, were commanded by God to enter and make atonement for all the people.

When the glory of God, the shekinah, seemed to lift itself, Moses turned to Aaron, who was wearing the ritual attire of the high priest. This consisted of a tunic and a girdle and the ephod, tied on with a skillfully woven waistband. Moses placed on Aaron's chest the breastpiece, which was woven in wool of gold, blue, purple, and vermilion, and placed a turban on his head with a sacred diadem on the front of it. He said to Aaron, "Come to the altar and sacrifice your sin offering and your burnt offering and make atonement for yourself and the people."

Aaron was trembling, but he turned and approached the altar and laid out the sacrifices as Moses had commanded him. Aaron then lifted his hands and blessed the people with the blessing that God had given to Moses.

What happened next was never forgotten by anyone who stood there that day. God accepted Aaron's offerings in a most dramatic way. Fire came out from the presence of the Lord and consumed the burnt offering on the altar. The people all shouted for joy and fell facedown to worship God.

Aaron's sons, however, were jealous of the honor given to their father by God. Having planned beforehand to upstage their father, Nadab and Abihu, each approached the altar with a censer filled with fire and incense, and offered this unauthorized fire before the Lord, contrary to God's commands.

Moses cried out a warning—but it was too late. As the two men raised their censers to cast the incense on the altar, mighty flames of fire suddenly roared out from God's presence and enveloped the two men. The horrified crowd watched as the flames swirled around them, consuming their garments and blackening their flesh. They fell to the ground dead, and the odor of burned flesh filled the air.

Aaron's face was ashen, and he trembled from head to foot. Moses turned to Aaron, his eyes flaming, and said, "Do not let your hair become unkempt, and do not tear your clothes, or you will die and the Lord will be angry with the whole community. Your sons have put strange fire on God's altar, and God has rained his judgment on them. Your other two sons, Eleazar and Ithamar, will serve in their stead."

Aaron stood looking at the two burned corpses of his sons. He swallowed hard and bowed over. "It shall be as you say, my lord."

Bezalel was standing beside Caleb, his kinsmen. "God is not to be tempted," Caleb said sternly. "Be sure you do not tempt the Lord your God."

"Never," Bezalel whispered. He knew he would never forget the sight and resolved more than ever to be faithful to his God.

CHAPTER

23

After the deaths of Aaron's sons, the tribes waited for God to speak. While they were waiting, Moses continued to wait upon the Lord to receive all the laws that would govern Israel. He knew it was no easy task to take a nation of slaves and make them into a nation of free-born citizens.

The incident of the golden calf and the defilement of Israel had sunk deep into Moses' heart. He began to issue, in the name of the Lord, laws that would govern not only the religious life of Israel but their social lives as well. Most of the peoples of that part of the world were given to incest, so Moses laid out strict commandments against such abominations. He also laid out the Lord's dietary commandments forbidding the consumption of certain animals and fish. But most important, he emphasized the heart of it all: *You shall love the Lord your God with all your heart and your neighbor as yourself.*

Some of the laws were not well received by many. The law that forbade a husband to be with his wife during her menstrual period shocked the men who were used to having their own way. Moses sternly commanded the husbands to respect the woman's state of body and mind and not to force himself upon her during those times. This was a tender and delicate thing for Moses to proclaim, and many men rebelled against it, but others saw that Moses was interested not only in men but in women. He was also interested in the strangers, the mixed multitude. Aaron and even Miriam had urged him to make the mixed multitude a secondary race, for they were not Hebrews, but Moses had insisted, "No. We shall be as one. The stranger will receive the same benefits as the children of Abraham."

Finally the cloud that had remained stationary for so long lifted, and Bezalel cried out to Miriam as he rushed back to their tent, "We must get ready to leave, Mother! The cloud is moving on." He turned and saw that Shani was sitting down sewing. "Aren't you excited, little lamb?"

Shani looked up. She had still not gotten over the hurt she had received when Bezalel had not even recognized or commented on her new garment. "It doesn't matter," she said glumly. "One place is like another."

Bezalel shot a glance at Miriam. "Is she sick?"

"You can talk to me," Shani said sharply. "I'm not deaf."

"Why, of course not, little lamb."

"Don't call me that!"

Bezalel felt terribly awkward. He saw that Shani was upset and had no idea what was going on. "I'm sorry you don't feel well," he said. "Would you want to come with me and help me load up some of my things?"

"No!"

"Well," Bezalel said, "you know where to find me if you change your mind."

As soon as he had left the room, Miriam said, "Why did you treat Bezalel like that?"

"He never sees me for what I am."

Miriam was a wise woman. She had dealt with young girls many times, and she knew exactly what Shani's problem was. "He's been very busy."

"I wish I were dead! I wish he had never saved me!" Shani cried bitterly.

Miriam came over and put her arm around the girl. "You don't mean that," she said quietly. "Growing up is hard, but look at how different you are. Why, you are a young woman now."

"I wish someone else could see that besides you!" Shani got up and left the tent, her back stiff.

Miriam shook her head sadly. "Poor child. She wants to grow up so badly, and that Bezalel, he's so blind."

She began gathering up materials getting ready for the move, and as she did, she wondered what it would be like to live in the land of milk and honey instead of in this desert.

The procession that left Sinai followed a strict military formation similar to that which Moses had learned during his service in the Egyptian army. At the head were the tribes of Judah, Issachar, and Zebulun. Following these three tribes, the tribe of Levi moved out from the camp where they had stayed so long. On wagons they carried the gifts of the tribe, and the tabernacle, which had been taken apart, was also carried by this tribe. It was a mighty host that made its way across the Sinai and into another type of wilderness. The road to the Jordan River presented many obstacles, and the tribes would be exposed to constant attacks.

Moses determined to avoid clashes with these people as much as possible. He did not know this country and had to depend totally on God. Each night the caravan stopped and camps were made. Campfires were started, food was cooked, and there was a great deal of excitement about approaching the Land of Promise. The days passed, and once again Moses saw that the people had not yet learned to trust God. Food was scarce, water was even more scarce, and the manna, which had been such a miracle at first, had lost its mystery. The people were ready for an easy life, and Moses was well aware that there would be no easy life for them in the near future.

Shani was winding her way back to Miriam's tent when she saw an argument going on. She drew forward and found that a group of Hebrew women had surrounded a dark-skinned woman who was crouched down with her head covered. Some of the women were even striking her. They were all shouting, and Shani heard them say, "Leave! Go back to where you came from!"

The woman lifted her head. She was a middle-aged woman with a worn face and tired eyes. "I have nowhere to go," she whispered. "Please don't beat me."

Shani's heart went out to the woman, and she waited until finally the Hebrew women shoved her and she stumbled away. Shani ran forward and said to her, "Come with me. I'll find you a place."

The woman turned and stared at the young girl. "There's no place for me," she whispered.

"What is your name?" Shani asked.

"Lamani."

"Where are you from?"

"Ethiopia."

"Is that far?"

"Very far."

"What are you doing out here in the middle of the desert?"

The woman seemed faint, and she shook her head sadly. "I heard that the God of the Hebrews loved other people, anyone who would love Him, so I came to find Him."

Instantly Shani knew what she must do. "Come with me," she said. "I'll take you to Moses."

Lamani seemed to hunch over. "The great leader? He would pay me no heed."

"Yes, he will. He's very kind. Come." Shani reached out and took the woman's hand. She drew her along until they reached Moses' tent. Her heart was beating fast. She had never spoken directly to Moses, though she saw him constantly. "Lord Moses," she whispered and then cried out louder, "My lord Moses!"

Moses stepped out of the tent, and his eyes set on the girl and on the woman. "What is it, child?" he said.

"This is Lamani. She comes from far away, but the women won't have her. The Hebrews were beating her, and they drove her out of camp."

"What are you doing here?" Moses asked the woman.

Lamani bowed down before Moses. "I came seeking the God who loves the stranger. The gods of my people are nothing but idols. When I heard of the Lord, I came to seek Him."

Moses' heart was touched. "Why are the women mistreating you?"

"I do not know, my lord."

Moses had been praying about the mixed multitude even before he heard the voice of Shani. The Hebrews were always jealous of them and disliked them, and he wanted to make some kind of statement. As he stood there, he said, "I will seek the voice of God about this. Meanwhile, child, take the woman to my sister, Miriam. She will feed her and care for her."

"Yes, Lord Moses. Come, Lamani," Shani said. "It will be all right."

The woman could not seem to rise. When Shani helped her to her feet, a light of hope was in Lamani's eyes. "All I want is to serve and worship and love the Lord, the God of the Hebrews."

"So it shall be. I must find a way," Moses said. "Now go with Shani."

Moses went before the elders to try to speak with them about the mixed multitude of strangers. He found no encouragement there and was saddened. "If the elders of Israel will not accept a lover of the Lord, what can we expect?" he said to them bitterly. He turned and went at once to Aaron's tent. He spoke with him briefly and found that Aaron was also opposed to paying any special attention to the woman.

"She's an Ethiopian, a heathen," Aaron said harshly.

"But we are all strangers until God makes us His own," Moses said quietly. He turned and left the tent, and for a long time he walked, thinking and praying. Finally he sent for the woman, and Shani brought her to his tent.

"Shall I go outside, master?" Shani said.

"No, you stay here," Moses commanded. He turned to Lamani and said, "I'm glad you have a love for the Lord, and I grieve that our people have not accepted you." He stood looking at the woman, and pity and compassion—always close to the surface of his heart—began to rise up. "I have decided to protect you," he said. "The only way I can do that is to make you my wife."

"Your wife!" Lamani was startled. "You cannot mean that, master!"

Quickly Moses said, "It will be merely a legal thing." He thought of Zipporah, who had gone back to Midian again. He had paid her so little mind that she had left him, and he knew now that he must make this matter very clear. "You will have a tent. You will have the protection of my name—but that is all. It will not be an ordinary marriage, but it will allow you to stay with our people. Will you accept this offer?"

Lamani bowed and whispered, "Yes, my lord, I will accept."

"I will find witnesses now." He marched to the door of the tent and called for Joshua and Caleb, who stood not far away. He called them inside and said, "You two will be witnesses. I take this woman Lamani as my wife. I will be her husband."

Both men were startled, but neither would ever think of challenging the word of Moses. "Yes, Moses. What are your orders?"

"Find her a tent. See that she has food. It will be a legal marriage and that is all, you understand? Protect her from those who would insult her."

Caleb grinned. "Yes, my lord, it shall be as you say."

"Go with these men, Lamani. We are now legally married."

"Thank you, my lord."

Moses watched the woman as she left and then turned to Shani. "Now I must tell my sister and my brother what I have done. They will not like it."

"Why not?" Shani said.

"They are jealous for my honor. I wish they were more jealous for the honor of the Lord! Come. Go with me while I speak to my sister."

Moses found no support at all from Aaron or Miriam. Both were angry and upset with him, and both tried to dissuade him from following such a wild course. Moses finally said, "It's something I must do. We must learn to love those who are different from us. She is a creature of God, as are all in the mixed multitude. Do you think God is interested only in one race?"

"We are the chosen race," Aaron said loudly, his face red with anger. "You have said so yourself."

"Chosen for a task, yes, but God chooses every man, woman, and child to love, so this is something I must do."

As Moses left the tent Aaron muttered, "My brother is not wise."

"No, he is not," Miriam agreed. "Sooner or later this will mean trouble. We must do what we can to ward it off."

"There's little one can do when Moses gets his head set that he's doing something for God, but we will try."

CHAPTER
24

"Bezalel, look—I brought you some cakes."

Bezalel straightened up, arched his back to ease the strain, and turned to face Shani. She was holding out two cakes, one in each hand, and her eyes were bright. He took one of them and said, "We'll share them."

"No. I've had some already. I baked them myself because I know you like them so much."

"You're too good to me, Shani." Bezalel bit into the cake and chewed it slowly, with obvious enjoyment. "This is good! You're getting to be a fine cook. Your husband is going to be a lucky man."

Shani laughed. "If all I know how to do is make cakes, he'll be pretty hungry."

"Maybe I'll have that other one after all." Bezalel took the cake and leaned back against the work table. He ate the second cake with obvious enjoyment, then said, "I've been meaning to tell you. That was a good thing you did for the Ethiopian woman."

"I felt so sorry for her."

"Well, you have a good heart, Shani."

"Do you really think so?"

"Of course I do."

Shani looked down at the ground and began to make a small line with her bare toe. She was silent for a long moment; then she looked up and asked, "Do you think I'll ever be pretty?"

"Why, you're pretty now, Shani."

"I don't think so."

"Nonsense. You're getting more beautiful every day. Look how much taller you are now and how your face has filled out, and you have the prettiest eyes I've ever seen."

"That's . . . that's the nicest thing you've ever said to me."

"Well, you'll hear lots of nice things like that, Shani." Grinning, he reached out and ruffled her hair. "I'll have to get a stick to beat off all the young men who are interested in you."

"I don't want any of them."

"Maybe not now, but you will." He licked his fingers and added, "My wife and I will be very careful of the young men that come courting you."

Shani looked up, a frown creasing her smooth forehead. "Your wife? You're going to get a wife?"

"Why, of course I will someday. A man needs a wife." He reached out and pinched her nose and laughed when she pulled back and slapped at his hand.

"I don't want you to get a wife."

"Well, you seem to have taken over my business, so I guess you'll have to help me find a wife too. You can pick out one for me."

He had spoken in jest, but Shani was deadly serious. "None of the young women I've seen around here are good enough for you."

"That's right." Bezalel gave her a hug, then kissed her with a loud smack on the cheek. "There, that's a reward. Go get me some more cakes and I'll kiss the other cheek."

"I'll go get them right now!"

Shani whirled and ran away, her feet flying across the sand.

"That's a sharp one," Bezalel said with a grin. "I won't have to make any decisions with her around."

He heard his name called and turned to see Oholiab hurrying toward him. "What's the hurry, Oholiab?"

"There's going to be trouble." He stopped before Bezalel, panting with the effort, and nodded as if he had said something very profound. "I knew nothing good would come of it. Didn't I tell you so?"

"You tell me so many things I can't keep up with them, Oholiab. What are you talking about now?"

"I'm talking about that Ethiopian woman Moses married."

"I think that was a good thing."

Oholiab snorted. "You're about the only one who does! Every-body's talking about how wrong it is."

"How could it be wrong? All Moses wanted to do was protect her."

"Why, she's a foreigner—that's what's wrong with it. Moses has already said when we go into the land of milk and honey, we can't take wives of the people there."

"That's because they're idolaters, and besides, this woman isn't from that land. She's from Ethiopia."

"Well, the people don't like it. A lot of them are muttering about how Moses chose to favor the mixed multitude."

"Oholiab, Moses just tells us to love the stranger because the Lord loves the stranger. Can't you understand that?"

"I suppose you're right." Oholiab rubbed his chin thoughtfully. "But what makes it worse is that Miriam and Aaron are both talk-ing against Moses."

Bezalel's eyes narrowed. "I can't believe that."

"It's so. I myself heard Aaron say that Moses had committed a sin."

"Aaron is wrong, and he'd better keep his mouth shut."

———————

The tribes were, for all their size, somewhat like a family. Almost everyone knew other people's business. Gossip was the only recreation some of them had, and they often concentrated on their leaders—Moses, Aaron, and Miriam.

One day a crowd of people saw Aaron and Miriam heading for Moses' tent. A big bushy-bearded Hebrew nodded as they went by and said to those around him, "Didn't I tell you? They're going to straighten Moses out about this foreign woman."

A murmur of approval went around as they all watched the two enter Moses' tent.

———————

230 ♦ GILBERT MORRIS

Moses looked up from where he was sitting and rose to his feet at once. "Good morning, brother, and you, sister."

"We've come to talk to you," Miriam said. "Your brother and I are unhappy with you."

"I suppose it's about the woman I married."

"Exactly that. You made one mistake marrying a woman from Midian, and now you've married another foreigner. The Lord cannot be pleased."

"That's right," Aaron said. "Don't you know she's of the mixed multitude?"

"I've told you many times there shall be one law for both the stranger and for Israel. We must love the strangers because we were strangers in Egypt."

Miriam shook her head. "Your brother and I feel you should cast the woman off. The people of the mixed multitude are nothing but trouble."

"Yes, they're trouble, but so are all of us trouble. It wasn't the mixed multitude alone that worshiped the golden calf." Moses fixed his eyes on Aaron, who suddenly flushed and dropped his head, unable to meet Moses' gaze. "I know they are not the seed of Abraham," Moses went on. "This means they haven't inherited the bloodline that the Hebrews have, but the Lord is their God also. Don't you know that God has even warned us against taking away the mother bird from her little ones when we find a nest in the field? He's caused a law to forbid us to muzzle the ox when it treads out the corn. If He cares for beasts like this, how much more does He care for people? He is a merciful and compassionate God."

Miriam was rarely angry with Moses. She had been his chief supporter and loved him ever since he was an infant, but she was deeply convinced that Moses had fallen into the snare of this woman.

"Because of you, all Israel will be troubled! Do you not know that other men will take strange women as their wives? Moses, you must declare at once that you have done a wrong thing, something which is forbidden of God!"

Moses stood there, his head slightly bowed, staring at the ground as Miriam and Aaron spoke at great length concerning his marriage. Aaron finally concluded by saying, "You must send her away, Moses. There's no other way."

Moses was quiet. He was the meekest of men, and it hurt him dreadfully that his brother and sister were angry with him and felt he had fallen into error. Still, he had heard the voice of God, and now he said, "The Lord has not prohibited Israel from taking wives among the mixed multitude, and He has told me not to exclude the stranger who acknowledges Him. This woman loves the Lord. I cannot turn away from the will of God."

Miriam's anger boiled over. "It is not God who says this! It is your own will. It is *you* who have made this decision—not the Lord!"

Aaron spoke up at once. "Has the Lord spoken only by Moses? Has He not also spoken by us?"

"You know He has," Miriam said, "and we will stand against you." She stood before him, her back straight and her eyes flashing.

Moses neither moved nor spoke. He was praying in his spirit, asking the Lord to give him wisdom, and even as he stood there, a presence seemed to fill the tent. Then they all stood transfixed as they heard the voice of God. *"Come out to the Tent of Meeting, all three of you."*

At once Moses left his tent and they followed him to the tabernacle. As soon as they reached it, a pillar of cloud came down and stood at the entrance to the Tent of Meeting and the voice of God summoned Aaron and Miriam. When they had stepped forward, God said: *"Listen to my words: When a prophet of the Lord is among you, I reveal myself to him in visions, I speak to him in dreams. But this is not true of my servant Moses; he is faithful in all my house. With him I speak face to face, clearly and not in riddles; he sees the form of the Lord. Why then were you not afraid to speak against my servant Moses?"*

The cloud lifted, and when Moses turned, he was horrified to see that Miriam had been stricken with leprosy. Great running sores covered her face, and her hands were curled together like the claws of a crippled bird. The sores filled her throat and even her eyes!

Aaron cried out and fell at Moses' feet. "Please, my lord, do not hold against us the sin we have so foolishly committed. Do not let her be like a stillborn infant coming from its mother's womb with its flesh half eaten away."

At once Moses began to cry out, "O God, please heal her!"

Again the Lord spoke audibly. *"If her father had spit in her face, would she not have been in disgrace for seven days? Confine her outside the camp for seven days; after that she can be brought back."*

Outside the people had gathered to see what would be the outcome of the conflict between Moses, his brother, and his sister. As they came out, they were shocked to hear Miriam's voice cry out in anguish, "Unclean . . . unclean . . . I am a leper!"

"She is a leper! It's because she has slandered Moses," one of the elders whispered. "God has punished her."

One of the mixed multitude said with satisfaction, "She has always hated us and called us less than lepers. Now she herself is a leper."

So Miriam was confined outside the camp for seven days, and Israel walked carefully before the man Moses. God had spoken, and it was evident that to criticize the Lord's servant was not safe!

CHAPTER
25

The sun beat down on Moses' bare head as he stood gazing away into the distance. Three months had passed since the Hebrews had left Sinai. It had not been an easy journey, for they had suffered hunger and thirst, but they had arrived at Paran, beyond which lay the wilderness of Zin.

Moses glanced to his right hand and thought of the tribes of Edom that occupied this territory. They were not a sophisticated people, mostly living in caves. They had some good land, however, and there were good roads through which Israel could pass. But the Lord had forbidden any invasion of Edom's territory.

The sound of laughter came to Moses, and he glanced back toward the camp. The people were content for the moment, but he himself was less so. He had thought much and prayed more on the journey from Sinai, and most of his thinking concerned the nation and what it would be like. It was like no other nation that had ever been, and now Moses had almost finished writing down the laws as they had been given by God. They would be a people of the law, a people of the Book. Other people had laws, but none handed to them by God himself!

Quickly Moses reviewed what had been accomplished up to this point. The elders now had been reorganized with various levels of overseers. It was like a military force, broken down into smaller units, each with its own officer.

But now at the very door of the Promised Land, Moses was

apprehensive. He had prayed all night, and God had spoken to him plainly, saying: *"Send some men to explore the land of Canaan, which I am giving to the Israelites. From each ancestral tribe send one of its leaders."*

Moses knew little about the land into which he was to lead the people. He knew he would encounter resistance, but how much or in what form he was not sure.

"Moses, we are here."

Moses turned and saw Joshua and Caleb approaching. His heart warmed, for these were the two men out of all of Israel he knew he could trust implicitly.

"I am glad you have come so quickly. I have much to say to you." Moses moved under the shade of a tree, where the two men joined him. They were both seasoned and mature men by this time, Caleb tall and lean with hawklike features and Joshua shorter but more muscular. He had hazel eyes that would blaze in battle, and though he was mild mannered during times of peace, he was a fierce warrior in combat.

"God has given me a commandment to scout out the land," Moses said. "I will choose one man from each of the twelve tribes, and you two will represent Ephraim and Judah." He named off the other scouts he had decided upon and then said, "I know little about this land, except that it is filled with Canaanites, Philistines, and Hittites. They are strong men and good warriors. Their hard work has toughened them, and they will not be easy to defeat."

Joshua nodded. "I have been talking with old Manon. He says there are walled cities in the land."

"I am sure he is right."

"It will not be easy," Caleb said, "but God will be with us."

"You will leave immediately. Over there is Edom, the descendants of Esau," Moses said, pointing. "They should rejoice to hear that we are free, but we cannot know until we ask. Moab lies over there—the descendants of Abraham through his nephew Lot. They also should welcome us."

"I doubt if any of these people will welcome us," Caleb said wryly, "but it doesn't matter. The Lord is with us, and we will win the victory."

"Yes indeed," Joshua said with a grin. "We've been waiting for this for a long time, and now our men are ready."

"I want you to go across the wilderness of Zin," Moses instructed them. "Take forty days and go to the borders of the countries all the way to the sea. I want to know all that you can find out before we cross over."

"We will bring you a good report," Joshua said, nodding. "God has brought us this far, and He will take us in. He has brought us out of Egypt, and now He will take us into the land of milk and honey as He has promised."

Moses was pleased. "If the other ten men were as good as you, I would have no fears. But come—you must set the example."

The three men hurried back to the camp, where Moses called the people together and gave them a preview of what would happen.

"These twelve men will search out the land. When they bring back the information, we will be ready to move at the command of God," he said. He held up his hands and cried, "The Lord is with us!"

A great cry of joy went up and Moses prayed, "Lord, let them keep their courage, for they will need it."

———————

Bezalel had washed himself at the small stream and had anointed his body with oil and his hair with another ointment.

"I take it you're going to the feast tonight," Miriam said.

"Of course. It's about time we had a little recreation. It seems like those scouts have been gone forever."

"Moses told us it would be forty days. It's only been two weeks."

"Then I will go and enjoy myself. Come along, Shani."

Shani was instantly at his side, wearing the green dress she had worn when the tabernacle was dedicated. She had washed herself, and her auburn hair caught the glints of the lamp. She waited for Bezalel to comment on her appearance, but he was talking with Miriam, loading up some food to take to the feast. She was disappointed, as she always was when he failed to notice her.

The two of them walked along toward the center of the camp,

where the food had been put out. There was already the sound of music, and Shani said, "Look, they're dancing."

"I expect they are."

"I don't know how to dance."

"Well, I'll teach you. I happen to be an excellent dancer."

"That sounds like bragging, Bezalel."

"No. Bragging is when you say you can do something, and you can't. If you can do it, it's not bragging."

Shani laughed. "You're funny, Bezalel!"

"You look out now for some of these young fellows. They take advantage of young girls."

"What do you mean?" Shani said, looking at him.

Bezalel was somewhat embarrassed. "You know what I mean. They will try to ask you to do improper things."

"What's an improper thing?" Shani knew very well what an improper thing was, but she saw that such talk made Bezalel uncomfortable, and it delighted her. He teased her constantly, and she was glad to give a little of her own back. "Now tell me about it. I need to know."

"Miriam will tell you."

"Miriam's not here."

"Well, I'm not going to give you a lecture right now. Just be nice, and if they ask you to do anything that sounds wrong, you come and tell me."

"What will you do?"

"I'll rattle their ribs with a staff."

"Are you going to ask any girl to do an improper thing?"

Bezalel turned and stared at her with astonishment. "What a question!"

"Well, it applies to you as much as to me, these improper things, whatever they are. Is it kissing?"

"Yes. Don't be kissing anybody except your aunt Miriam and me."

"Just you two?"

"We're your family. You can kiss us."

"All right," Shani said, then added with a glint of humor in her eyes, "and you can kiss me and Miriam but nobody else."

The sound of the music grew louder. There were pipes and timbrels and harps of various kinds, and already people were spinning around doing the dances that went back centuries.

"Teach me how to dance."

"Later. We've got to put this food with the rest of it."

They went over to where the food and drink was being collected, and as he put it down, a young woman turned and said, "Why, hello, Bezalel."

"Oh, Yona, it's you!"

"I thought you were too serious to come to frivolous things like celebrations and feasts."

Yona was the daughter of Elhanan, of the tribe of Dan. Her father had served as a slave in the home of a wealthy Egyptian, and she was richly arrayed in some of the silks and jewelry they had carried out of Egypt. She was not a tall woman but was well shaped and knew how to make the best of her appearance. Her mouth was broad and rather sensuous, and her eyes were large and lustrous.

"Why, I'm as frivolous as the next fellow."

"Are you frivolous enough to dance with me?"

"I should think so," Bezalel said with a grin. He put the food down and took Yona's hands, and the two of them went out to join the dancers. Shani stood there and watched them, her face clouded with disappointment.

Oholiab stopped by and said, "You look like you just bit into a sour pickle. What's the matter?"

"Nothing."

"Well, I think there is." He looked out and saw Bezalel dancing with Yona. "They make a good-looking couple, don't they?"

"I think she's ugly."

"Ugly! You must be blind. She's a beautiful young woman. I wouldn't mind dancing with her myself."

"Her nose is too big."

Oholiab peered sharply at the young girl and laughed. "Well, it looks like Bezalel's busy, so you can dance with me."

"I don't know how to dance."

"Well, you've got the best teacher in all of Israel. Come along!"

———————

"I don't think I've ever danced so much in my whole life," Bezalel said. He was strolling along under the light of a full moon with Yona. The festival had gone on for a long time, and they had stayed until the very last of the musicians had left. Now as he walked back to her tent with her, he was stirred by her appearance. He had always been easily influenced by pretty girls, and this one was much more than that.

"I can't tell you how much I admire your work, Bezalel."

"Do you really?" Her words pleased him, for he took great pride in what he did.

"I used to come around when you were working on the furnishings for the tabernacle. Of course, I knew no one could see it once it was taken inside. That candelabrum you made was a stunning work of art."

"It was very difficult. Moses told me exactly what it was to look like, but it was hard to get it just right."

"You did a beautiful job. I never saw the ark, but I know it must have been beautiful."

"I don't suppose anyone will ever see it again except for Aaron or the next high priest."

Indeed, no one except Aaron did see the ark after it was finished. As soon as Bezalel had finished it, it was carried into what was called the Holy of Holies, which was separated from the Holy Place. All that was in there was the ark. As soon as Bezalel had placed it there and left, Moses said, "No man will see the ark except the high priest."

So it was. Whenever the tabernacle was to be moved, Aaron went in and covered the ark; then young men of the tribe of Levi put poles through the rings on the side, and they carried the covered ark to the next camping place. Aaron himself was commanded only to go in once a year on the most holy day of all and sprinkle the ark with the blood of a sacrifice.

"Everyone is talking about how clever you are to make all those things and the tabernacle as well."

"Well, Oholiab had a lot to do with it. He's a clever fellow, and Moses gave all the details of the work, exactly as God gave them to him on the mountain."

They walked along, and Yona continued to speak of how beautiful Bezalel's work was. When they reached her tent, she turned and faced him squarely. She smiled and Bezalel was suddenly aware of the perfume she wore and found himself drawn toward her.

"You're so beautiful, Yona!"

"Come, now. You're much too serious a man to be making pretty speeches to girls."

"Not at all." Bezalel was admiring the strong lines and planes of her face, the smoothness of her cheeks in the silver glow of the moonlight, and the way her head smoothly joined her strong but graceful neck. Her lips were well shaped, and he could not seem to take his eyes off of them. Suddenly, without really meaning to, he reached out and pulled her to him. She came to him easily, and he was acutely conscious of the pressure of her soft body against his. To his surprise she did not pull away. Her lips were soft beneath his own, and suddenly long-hidden feelings stirred him, deepening his sense of loneliness.

Yona drew back and whispered, "You shouldn't have done that."

"I'll probably do it again." He made an attempt, but she laughed and put her hand on his chest. "That's enough. I enjoyed the dancing."

"I'll come and see you again."

"That would be nice," Yona said with a smile. She touched his cheek, turned, and went into the tent.

Bezalel made his way back to his own tent as if he were treading on air. When he went inside, he was grinning foolishly, and Shani, who was sitting on the mat she used for a bed, stared at him without expression. "Hello, Shani."

She did not answer but got up and stalked out of the tent.

"What's the matter with her, Miriam?"

"She's jealous, Bezalel."

"Oh, that's foolish! Young girls often get attracted to older men. She'll get over it. She's just a child."

Miriam turned to face Bezalel and shook her head scornfully.

"She's at least fourteen years old, maybe more. Many of our maidens are married when they're that age."

Bezalel was still living in the memory of Yona's soft lips. "Well," he said absently, "I'll look around for a husband for her."

Miriam threw up her hands and gave a short, bitter laugh. "It's a good thing you can makes things, son, because you are ignorant beyond belief!"

CHAPTER
26

"Come on, everybody—the scouts are back!"

Miriam looked up from where she was working on a pair of sandals, a light of pleasure in her eyes. She got up, saying, "Come along, Shani. You wouldn't want to miss this."

Shani had been cooking over the fire. She put the pot to one side and joined Miriam.

Bezalel reached out and pulled her hair. "Try to look a bit more excited, little lamb. This means we're going to the Promised Land, the land of milk and honey."

Shani did not answer. She saw that everyone was hurrying toward the east end of the camp. There were shouts and calls and laughter, and Bezalel caught her by the hand and said, "Come on let's run."

"I don't want to."

Bezalel stared at her. "You always like to run."

"I don't feel like it today."

Bezalel had done his best to make up with Shani, but during the past days he had spent a great deal of time with Yona. He knew this did not meet with Shani's approval, but he was a young man in love and could not help himself. "Well, I'll just walk along with you, then."

"Go ahead. Don't wait for me," Shani said shortly.

The two approached the crowd and pushed their way toward the front. "Look, Shani, there's Joshua and Caleb, and look at the size of that bunch of grapes they're carrying. Why, it takes both of them!"

The scouts arrived in single-file, all of them carrying some evidence of the fruitfulness of the land—grain, fruit, green vegetables. The cluster of grapes that Joshua and Caleb carried was enormous. "They make your mouth water just to look at them, don't they, Shani?" Bezalel said with excitement. "I can't wait until we get there."

Moses was waiting, and when he examined the fruits of the land, he was smiling. "These are wonderful fruits. Now give us your reports."

Gaddiel, of the tribe of Zebulun, spoke up. He was a short, muscular man with a stolid expression, and now he was scowling as he spoke. "We went into the land to which you sent us, and it does flow with milk and honey! Here is its fruit. But the people who live there are powerful, and the cities are fortified and very large. We even saw descendants of Anak there."

Geuel, of the tribe of Gad, interrupted. He was a tall, lanky man and ordinarily pleasant enough, but now he was scowling. "The Amalekites live in the Negev," he said. "The Hittites, Jebusites, and Amorites live in the hill country, and the Canaanites live near the sea and along the Jordan."

A muttering went through the crowd, but Caleb raised his voice and silenced them. "We should go up and take possession of the land, for we can certainly do it."

Shaphat, of the tribe of Simeon, glared at Caleb. "We can't attack those people; they are stronger than we are."

Then the voices of the scouts grew louder as they overrode the opinions of Caleb and Joshua. Nahbi, of the tribe of Naphtali, stepped forward to speak. He was a spare man with a cavernous face and a lantern jaw. "The land we explored devours those living in it," he declared. "All the people we saw there are of great size." His jaw set stubbornly as he added, "We saw the Nephilim there. We seemed like grasshoppers in our own eyes, and we looked the same to them."

The crowd's mutterings and complaints turned to cries of dismay.

"We are like grasshoppers, the men say ... they are like mountains ... there are fortified cities!"

The complaints and weeping of the people overwhelmed the congregation as they lamented, "Woe and misery to us! What will happen to us?"

Joshua lifted his voice and called out, "Do not despair! The Lord is God. He has delivered us from Egypt. He will take us into the land."

But the crowd would not be convinced. A woman with a child in her arms cried out, "Why did you take us out of Egypt, Moses? We had bread to eat there."

"Yes, back to Egypt!" cried a voice behind her.

"Back to Egypt! We should choose a leader and go back to Egypt!"

As the voices of the crowd grew tumultuous, Moses pleaded with them, "Only remember what the Lord has done for you. He will win this battle for you as He has won other battles."

Joshua then leaped forward. His hazel eyes were burning, and he shouted like a trumpet, "The land we passed through and explored is exceedingly good. If the Lord is pleased with us, he will lead us into that land, a land flowing with milk and honey, and will give it to us."

Caleb added his voice, "Only do not rebel against the Lord. And do not be afraid of the people of the land, because we will swallow them up. Their protection is gone, but the Lord is with us. Do not be afraid of them."

But the voices of the two were drowned out with shouts, and many took up stones to kill them. But even as stones were grasped, there was a cry and everyone froze. Bezalel looked up and saw a cloud descending. It was a terrible cloud, dark and ominous, like a mountain settling down on the heads of all the congregation. Many fell to their feet. Others tried to run and hide, but Moses stood still, for he knew that this was Israel's time of testing.

The voice of the Lord spoke to Moses: *"How long will these people treat me with contempt? How long will they refuse to believe in me, in spite of all the miraculous signs I have performed among them? I will strike them down*

244 ❖ GILBERT MORRIS

with a plague and destroy them, but I will make you into a nation greater and stronger than they."

Moses cried out to God, "Then the Egyptians will hear about it! By your power you brought these people up from among them. And they will tell the inhabitants of this land about it. They have already heard that you, O Lord, are with these people and that you, O Lord, have been seen face to face, that your cloud stays over them, and that you go before them in a pillar of cloud by day and a pillar of fire by night. If you put these people to death all at one time, the nations who have heard this report about you will say, 'The Lord was not able to bring these people into the land he promised them on oath; so he slaughtered them in the desert.'"

On and on he pleaded, and finally Moses used the words that God had given him when he asked to see the glory of God. They had never departed from Moses' mind, and now he cried out the words with a loud voice: "The Lord is slow to anger, abounding in love and forgiving sin and rebellion."

And then the Lord replied, *"I have forgiven them, as you asked. Nevertheless, as surely as I live and as surely as the glory of the Lord fills the whole earth, not one of the men who saw my glory and the miraculous signs I performed in Egypt and in the desert but who disobeyed me and tested me ten times—not one of them will ever see the land I promised on oath to their forefathers. No one who has treated me with contempt will ever see it. But because my servant Caleb has a different spirit and follows me wholeheartedly, I will bring him into the land he went to, and his descendants will inherit it. Since the Amalekites and the Canaanites are living in the valleys, turn back tomorrow and set out toward the desert along the route to the Red Sea."*

The Lord then addressed both Moses and Aaron: *"How long will this wicked community grumble against me? I have heard the complaints of these grumbling Israelites. So tell them, 'As surely as I live, declares the Lord, I will do to you the very things I heard you say: In this desert your bodies will fall— every one of you twenty years old or more who was counted in the census and who has grumbled against me. Not one of you will enter the land I swore with uplifted hand to make your home, except Caleb son of Jephunneh and Joshua son of Nun. As for your children that you said would be taken as plunder, I will bring them in to enjoy the land you have rejected. But you—your bodies will fall in this desert. Your children will be shepherds here for forty years, suffering for your unfaithfulness, until the last of your bodies lies in the desert. For forty years—one year for each of the forty days you explored the land—you will suffer for your sins and know what it is like to have me against you.' I, the Lord, have spoken, and I will surely do these things to this whole wicked community, which has banded together against me. They will meet their end in this desert; here they will die."*

The voice of the Lord faded, and the people began to get to their feet. Moses was sick at heart and knew that his great dream was now no more. He looked out over the congregation and knew that not one of those men and women who were twenty or older would ever see the land of milk and honey. Only the children and those under the age of twenty would be able to enter it.

Shani turned to Bezalel and whispered, "What does it mean?"

"It means, Shani, that no one over twenty can ever go into the Promised Land."

"I'm not going if you're not."

Bezalel had been shaken, and now he said slowly, "I'm exactly twenty. I don't know whether I'll be permitted to go in or not."

Shani reached for his arm and clung to it. When he looked down at her, she whispered fiercely, "I'm not going to the Promised Land if you're not!"

Bezalel tried to smile, but it was difficult. He caressed the girl's shiny red auburn hair. "We'll see," he said, but his heart was sick. He knew that Aaron and Miriam and even Moses himself would never go into the Promised Land, according to the word of God. "It hasn't worked out as Moses dreamed it would," he said.

"It'll be all right. You and I will go in with the younger ones."

The two stood there uncertainly, thinking of the long years that would pass before anyone could go into the Promised Land.

PART FIVE

THE PROMISED LAND

CHAPTER
27

Caleb and Joshua had been sitting outside Moses' tent for hours. From time to time they spoke quietly of all that had taken place, but for the most part, silence reigned between the two. Finally Joshua straightened up and touched Caleb's shoulder. "Listen, I think I hear Moses."

Caleb, whose hearing was somewhat better than Joshua's, nodded. Wearily he said, "Yes, he's been praying all night long. I don't know how he has the strength for it, strong man though he is."

The two men sat there for another half hour, and then the curtain was parted and Moses stepped outside. The younger men at once rose and bowed before Moses.

"What are the people saying?" Moses' face was lined with deep creases, and the glory of God that had once suffused his face had faded. His shoulders were slumped, and he moved slowly, like a very old man.

Caleb hesitated, then said, "The ten men who were with us on the mission to spy out the land are dead. The Lord killed them."

Moses shook his head, and his lips drew into a white line. "I grieve for them. Their name will have a bad reputation forever. Why could they not believe the Lord God as you two do?"

Neither Joshua nor Caleb had an answer for that, and finally Joshua said, "Some of the people have said they are now ready to enter the land and fight."

"It is too late for that," Moses said. "We must think of other things."

"What is your command?"

For a time Moses did not answer, and as he stood there silently, both Caleb and Joshua realized, perhaps for the first time, exactly how lonely this big man was. He alone bore the burden of being a spokesman of the Lord to the people. He had to bear the criticism, the mutterings, the complaints of the people.

"My heart is broken, and the people—the poor people—they are confused and will be scattered in a moment like sheep. God has given me His word. We are to turn back into the wilderness."

Joshua's eyes opened. "How soon?"

Moses appeared not to have heard him. He said in a low voice, "The generations that we led out of Egypt will perish in the wilderness, as God has sworn. I was wrong about the people. I thought they could be transformed into a nation of strong warriors, but the shackles of slavery were too strong, and the idolatry that was part of that old life has sunken into their souls. God is wise, for it will take another type of nation to overcome the inhabitants of Canaan."

"The people are weak," Caleb agreed, nodding. "They are not warriors."

"They will have to become warriors—not the men of your generation, but your children and your grandchildren. They will have to become hard, and they will have to learn to trust in the Lord."

"How will the people live in the wilderness?" Joshua asked.

"By the hand of the Lord. Do you not remember the manna that He provided, and that He gave water out of a rock? This generation must die, and a new nation must be born before Israel receives its inheritance into the Promised Land."

For a long time the two men listened as Moses spoke of the plans to turn back into the wilderness. Finally he dismissed them, giving them instructions to speak to the people.

Joshua and Caleb left the great leader and went their separate ways. Caleb, on his way back to his own tent, encountered Miriam.

She came to him at once. "Have you spoken to my brother?"

"Yes. We will turn back into the wilderness very soon."

Miriam did not speak, but tears came into her eyes. "I will never see the Promised Land," she whispered.

Before Caleb could reply, she whirled and went back to her tent. She found Shani cooking breakfast, and the girl asked, "What has happened?" She listened as Miriam told her, and then her hands trembled. "I am afraid, Miriam."

Miriam forced herself to straighten up. She went over to Shani and put her arm around her. "You must trust in the goodness of the Lord. I will not see the land of milk and honey, but you will see it, as will your children."

CHAPTER
28

Shani struggled to pull the green dress down over her head, but she soon discovered that there was no chance at all of wearing it. The months that had passed since Israel left Sinai and wandered in the wilderness had been a time of development for her. She was now about sixteen, as well as she could guess, and she had grown taller and her figure had grown fuller.

With a muffled cry she yanked the dress off, threw it aside, and picked up the simple cotton dress she had been wearing every day. It was worn thin and shapeless from many washings.

She heard a sound in the camp and she looked out the door of the tent. Bezalel was leading a dozen sheep through the middle of the camp. He was laughing and his teeth flashed white against his bronzed skin. He was looking down at Yona, who was beside him—as she usually was.

"Can't she even leave him alone long enough for him to do his work?" Shani muttered bitterly. She watched as the pair moved out of sight and noted that Yona missed no opportunity to reach out and take Bezalel's arm. With a quick motion Shani went back into the tent and began grinding the wild oats she had gathered, breaking them into a coarse flour in a hollowed-out stone and using a rock to crush the seeds.

Miriam came in bearing a small goatskin flask of milk and said, "I've asked Bezalel to kill one of the sheep. We'll have fresh meat tonight." Coming over, she stood beside Shani and let her hand rest slightly on her head. A light of affection came into her eyes. She had aged much during the long, tiresome wanderings in the wilderness. It was harder for her to get around now, but she hated to admit it. More and more she had come to rely on Shani. The girl had become like a daughter to her, the daughter she'd never had, and now she sat down and began talking about household matters and what was happening in the nation.

Shani listened, amazed that Miriam knew so many of the Hebrews. Sometimes it seemed that Miriam knew every woman and child in the camp, but this, of course, was impossible. Finally Miriam mentioned Bezalel's courtship of Yona. "I'm surprised he's been chasing her for as long as he has. His love affairs have never lasted very long."

"Has he had a lot of them, Mother?"

"Oh, he's always been chased by girls. He's such a handsome young man. He's been in love a dozen times—or what he thinks is love. But no one's ever been able to pin him down."

"Yona's trying hard enough to get him. . . . I think she will."

"I hope not."

Shani looked up quickly. "You wouldn't want them to marry?"

"No. She thinks his gift for making things is going to make him rich—and it would, under different circumstances."

"He'll never get rich out here in the wilderness. Who would he sell things to? No one has any money."

"I didn't want to mention it, but Yona's trying to get him to go back to Egypt."

Startled, Shani said, "Back to Egypt! Why, he would never do that."

"I hope not, but she keeps talking about how much money he could make working for the rich Egyptians." Distaste came into her eyes. "I don't think she'd care if he made idols for those awful people."

"You don't think he'd do it, do you?" Shani asked quickly.

"I think he has better sense than that."

"I'm not so sure. Men don't have much sense when a woman sets out to get them."

Miriam leaned over and took Shani's hand. She held it in both of hers, and her eyes grew soft. "Don't be bitter, Shani. You're such a sweet girl. You have such a good spirit. Try not to be upset with Bezalel. He has so much talent, but as you say, he's a man, and men are weak where women are concerned. We just have to pray that he'll have wisdom to see beyond that woman's seductive ways."

The two sat for a time talking, and Miriam's old eyes were sharp as she studied the girl's face. Shani had blossomed into an attractive woman, and Miriam thought, *Bezalel's a fool not to see what's before his very eyes!*

———

"Tell me some more about the Promised Land, Caleb."

Caleb had stopped by to watch Bezalel, who was making a sword for him. It was to be a better sword than most of the Hebrews possessed. Bezalel had been experimenting with a new kind of metal that was much harder and stronger. Caleb was sitting with his back against a tree watching the young man work. "What do you want to know?"

"Everything. What does it look like? Are there many trees, forests, valleys?"

Caleb laughed. "It's a land flowing with milk and honey. That's what the Lord promised us and that's what it is." He went on to describe the fruitful land of Canaan. He himself was not a farmer, but he had a quick eye for such things. He spoke for some time about how the dwellers in Canaan had laid out their farms close to the River Jordan and how bountiful the crops were.

"You saw the grapes we brought in. They were huge, and they were delicious too."

Bezalel held up the shining blade and examined it critically. "Almost through here." He took the sword by the hilt and made passes in the air. "It's well balanced. Try it out, Caleb."

Caleb stood up, took hold of the sword, and exclaimed, "It seems to fit in my hand as though it were made for it!"

"Why, it *was* made for it! Don't you remember I made that cast of your grip?"

"You've done a magnificent job." Caleb cut through the air with the blade and then stared at the sword in admiration. He put his hand on the young man's shoulder. "You'll see that land one day."

"Not me. Only those under twenty will go in. I was twenty just before you left."

"The Lord wasn't absolutely clear on that point. Surely He is pleased with your devotion to Him—and the work that you did on the tabernacle."

"Well, that work's done now."

"But Israel's going to need good men, sound solid men, fighters."

"I'm not all that great a warrior, Caleb, not like you and Joshua. Besides I'll be an old man if I do get to go in."

"You'll be about sixty. That's not old. I'll be over eighty. Joshua will be older too, but you know God has given me a promise that my physical strength will remain."

Bezalel smiled. "You two are different. I'm just not sure about myself."

Caleb ran his hand along the gleaming length of the blade and said sadly, "I've wondered about Moses and Aaron and Miriam. They've been our leaders since we left Egypt."

"Will they be allowed to go in, do you think?"

"I have no idea. But by the time we enter the land, Bezalel, you'll have a wife and a tent full of children. Maybe even some grandchildren." His eyes lit up then, and he held the sword up firmly, gazing at it as he murmured, "And you will be free. That's the important thing—free."

"Forty years is a long time."

Caleb reached down and pulled the medallion from beneath his garment. He held it out and said, "Look at this. A lion on this side and a lamb on that side. I have no idea what it means, but it means something. I think it has to do with Shiloh, who is to come."

"Quite a difference between a lion and a lamb."

"I know. I lay awake sometimes at night wondering about what kind of man could combine the courage and the strength of a lion with the meekness of a lamb, but I can't picture it."

The two men stood there, and Caleb spoke for some time about the days that were to come. Finally he left, and Bezalel turned and went to his tent. It was late afternoon now, and the shadows were long. He was not conscious of the sounds of the camp, the lowing of the cattle kept in herds out at the borders, the yells and laughter of children playing and women calling to them. These were all familiar sounds, but Bezalel was thinking now of the long years that seemed to stretch out into eternity. At his age, forty years seemed like forever, and the idea of being sixty years old ... Well, he could not even imagine that.

As he moved around through the tents, he came in sight of his own and suddenly stopped dead-still. There in front of his tent, Shani was standing with a tall, well-built man somewhere in his midtwenties. Bezalel tried to remember where he had seen him, thought perhaps he was a member of the tribe of Simeon, but he could not be sure. He was a strong-looking fellow, lean but muscular. His garments were well made, and his beard was black and glossy, as was his hair.

Suddenly the man reached forward and pulled Shani to him. He laughed and kissed her, and at that moment Bezalel, the maker of beautiful objects, the architect of the tabernacle and of the ark of the covenant, lost it!

With a growl deep in his chest, he threw himself forward, ran up to the two and grabbed the man by the arm. It was like grabbing an oak tree, but he jerked him away so hard the man staggered backward.

"You get out of here and don't come back!"

"What are you doing, Bezalel?" Shani cried. "Hiram didn't mean anything."

The man called Hiram caught his balance. He stood there at least three inches taller than Bezalel and much stronger. "Is this your father?"

"Yes!" Bezalel said.

"No, he's not!" Shani snapped. "He's not kin at all."

"I'm her foster father," Bezalel said, inventing the office on the spot. "And I'll thank you to leave and not come back."

"We're not kin at all, Hiram," Shani said, her face rosy with anger. "Bezalel, what do you mean acting like a wild man?"

"I'll not have you dallying with this kind of fellow!"

Hiram's face grew tense. "This kind of fellow? If you're not her

258 ❖ GILBERT MORRIS

father or her kin, I don't have to take that kind of talk."

Bezalel stepped forward and gave the big man a push. "Get out!" he shouted. "I don't want to see you around here again."

Hiram returned the push, saying, "I'll leave when she asks me to leave and not before."

Bezalel struck out, and his fist caught the big man high on the cheekbone, merely grazing it. Hiram had struck back at the same moment, his big, hard fist catching Bezalel right in the mouth. As he reeled backward onto the ground, he knew he was making a fool of himself, but he could not help it. He had lost control as he never had before in his entire life. With a yell he scrambled to his feet and threw himself at the bigger man. He threw many blows, some of which Hiram caught on his forearm, and none of which did any damage.

Hiram's blows, however, *did* do damage. He struck quickly and hard, and Bezalel seemed to take a perverse delight in the pain they brought. Time and again he was knocked into the dust, but he always came to his feet and threw himself forward. He was dimly aware that Shani was calling at him to stop, and that Miriam's voice was also somewhere calling to him, but he did not care. He was determined to drive the man away.

Finally a tremendous blow caught him right on the temple, and the whole world seemed to turn into thousands of red and green specks that swirled around him. He felt his back hit the dust and he tried to rise, but he could not. He was aware of something running down his face, and when he blinked, blood filled his eyes.

He felt hands on him and, blinking, managed to see that Miriam was bending over him. He raised his head and saw Hiram looking at him curiously. There wasn't a mark on him, and the big man shook his head and turned. "I'm sorry. It was not of my doing."

Shani stepped toward the big man. "You did nothing wrong, Hiram, but you'd better go now."

"May I come back later?"

"Yes. Certainly."

Bezalel was beginning to feel the pain from the hard blows he had taken. His ribs felt like they were coming apart, and when he tried to lift himself, he gasped.

"Come and help me with him, Shani."

The two women got Bezalel to his feet and then inside the tent. "Here, lie down, you fool," Miriam snapped. "We'll have to clean him up," she said to Shani, "and I think that cut in his eyebrow is going to have to be sewn up."

"I'll get a needle and thread."

Bezalel lay there, shocked at what had happened. He was not a man of hot temper and had never felt the explosive anger that had been released in him. While the two women anointed his cuts and bruises with oil, he watched Shani's face, but it was like a mask.

"This is going to hurt," she said calmly, as she began stitching up his eye. He gritted his teeth against the pain. When she was finished, he muttered, "I want to sit up."

"Better lie down," Miriam said. "I'm going to give you some strong wine, something to kill the pain." She brought a bitter-tasting drink to him, forced him to gulp it down, and then said, "You lie there, and while you're there, pray that the Lord will give you better sense."

Whatever it was that Miriam gave him soon began to work. His limbs began to tingle, and his eyelids grew heavy. The more he lay there thinking about what he had done, the more foolish he felt. "Shani," he called out, and she came to stand over him.

"What is it?"

"I don't want you to do that again."

"I'm a grown woman, Bezalel."

"You're too free and easy with that man. Who is he, anyway? I can tell he's no good."

"No good! Why, he's one of the finest young men in the tribe of Simeon."

Bezalel's lips closed firmly, but that hurt, so he let them relax. "Well, I'll talk to him, and I'll find out what his intentions are."

"You stay away from him," Shani said sharply. "He hasn't done anything with me that you haven't done with Yona."

Sleep was coming fast, but Bezalel opened his eyes and protested, "Well, that . . . that's different."

"No, it's not different. Now go to sleep, and I hope this will give you a little more sense."

———

Bezalel was so stiff and sore the next morning he could hardly move. Groaning, he got out of bed, but his mouth was so sore, he could barely eat the mush Miriam fixed for him.

All day he kept to his mat, and after more of Miriam's bitter medicine, he had another good night's sleep. The next day he still was in considerable discomfort, but he had had time to think. *I was a fool! Why did I have to act like that?* He began to consider what he might say to Shani to make it up to her. It was late in the morning when he heard a voice outside, and after a few moments Hiram came in. He seemed to fill the whole tent, and Bezalel got to his feet, trying to ignore the pain.

"I have come to ask your permission to speak with Shani."

Everything in Bezalel urged him to cry out "No!" but he knew that was useless. "You have my permission," he said. But then he added, "I'm . . . I'm sorry I thrashed you. I hope you'll forgive me."

Hiram, who did not have a mark on his face, looked at the battered countenance of Bezalel, the maker of beautiful things. "Oh, that's all right," he said, turning aside to hide his smile.

———

Shani was gone most of the day, and Bezalel knew she was staying away to avoid speaking to him. Finally that night, after the evening meal, he had a chance to speak to her alone. She was making a new dress, sewing by the light of the small oil lamp. The dim yellow light cast its glow over her features, and Bezalel cleared his throat. "I'm sorry about what happened."

"It's all right." Her tone was stark, without compassion.

"I just don't . . . I just don't want you to make a mistake."

"We all make mistakes, Bezalel."

"Not you."

"Yes me. My mistake is wanting a home and a husband and children. That's a terrible thing, isn't it?"

Bezalel met her gaze, and he thought he'd never seen her green eyes more beautiful—or more angry. "We all want that," he muttered.

"Is that what you want?"

"Well, of course."

"When are you going to marry Yona?"

The question caught Bezalel off balance. "Oh, I don't know. We haven't talked about it much."

"If you love her, what are you waiting for?"

"Well, I don't want to make a mistake."

Shani looked at him and said again, "We all make mistakes. Now, leave me alone."

Miserable and sore, both inside and out, Bezalel went over and lay down on his mat. He reviewed all that had happened and finally came to a firm conclusion. "Bezalel, my boy, you've always been a fool, but you're getting worse. You've got to start acting like a grown-up instead of a child."

The days passed and then weeks after the beating that Bezalel took. Slowly the pain left, and the bruises, which had been a magnificent rainbow of orange, purple, and green, had faded. Hiram was a frequent visitor to Shani, and so were two other young men.

Bezalel was shocked by this, and he mentioned it to Oholiab. "I wish all those young fellows would stay away."

"What are you worried about? They're all nice enough, aren't they?"

"I'm not sure."

"You know they are. Hiram will be a leader in the tribe of Simeon one of these days. Why don't you mind your own affairs?"

Caleb gave Bezalel the same advice. He stopped by early one morning and delivered his counsel. "I've heard about this foolishness. I hope Hiram managed to beat some sense into you. He's a good young man, responsible. Shani could do no better."

"Well, I just lost my temper."

Caleb scowled. "Lose it over a better cause. If you want to lose your temper, lose it with the elders."

Bezalel looked up quickly. "What's the matter with the elders?"

"The same old thing," Caleb said. "They're all unhappy with Moses."

"What is it this time?"

"It's that Korah faction. Korah's always seen himself as the true leader of Israel."

"That's ridiculous. He couldn't lead a sheep to water."

"But he can influence people. I don't know why, but maybe because he's wealthy, people like Dathan and Abiram, from the tribe of Reuben, listen to him, and now he's got them all stirred up."

"What do they want?"

"I don't think they know. They just want to get rid of Moses."

"Get rid of Moses! That can never happen."

"I wish Korah knew that. They're having a meeting with him this afternoon. You be there."

"All right. I don't know what I can do, though."

"You love Moses. He'll need all of his friends."

The meeting between Moses and the elders was a stormy one. The essence of it was that the elders wanted to take over the leadership of Israel and, of course, Korah, the most influential elder, would be, in effect, the ruler of the Hebrews.

At one point Joshua cried out, "You elders, give heed to me. The Lord himself has chosen Moses, not you, to be the leader. You are rebelling against the Lord."

"We don't rebel against the Lord!" Korah shouted. "The Lord's curse is on us because of the sins of Aaron, who made the golden calf."

"Yes," Abiram agreed, "and He commanded the Levites to kill the idolaters. Why didn't Moses kill his brother? It was Aaron who made the golden calf."

"You have gone too far!" Korah went on. "The whole community is holy, every one of them, and the Lord is with them. Why then do you set yourselves above the Lord's assembly?"

When Moses heard this he fell facedown and said to Korah and his followers, "I have only done as God has directed me. Is it not honor enough for you that God has chosen you to be the elders of Israel? In the morning the Lord will show who belongs to Him and who is holy, and He will have that person come near him. The man He chooses He will cause to come near Him. You, Korah, and all your followers are to do this: Take censers and tomorrow put fire and incense in them before the Lord. The man the Lord chooses will be the one who is holy. You Levites have gone too far!"

Bezalel murmured to Caleb, "What will happen, Caleb?"

"Nothing very good for Korah." Caleb's lips were drawn in a tight, angry line. "And it is time that he discovered it is Moses, not he, who is the true leader chosen by the Lord. Tomorrow," he said angrily, "we shall see!"

The camp rose at dawn, and all were ready for the confrontation between the elders and Moses. Korah and his men, some two hundred fifty of them, filled their fire pans and added incense. They came to stand before the sanctuary waiting for Moses.

As for Moses, he and Aaron stood and watched, not knowing what would happen, and then the glory of the Lord appeared to the entire assembly, and the voice of God spoke: *"Separate yourselves from this assembly so I can put an end to them at once. Say to the assembly, 'Move away from the tents of Korah, Dathan and Abiram.'"*

Moses rose up and moved forward, speaking stridently to the congregation. "Move back from the tents of these wicked men! Do not touch anything belonging to them, or you will be swept away because of all their sins."

The people who had been close to the tents of Korah, Abiram, and Dathan immediately fled, and when they were clear, the three leaders of the rebellion, with their wives and children, stood their ground, staring defiantly at Moses.

Moses cried out with a powerful voice, "This is how you will know that the Lord has sent me to do all these things and that it was not my idea. If these men die a natural death and experience only what usually happens to men, then the Lord has not sent me. But if the Lord brings about something totally new, and the earth opens its mouth and swallows them, with everything that belongs to them, and they go down alive into the grave, then you will know that these men have treated the Lord with contempt."

Even as Moses finished his speech, the ground underneath the tents of the three rebels was split, and the earth opened its mouth and swallowed them up with their tents, all their families, and all their goods. They went down alive into the pit, screaming. Bezalel saw Korah meet his doom, screaming with a high-pitched voice like a woman, even as the earth swallowed him up.

Terrified, the congregation scattered, crying out, "The earth is going to swallow us too!" and as they fled, a fire from the Lord came down and consumed the two hundred fifty men who had offered their incense.

Caleb had not moved, and now he gripped Bezalel's arm with an iron grip. "So may it be with all who rebel against the Lord God of Israel. Come! Now that those troublemakers are out of the way, perhaps we will have some peace!"

CHAPTER
29

The terrible punishment of Korah and his followers did not stop the murmurings of the people. Instead they blamed Moses for the deaths of the leaders and the elders. Many of them were bitter at what they felt was God's refusal to honor His promise.

A burly member of the tribe of Gad spoke plainly. "I want to live as well as my children and my grandchildren," he cried out.

Others joined his cry and said, "I want to have my own farm, grow my own grapes. Instead the Lord has condemned us to wander in this desert. Only our children will go into the land."

"Yes, and who knows whether even they will go in?" a man answered him. "The Lord might break His promise to them too, as He has to us."

Moses, of course, was fully aware of all of the murmuring and complaining. It had been like this since they had left Egypt. Moses was terrified that the people might turn again to idolatry, or join themselves to the desert tribes, all of whom were idolaters.

He was constantly burdened by indecision. Where was he to lead Israel? The desert was a terrible place, and he lingered in Kadesh-Barnea as long as he dared, for the cloud had moved on. The wanderings were wearing the people down, at least the people of the older generation. Moses was desperately trying to find an answer to this when Shani came running up to him.

"Master," she said breathlessly, "Miriam is very sick. I think she's dying."

Moses' heart filled with anguish, and he turned at once. "I will go to her," he muttered.

The two hurried back to the tent, and Moses, at his first glance, saw that his sister was indeed dying. She had been ill for some time, but now the shadow of death lay on her. She opened her eyes, and her voice was weak as she said, "My brother, why are you so disturbed?"

"I cannot bear the weight that is on me, my dear sister. It's more than I can bear to lead my people in the desert for forty years."

"Moses, I put you in the basket and watched God's hand on you. He has used you as a mighty deliverer, but now where is your faith? Think of the generations yet to come, the seed of Abraham who will multiply and live because Israel was led out of bondage."

"God's judgment is always true," Moses murmured. He took Miriam's hand and knelt down beside her. He kissed the thin hand and began to weep.

"I remember," Miriam whispered faintly, "how I put you in the little basket boat and how the waters carried you over the crocodiles straight to the Princess Kali. It seemed like death at the time, but it was life. So let it be with you, my brother."

Miriam lived long enough to bless her family. She prayed for Aaron, for Moses, and then for Bezalel and Shani. "Love God and all will be well," she whispered.

Shani's eyes were filled with tears. "You cannot leave me, Mother."

"I must go, but God will lead you and put His hand on you, and on you too, my son, Bezalel. God is all."

She passed away an hour later without saying another word, and Moses, his face contorted with agony, took her dead hand and held it to his cheek. "She was a mother in Israel and my comfort," he whispered.

———————

After Miriam's funeral, Shani went back to her tent. It seemed very empty without Miriam, and she knew it would be so for a long time. She was startled at the sound of her name being called.

It was a woman's voice, and when she went to the door of the tent, she saw Yona standing there. "I must speak with you," Yona said.

"Come in."

Yona stepped inside but refused to seat herself when Shani invited her. "You must forgive me for coming so soon after the burial of your mistress, but something must be settled."

"What is that?" Shani asked.

"As long as Miriam was alive," Yona said, "it was good that you lived here with her and with Bezalel. But now an unmarried maiden and an unmarried male must not live together."

"Of course not. I will be leaving at once."

Yona's jaw sagged. She had expected an argument, and now she glared suspiciously at Shani. "It must be done at once."

"It will be done today, and now if you will excuse me—"

Yona stared at Shani, who turned and was evidently packing her things. "I'm glad you have the sense to see it!" she said sharply and turned to leave. A smile touched her lips. "Now, that's one problem out of the way," she murmured.

Yona went at once to Bezalel and said, "I have spoken with Shani."

"With Shani? About what?"

"Why, about your new arrangements, of course," Yona said. "Surely you know something has to be done."

"I don't understand you, Yona."

"You can't live with Shani. She is an unmarried woman and you are an unmarried man. It's not fitting."

His anger flared. "I think I'm capable of taking care of my own affairs."

"Don't be angry. I've already arranged it. She's leaving today."

"Leaving today! Did you tell her that?"

Yona opened her mouth, but she had no time to answer, for Bezalel whirled and ran away, leaving her standing there.

————

Bezalel paused outside the tent, took a deep breath, and tried to calm himself. He was confused and angry with Yona, but did not want to let that show. He stepped inside and, in once glance, saw that Shani was packing her things. "You're leaving?"

Shani turned and nodded, her eyes fixed on him. "Yes. You must see I can't stay here."

"Yes, you can."

"We can't live together, Bezalel."

"Of course not. I realize that. This is your tent, Shani. It belongs to you, along with all of Miriam's things. I've already been invited to stay with Caleb. He has plenty of room."

Shani's eyes suddenly filled with tears. "That . . . that would be kind indeed."

"There's no kindness to it," Bezalel said with a shrug. He came forward and took her hand. "We've always been close, you and I, haven't we, little lamb?"

The use of the old nickname seemed to break through Shani's emotions, and she began to sob. She was trembling uncontrollably, and without thinking, Bezalel reached out and pulled her into his arms. She began to cry with great, heaving sobs, and he stroked her hair and murmured soft words of comfort. "I know you'll miss her, and so will I. It's like having a limb torn off, but we must go on."

Slowly the sobbing ceased, and finally Shani stepped back. She wiped the tears from her eyes with a cloth she carried in her belt and said, "Thank you for your kindness."

Bezalel struggled to say something, but he could not think how to put it. "You and I, we are all that's left of our family."

"Yes."

The word was short, but Bezalel could see that she was struggling not to weep anymore. "We'll talk later. It will be all right, Shani. You'll see."

Later in the afternoon Hiram came to speak to Bezalel. Even before he opened his mouth, Bezalel knew what he would say, and he had to force himself to listen.

"I would like your permission to marry Shani," Hiram said.

"I am not her father. We've been through that," Bezalel replied tersely.

"I know. You're not even her blood kin, but she says she won't marry me unless you agree to it."

An incredible temptation came to Bezalel at that moment. *All I have to do is say no and it'll be over.* He knew, however, that he should not do that, and he said, "I will talk to her, Hiram. Come back tomorrow."

"Very well." Hiram nodded and added, "I will be a good husband to her, Bezalel. I want you to know that."

"I believe you, Hiram. Your reputation is good. Come back tomorrow."

Bezalel immediately went looking for Shani and found her by a small creek, washing clothes. He sat down beside her but could not speak.

After a time of silence, Shani asked him, "What is it? Something's bothering you."

"I've just had a visitor."

"A visitor?"

"Yes. It was Hiram. He asked permission to marry you."

Shani did not look at him, seeming preoccupied with washing one of the garments. She dipped it again and again in the water, and finally she turned to face him. He noted how widely spaced and beautifully shaped her eyes were, colored with a green that seemed to have no bottom. She had a woman's wide, clean-edged lips, and her hair had glints of gold in it from the sun. He also could not help noticing her figure as she bent over the stream. She had indeed become a woman. He thought about how homely she had been as a child, but now all that had changed. He saw in her eyes and in her lips the hint of her will and pride, and even as he watched, her lips changed slightly at the corners, becoming soft with interest.

"What did you tell him?"

"I told him I would talk to you."

"And what do *you* say, Bezalel?"

"You're too young. Wait awhile."

"I'm not much younger than Yona. Most girls my age are already married."

"I know all that, but still I . . . I wish you'd wait."

"Why, Bezalel? What is there to wait for?"

"I don't know." He suddenly picked up a rock and heaved it as far as he could throw it. He watched it hit the ground and then turned to face her. "I'm confused. Miriam's death has been a blow. It's not the right time to make such a big decision. Will you wait for a while?"

Something passed behind those green eyes that Bezalel could not understand, but she said softly in a whisper that he barely heard, "I will wait, Bezalel . . . until you know what you want."

"I want you to be happy," Bezalel insisted. He took her hand and held it in both of his. "Just for a little while," he promised.

"All right, if that's what you want."

———

Shani did wait—for much too long a time in Hiram's opinion. The weeks rolled by and then the months, and still she put him off. He grew short with Bezalel, for he was confident that it was Bezalel who was holding up his marriage, but he loved Shani deeply and did not press the issue.

During months of travel, the people of Israel dragged themselves from one end of the desert to another. Finally they came once more to Kadesh-Barnea. Despite the hardships, the young men and women of the new generation were growing stronger. Their diet was healthy, even though it was spare, but water was hard to find. They began to cry out to Moses as they had cried out before when leaving Egypt. Some of them said, "If only we had died when our brothers fell dead before the Lord! Why did you bring the Lord's community into this desert, that we and our livestock should die here?"

Moses at once went before the Lord, and God said to him, *"Take the staff, and you and your brother Aaron gather the assembly together. Speak to that rock before their eyes and it will pour out its water. You will bring water out of the rock for the community so they and their livestock can drink."*

Moses was weary almost to death. He gathered the people together, but then, for the first time in his life, he did not obey the words of the Lord. He cried out, "Listen, you rebels, must we bring you water out of this rock?" Then, instead of speaking to the rock as God had commanded, he lifted his staff and struck the rock twice. Water gushed out, and the people cried out in delight. They crowded together before the stream, filling their jugs, some falling on their faces to drink.

But suddenly Moses heard God's voice, and there was no gentleness in it, striking fear into him. *"Because you did not trust in me enough to honor me as holy in the sight of the Israelites, you will not bring this community into the land I give them."*

Moses could not speak. He knew he had heard his doom pronounced. Aaron also was included, and the two of them stood before the Lord and bowed low. Moses could not speak a word. For once he could not think of anything to say to his God.

Moses led the people into the kingdom of Edom, but the Lord had forbidden him to do battle with the people of that land. Instead the Lord spoke to Moses and Aaron at Mount Hor, near the border of Edom: *"Aaron will be gathered to his people. He will not enter the land I give the Israelites, because both of you rebelled against my command at the waters of Meribah. Get Aaron and his son Eleazar and take them up Mount Hor. Remove Aaron's garments and put them on his son Eleazar, for Aaron will be gathered to his people; he will die there."*

Moses did as the Lord commanded. He took the two men up to Mount Hor in the sight of all the congregation, and Moses stripped Aaron of his garments and put them on Eleazar, his son.

Aaron stood there shivering, and Moses' heart broke, but God had spoken. "Good-bye, my brother," he said. He embraced Aaron, who clung to him. Finally Moses tore his arms away and fled. He could not bear to think of losing his brother on top of the barren mountain.

Eleazar stayed, and when he came down later saying that his father was dead, all of Israel mourned for thirty days for the high priest.

Moses wandered outside the camp during the period in which the people were mourning for Aaron. Once Bezalel brought him food and drink, and he ate a little of it, but his eyes were filled with sorrow. "I am all alone now. My brother and my sister are both gone, and I will never enter the Land of Promise."

Bezalel's eyes glimmered with tears. "I am sorry, my lord Moses."

"It is the will of the Lord." Moses put his hand on the young man's shoulders. "Strong men like you will enter in. Follow the man that God raises up to take my place."

Bezalel made his way back to the camp, where he met Caleb and told him what had happened.

Caleb bowed his head. "It is not what I would have done, but our ways are not God's ways. Moses will never complain." He turned and walked away, leaving young Bezalel looking after him, wondering what would happen in the years to come.

CHAPTER

30

Hiram tried to be as gentle as he could, but there was a stubbornness in his full lower lip as he stood before Shani. He had followed her outside the camp, where she had gone to search for herbs among the wild flowers. She knew what was on his mind, and as soon as he spoke, she saw that she was right.

"I've waited for a long time, Shani, as long as I can wait. You must give me an answer."

"You've been very patient, Hiram, more patient than most men would have been."

"You must know how much I care for you."

"You've certainly been faithful," Shani said, smiling. She was troubled in her mind, for she had known this was coming for some time and was prepared for it. "I think I've been very unfair to you."

"You've made me wait a long time." But Hiram suddenly smiled. "But now you're ready to marry me?"

"No. I was unfair because I should have released you a long time ago."

Hiram could not believe what he was hearing. He knew well his own worth, and there were many young women who wanted his attention. Now he said incredulously, "You won't have me, Shani?"

"I'm not the woman who can make you happy. I'm really doing you a favor."

Hiram threw his hands up and cried, "Well, I don't understand you in the least! And you're right, you should have told me this a long time ago."

"I'm sorry. I hope you'll forgive me."

Hiram stared at her, then shook his head. "All right. That's it, then. Do you think you'll ever marry?"

"Who knows about things like that, but I wish you well."

Shani watched him go and felt instantly released from the pressure his courtship had put on her. Now she finished filling her basket with herbs and started back toward the camp.

She met Yona on the way, who said, "I must talk with you, Shani."

"This must be my day for having talks. What is it?"

"It's about Bezalel."

"What about him, Yona?"

"I want you to let him go." Yona's face was flushed, and she was obviously upset.

"Let him go? Why, I haven't tied him down. He's free to do as he pleases."

"You know that's not true."

"Yona, you shouldn't be jealous."

"I'm not jealous!" Yona exploded. "It's just wrong, that's what it is. He and I would have been married long ago if you hadn't kept after him."

"I haven't kept after him at all. He's been very kind to me and a good friend."

"He can't think of any other woman as long as you're around. I want you to go to him and tell him that you're not interested in him."

"Why don't *you* tell him?" Shani said, smiling suddenly. "I think you know what to say."

Yona flushed. "I have told him, but he needs to hear it from you."

"You're mistaken. Bezalel is more interested in his work than he is in anything else. If you want my advice, find yourself another man."

"So you can have him for yourself?"

"You're an ignorant girl, Yona," Shani said calmly, then turned and swept her aside as she continued on her way back to camp. She heard Yona cursing after her and murmured to herself, "Bezalel, you'd be wise not to take her. If she acts like this toward me, she'll do the same toward you." She suddenly felt lighter and happier than she had in a long time, as if she had finally stepped out of prison. She began to sing and stopped to do a little dance on her way back to her tent.

The fighting had begun abruptly when Arad, the Canaanite, struck out against Israel and took some of them prisoner. Moses had immediately commanded Caleb and Joshua, his two fighting generals, to strike back and recapture those taken into captivity by Arad. At the head of the army was Joshua. His black hair was streaked with gray now, but his shoulders were still broad and strong. Caleb was also gray but was as strong as any man among the Israelites. These two led the Hebrew warriors against Arad, the Canaanite, and soundly defeated him.

Almost immediately Sihon, king of the Amorites, bluntly refused to let the Hebrews pass through his land, although Moses had offered to buy water and promised that they would harm no one.

Once again Joshua and Caleb summoned the fighting men of Israel to battle.

Bezalel had not fought in the first of the battles, but he now armed himself and marched alongside Caleb. They met the armies of Sihon in a fierce battle. Israel moved forward inexorably, and Bezalel fought valiantly. It was in the midst of the battle that he was overwhelmed by a giant of a man who wounded him three times in spite of all he could do. Caleb came to his rescue, cleaving the head of the enemy soldier from his body in one stroke. He knelt down beside the wounded Bezalel and cried for help. "Bind up his wounds! Carry him back to the camp!" he shouted.

Helping hands arrived at once, and Bezalel, weak from loss of blood, knew no more.

Time had ceased to have any meaning for Bezalel. He seemed to be trapped in a box, black and hot. He felt his body burning, then came times of soothing coolness when wet cloths were pressed against his wounds. He heard many voices, and one he came to identify with a soft touch. The voice was softer and the touch was so gentle that it was almost like a feather.

At times he almost broke through the darkness, but then he would drop back into the blackness of the pit.

Finally he awoke, knowing that he was lying flat on his back. He could hear the sound of a woman singing and smell the aroma of food cooking. He tried to move and cried out, for the pain was sharp and instant.

"Bezalel!" Shani's face appeared above him. She knelt down, stared into his face. "You're awake!"

"Yes. Where am I?"

"You're back home again. You've been so ill."

"I feel terrible!"

"You almost died," Shani said. "You got a fever. We had to keep you cooled down with fresh water to keep you from dying." Her face was filled with concern, and she put her hand on his cheek. "I'm so glad you're awake. You must eat something. You've lost so much weight."

"I could eat a little."

"You lie here and I'll fix it."

Bezalel lay there and looked down at his body. It was as if it belonged to somebody else! "Why, I'm nothing but skin and bones!" he whispered.

Shani was back then with a bowl. "Sit up and I'll feed you." She helped him sit up and then began spooning warm, sweet mush into his mouth. He suddenly realized he was ravenous, but she gave him only a little. "You can have all you want but only a little at a time."

Bezalel whispered because his voice was creaky with disuse. "What about the battle?"

"Joshua and Caleb have won. The war is over. That one, anyway. Here, I must change the bandages."

Bezalel was shocked at the sight of his wounds.

"I sewed you up as well as I could, but you're going to have some bad scars."

Bezalel touched the huge scar across his chest. "You're a good seamstress," he said and managed a smile. "Thank you, Shani."

Shani hesitated, then brushed his hair back. "I'm going to have to cut your hair. You're getting shaggy as a mountain goat!"

"How long have I been here?"

"Over two weeks."

"It's a wonder I didn't starve to death."

"I managed to get a little food and water down you, but it was a struggle."

"I didn't prove to be much of a soldier."

"Caleb says you were."

"Seems all I did was get chopped up."

"Caleb said you fought bravely until you were wounded. You couldn't help that." She hesitated, then said, "Do you want me to go get Yona to visit you?"

"Yona? Hasn't she been here?"

"She came once, the third day you were home."

"I guess that tells me something."

Shani caught something in his voice. "I'll go get her if you'd like."

"What good would it do? If she truly loved me, she would have been here taking care of me herself. What about you and Hiram?"

"Oh, he's found a new love. Hannah, the daughter of Jemon. They're going to be married right away."

"I'm sorry, Shani. It's my fault for making you wait."

"No, it's not." She reached for a cup of water and held it to his lips. "You need to drink all the water you can. In a little while I'll give you another few bites of porridge with lots of honey."

"Well, I think I would have died if you hadn't taken care of me." He reached out and caught her hand. "That means you have to take care of me for the rest of my life."

Shani colored. "What are you talking about?"

"I rescued a dog once. He was old and was being attacked by some wild desert dogs. I fought them off and brought him home. He never did amount to much, but I couldn't turn him out after I'd saved him. So"—he smiled faintly—"I guess you've taken me in to raise. I feel about like that old dog looked, not worth much."

"Don't talk like that," Shani said quickly. "You're going to be fine." She touched his cheek and smiled. "I'll get you another bite or two of the mush."

"I'd like to have something solid—like some mutton."

Shani laughed. "No, not now. When you're better I'll make you some of that mutton dish you like so well."

———

Bezalel healed very slowly. He had received terrible wounds and knew that he would carry the scars for the rest of his life. Shani cared for him as if he were a child.

After a time he was able to get up and move around and began to complain.

"You must be getting better," Shani smiled. "You're well enough to mutter about your bad treatment."

"Oh, it's not that, Shani. I just don't know what's going on."

"There's a battle going on against King Balak of Moab. He has brought in a prophet called Balaam to prophesy against Israel. But from what I hear, all he does is prophesy good things of us."

"Tell me all about it."

"I don't know much. Caleb will be coming today. He can tell you more than I can."

Caleb did come and filled Bezalel in about King Balak. "He got more than he bargained for," Caleb said, laughing. "That Balaam is not much good. He specializes in curses, but the way I hear it, God told him not to say anything bad about Israel. So when he prophesied, it was always a blessing on Israel. I've been told Old Balak was livid."

Caleb seemed to be withholding something. He was sitting beside Bezalel, and finally Bezalel said, "Is something troubling you, Caleb?"

"I have been a little troubled. Actually, not troubled so much as uncertain."

"Is there anything I can do?"

"As a matter of fact, there is." Caleb slowly pulled his garment back from his chest and, grasping the leather thong from around his neck, pulled the medallion over his head. To Bezalel's astonishment he leaned forward and put the leather thong over Bezalel's head. "The Lord has told me to give you the Shiloh medallion."

Bezalel could not move. He stared at Caleb for a long moment, then shook his head. "Surely not me. A better man than I needs this."

"We never know how good a man we are until we're put in the furnace. You know that from working with metal. It takes heat to make good, strong metal. I don't know what God is going to do to make good, strong metal out of you, my son, but in any case you will carry the Shiloh medallion until God tells you to pass it along."

Bezalel's fingers trembled as he took the medallion and ran his thumb over the image of the lion. "I wish you hadn't given this to me."

"Because it means responsibility?" Caleb clamped his hands on Bezalel's thin shoulders. "Responsibility is what makes a man. It's hard times that make men strong, not easy times. Someday we'll be going over to possess the land. Joshua will lead us, I feel sure. But you and I will be in his army. God will use the gift that's in you of making things." He looked down and said, "Somehow I feel naked without that medallion. I've worn it a long time." He got up and looked down at Bezalel, who seemed stunned by the news. "Remember that Shiloh—the man who will come to redeem Israel, and some say the world—will be of our tribe. Be sure, my boy, that you marry well, because you and your wife may be in the line that will produce the coming Savior."

Caleb left abruptly, and Bezalel could not move. He was still sitting there when Shani came in later. "What's wrong?" she asked. "Do you feel bad?"

"No. Look, Caleb gave me this."

"What an odd medallion! I never saw anything like it."

Bezalel explained the significance of it to her, then added, "I think he's made a mistake. Caleb doesn't usually make many mistakes, but this time he has."

"Why would you say that?"

"Because I'm not worthy to be the bearer of this."

"Then you must make yourself worthy, Bezalel."

"How can I do that?"

"Love the Lord. Obey Him. Love your fellow men. That's all any of us can do."

The two sat talking for a long time, and finally Bezalel reached out and took her hands. "You're the true one, Shani." He kissed her hand and saw her face redden. "I didn't mean to embarrass you, but you're such a fine woman. There's none finer."

Shani was flustered and laughed uncertainly. "If you think that's going to get you more sweet cakes, you're wrong."

She got up and left, but he called after her, "You're the only true one, Shani!"

Receiving the medallion from Caleb seemed to have quieted Bezalel. For several days he said little, and Shani noticed that he was often fingering the medal. She said nothing to him but simply saw to it that he had plenty to eat and that he got his rest.

Five nights after he had received the medallion, she was surprised when he got up and said, "Come take a walk with me."

"All right, but just a short one. You don't want to tire yourself."

The two left the tent and walked under the glittering stars. The moon was full and cast its silver beams down on the camp. Many were asleep, but there were still sounds of people stirring.

"We'll be going into the Promised Land someday, but it won't be for a long time," Bezalel said.

"I can't wait to see it, even though I'll be an old woman."

"You'll never be old."

"Don't be foolish. All of us get old."

They reached the edge of the camp and stood there silently, soaking in the sounds of the night and the cool breeze that the earth gave off. The moon bathed their faces with the silver light, and she finally said, "I think it's wonderful that Caleb has given you the medallion. You'll be a great man in Israel."

"I don't feel like I'm worth anything."

"You must never say that, Bezalel, never. God has given you a great gift. You have offered your life in battle, and Caleb has passed the medallion on to you."

Bezalel suddenly knew what he had to do. He turned to face her and took her arms. "Caleb told me something else about being the bearer of the medallion."

Shani was very aware of his hands on her arms. "What did he say?"

"He said that the bearer of the medallion had to be careful to find a good wife, because her blood may also be in the line that will produce Shiloh."

He pulled her forward, and she came willingly. She was smiling now, and there was a sweetness in her that hard times had not destroyed, which gave her a faint fragrance and desirability. Bezalel knew at that moment that no other woman could ever stir him as this one. She had an outward beauty and an inward grace. She was rich in a way a woman should be rich—at times in high spirits and reckless, and at times showing the mysterious glow of a softer mood. She was as beautiful to him as inspiring music or a gentle wind. She had the power to stir him deeply and fulfill his sense of longing. He kissed her and then whispered, "I want you to share your life with me."

"My dear, I thought you'd never ask! I've loved you all my life—ever since you saved me." She held on to him and put her head on his chest.

He smelled the fragrance of her hair, and after a time he murmured, "We will have our children in the wilderness, perhaps even grandchildren, but they will enter with us into the Land of Promise, and we'll have each other."

"Yes," she said and lifted her face, and he saw tears glistening in her beautiful eyes. "We'll have each other."

EPILOGUE

Bezalel looked around at those sitting down to enjoy the meal. "Six sons, three daughters, and four grandchildren," he said aloud. "That's not nearly enough." He grabbed at Shani, who was passing by, and said, "I need six more sons and a passel of daughters."

Shani's auburn hair had gray in it now. She smiled at him and winked at the children. "Somebody has been feeding you raw meat, old man."

"Old man? I'll show you old man. You just wait until I get you alone," Bezalel cried.

Shani laughed, accustomed to his teasing. "Everybody eat, because big things are going to happen today."

Eli, their oldest son, was a taller, bigger man than his father. His eyes were dark and glistening, and his muscles were corded with strength. "It's the day we've been waiting for, Father, isn't it?"

"Yes, it is."

"That was a long speech Moses made," Eli said with a shrug, "but it was good to hear the history of our people."

Moses had stood before Israel and read the entire law to them. He had given the history of the Hebrews, and he had announced that he was leaving to go up onto Mount Nebo to die as Aaron had.

"What will we do?" Micah, the second youngest son, said. He was a smaller man than Eli, but he had his father's clever hands and inventive way. "Who will lead us?"

"You know that, son. Joshua is the man God has chosen to lead us. It was Moses who brought us out of Egypt, but it's Joshua who will lead us into the Land of Promise."

The sun was shining brightly, and Moses was preparing to leave. He put his hands on Joshua and once again made it clear to

Israel that Joshua was now their leader. He had bidden farewell to those closest to him—to Caleb first, and then to Bezalel and his family. He stood looking at Bezalel and said, "You are the bearer of the medallion, my son. Keep yourself from sin and love the Lord as He loves you."

"I will do my best, master."

Moses turned slowly, and a silence fell over Israel as he climbed up the mountainside. No one moved until his figure grew smaller and smaller and he finally disappeared into the clouds.

Bezalel sighed. "What will we do? What will we do? There will never be another man like Moses."

Shani was standing beside him. She put her arm around his waist and looked up at him. "The spirit of the Lord is on Joshua, husband. He will lead us to our new home. We will sit under the shade of our own fig tree and drink the fruit of our own vine, and our children will be free."

"What a woman," Bezalel whispered. He hugged her; then his free hand went to finger the medallion. "We will have to fight for the land, but the Lord is with us." He looked at the medallion and asked softly, "I wonder what He will be like, the Messiah who is to come?"

"He will be like no other man," Shani said. "He will not only save Israel but the whole world."

Eli suddenly cried out, "Joshua is calling, Father! We must prepare to cross over the Jordan."

"Yes," Bezalel said, smiling and taking Shani into his arms. "Into the Land of Promise. It's God's own gift to the people of Israel."

"Yes," Shani said, "and it will be our land forever."

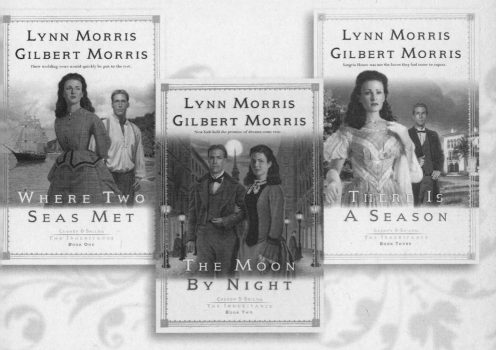